KB113507

청암 박태준

Park Tae-joon: A Memorial Issue

ASIA
PUBLISHERS

차례

Contents

책을 내며
Preface

'박태준'을 말하다
Memories of Park Tae-joon

2011년 12월 13일 향년 84세로 타계한 세계 최고 철강인 박태준 선생의 정신과 실천을 추모하고 그 귀중한 공적 자산을 더 널리 공유하기 위한 하나의 시도에 이바지하기를 바라면서 삼가 고인의 영전에 '특별한 꽃'으로 이 책을 바친다.

This special issue is dedicated to the late Mr. Park Tae-joon, the world-renowned "man of steel." This issue is conceived as a "special flower" that we offer to his spirit, cherishing our memories of that spirit and his practice and hoping to contribute to a wider sharing of these precious public assets.

이대환 **Lee Dae-hwan**
작가, 《ASIA》 발행인 Novelist; Publisher of *ASIA*

'박태준'을 말하다

1953년 여름 한국전쟁이 휴전으로 멈추려는 즈음에 멀쩡히 살아남은 한 청년 장교가 자신의 영혼에다 조각칼로 파듯이 '짧은 인생을 영원 조국에'라는 좌우명을 새겼다. 1977년 5월 조업과 건설을 동시에 감당해 나가는 영일만 포항제철에서 절박한 목소리로 단호히 외치는 한 중년 사내가 있었다. "우리 세대는 희생하는 세대다. 이것저것 개인을 위해서는 생각할 수 없고 다음 세대를 위해 희생하는 세대다." 그가 박태준이었다. 그리고 그는 도무지 낡을 줄 모르는 그 좌우명과 그 신념으로 삶의 길을 개척하면서 다른 쪽으로 한 치 벗어나지 않는 일생을 완주했다. 그래서 동시대 사람들, 후대 사람들이 박태준에 대해 다음과 같이 말할 수 있었다.

"박태준은 후세의 경영자들을 위한 살아있는 교본이다." 삼성그룹 창업자 이병철

"나는 재일 동포로서 박태준의 뜨거운 애국심과 사업가다운 일에 대한 높은 사명감에 감동을 받았고, 그런 사람이 한국에 있는 한 한국의 경제 발전은 보장돼 있는 것과 마찬가지라는 믿음이 생겼다."

롯데그룹 창업자 신격호

"박태준은 철강 산업에 국한된 인물이 아니라 국가 전체를, 적어도 동북아 내지는 태평양시대를 생각하고 있었다. 무엇보다 그는 청렴했다."

전 일본 수상 후쿠다 다케오

"한국에 봉사하고 또 봉사하는 것, 그것이 박태준에겐 지상명령이었다."

전 프랑스 대통령 프랑수아 미테랑

"박태준은 한국의 진정한 애국자다. 냉철한 판단력, 부동의 신념과 정의감, 깊은 사고력을 겸비한 그의 인품이 일본의 대한(對韓) 협력을 성공으로 이끌었다." 전 일본 수상 나카소네 야스히로

"박태준은 의외로 청소년 문제에 관심이 깊었다. 특히 개발도상국에서 종종 나타나는, 재벌 기업이 부를 독식하고 재분배를 하지 않는 것에 대한 청소년들의 불만을 매우 걱정했다."

전 세계철강협회 사무총장 레너드 홀슈

"한국에서 사원 복지 제도가 가장 훌륭한 곳이 포스코가 아닌가 한다. 사원들이 그(박태준)를 진심으로 존경하고 있음을 피부로 느낄 수 있었다."

전 유에스스틸 회장 데이비드 로데릭

"박태준은 위대한 사람이다. 유럽인들 중에서 그처럼 자기 나라의 경제에 헌신적으로 일한 사람은 없다." 전 오스트리아산업주식회사 회장 유고 세키라

"박태준은 선견지명으로 이상(vision)을 현실화 할 줄 아는 지대한 능력의 소유자다." 브라질의 저명한 기업인 엘리저 바티스타

"가장 신뢰할 수 있는 파트너인 박태준은 조국을 근대화하겠다는 일념으로 일하는 사람이다." 전 오스트리아 국립은행 총재 헬무트 하세크

"박태준은 헌신적이고 목적의식이 뚜렷한 전문적인 관리자이며 지도자라고 느꼈다. 그는 내가 가장 존경하는 사람이다." 전 호주 BHP그룹 회장 브라이언 로톤

"그분(박태준)의 리더십의 근간은 청렴결백이었다." 전 포스코 회장 황경로

"고인(박태준)은 우리나라 경제의 토대를 만드신, 우리 시대의 거목이시다." 새누리당 비상대책위원장 박근혜

"고인(박태준)은 일본인을 포함해 내가 가장 존경하는 분이다. 그만큼 훌륭한 분을 뵌 적이 없다." 전 신일본제철 임원 스즈키 노리오

"당신(박태준)은 제철보국, 선공후사의 정신을 후배들에게 일깨우고 그것을 포스코의 DNA로 심어주신 분이다." 포스코 회장 정준양

"우리 민족사에서 수난의 식민지 시대를 지울 수 없듯이 경제발전사도 지울 수 없다. 그 보람찬 경제 발전사 위에서 가장 크고 밝게 빛나는 인물이 박태준이다." 소설가 조정래

"고인(박태준)은 강철같은 이미지이지만 마음은 따뜻하고 넓은 품을 가진 분이다." 서울시장 박원순

"스티브 잡스가 정보기술(IT) 업계에 미친 영향보다 고인(박태준)이 우리나라 산업과 사회에 남기신 공적이 몇 배 더 크다." 삼성전자 사장 이재용

"1998년 초 이른 새벽부터 연구를 하고 있었는데 학교(포스텍)를 둘러보시던 박 회장님과 우연히 만났다. 그때 나라를 위해 큰일을 해달라며 따뜻하게 격려해 주시던 모습이 잊혀지지 않는다."

성균관대 신소재공학부 교수, '2011 젊은 과학자상' 수상자 안종현

"박태준이 작고하고 영결식 날까지 닷새 동안 일반 시민을 포함해 각계 조문객 8만7천여 명이 서울, 포항, 광양 등 전국 일곱 곳의 분향소를 찾았다. 우리 사회는 '세종대왕이 다시 와도 두 손 들고 떠날지 모른다'라는 자조적 농담까지 나올 만큼 갈등과 반목이 심하다. 김수환 추기경, 성철 스님, 한경직 목사 등 극소수 원로를 빼면 이번만큼 범국민적 추모 열기가 뜨거웠던 적은 드물었다." 《동아일보》, 2012. 1. 5. 저널리스트 권순활

포스코는 2012년 1월 25일 캐나다 경제 매거진 《코퍼레이트 나이츠》가 스위스 다보스포럼에서 발표한 '글로벌 지속가능경영 100대 기업' 중 30위에 올랐다. (아시아권에서는 일본 도요타자동차 21위, 히타치화학 28위, 한국 삼성전자 73위)

포스텍은 2010년 영국 《더타임스》가 발표한 세계 대학평가에서 28위에 올랐다.

POSCO was ranked 30th in the Global 100 Most Sustainable Corporations in the World announced by *Corporate Knights*, a Canadian economic magazine in the World Economic Forum in Davos, Switzerland on January 25, 2012. (Among Asian companies, Toyota Motor was ranked 21 th, Hitachi Chemical 28 th, and Samsung Electronics 73th.)

In 2010, *The Times Higher Education* of Britain ranked POSTECH as the 28th best university in the world.

Memories of Park Tae-joon

A young officer who survived the Korean War carved a motto, "Let me devote my short life to my eternal fatherland!" into his soul in the summer of 1953, as the war neared its end. In May 1977 at POSCO on Young-il Bay, which was already operating though still under construction, a middle-aged man urgently and firmly declared, "Ours is a generation of people that sacrifice themselves. We cannot think about our individual interests but have to sacrifice ourselves for the happiness of posterity." That man was Park Tae-joon. For the entire course of his life, he followed his destiny armed with that same motto and that same belief, never straying an inch, which is why his contemporaries and successors could say these things about him:

"Park Tae-joon is a living textbook for future executives."
Lee Byung-chull, founder of Samsung Group

"I was deeply moved by Park Tae-joon's ardent patriotism and passionate sense of mission towards his work as a businessman. I came to believe that Korean economic development is guaranteed as far as Korea has a businessman like him." Shin Kyuk-Ho, founder of Lotte Group

"Park Tae-joon thought not just about the steel industry but about the entire country and the age of Northeast Asia or the Pacific Rim. Above all, he was a man of integrity."

Fukuda Takeo, former Japanese prime minister

"To serve Korea again and again—that was Park Tae-joon's most urgent imperative."

François Mitterrand, former French president

"Park Tae-joon was a true Korean patriot. His character, which combined level-headed judgment, firm belief, a sense of justice, and thoughtfulness, led to the success of Japan's collaboration with Korea.

Nakasone Yasuhiro, former Japanese prime minister

"Surprisingly, Park Tae-joon was deeply interested in youth. In particular, he was very concerned about the dissatisfaction the young feel about the conglomerates' monopoly of wealth, which is very common in developing countries." Lenhard Holschuh, former secretary general of International Iron and Steel Institute

"POSCO offers probably the best benefit packages to its employees in Korea. I could feel the genuine admiration his employees have for him."

David M. Roderick, former chairman and CEO of the US Steel Corporation

"Park Tae-joon is a great man. No European devoted his life to the economy of his country as sincerely as Park did."

Hugo M. Sekyra, former CEO and chairman of Austrian Industries

"Park Tae-joon is a man of great ability who had foresight and vision which he knew how to turn into reality."

Eliezer Barista, renowned Brazilian businessman

"Park Tae-joon, the most reliable partner, works only for the modernization of his country."

Helmut Haschek, former chairman of the board, Austrian National Bank

"I could sense that Park Tae-joon was a professional manager and leader who was devoted to his clear mission. I have the greatest respect for him."

Brian T. Loton, former chairman of BHP Group in Australia

"The basis of his leadership was his integrity."

Hwang Kyung-ro, former chairman of POSCO

"The deceased (Park Tae-joon) is the giant of our times, who laid the groundwork for our country's economy."

Park Geun-hye, chair of the emergency committee, Saenuri Party

"The deceased (Park Tae-joon) is someone I admire above all

others, including Japanese. I have never met anyone else as upright."

Suzuki Norio, former executive of Nippon Steel Corporation

"You (Park Tae-joon) instilled the spirit of 'patriotism by steel manu-facturing' and 'public affairs before personal interests' in your juniors."

Chung Joon-yang, chairman of POSCO

"As we cannot erase the ordeals of the colonial period from the history of our nation, so we cannot erase the period of economic development. Park Tae-joon is the character who shines most brightly and greatly in that rewarding history of economic development." Jo Jung-rae, novelist

"The deceased (Park Tae-joon) has an image of steel, but a warm heart and generous hands." Park Won-soon, mayor of Seoul

"Park Tae-joon's achievements for the industry and society of our country are many times greater than Steve Jobs' influence on the IT industry." Lee Jae-yong, CEO of Samsung Electronics

"I was doing research at school one morning in early 1998 when I happened to run into Chairman Park who was looking around the school (POSTECH). I will never forget how he warmly encouraged me to work hard for our country." Ahn Jong-hyun, recipient of the "2011 Young Scientist Award" and professor at the School of Advanced Materials Science and Engineering, Sungkyunkwan University

"For the five days from when Park Tae-joon passed away to his funeral, about 87,000 people, including ordinary citizens as well as leaders of various fields, visited seven memorial altars all over the country including Seoul, Pohang, and Gwangyang. Our society is so divided and contentious that some people self-deprecatingly joke, 'Even King Sejong would give up and leave if he visited our country now.' Except in the case of Cardinal Kim Sou-hwan, Buddhist priest Songchul, and Pastor Han Kyung-chik, our people rarely have shown this level of passionate nationwide respect and love for the deceased. *The Dong-A ILBO* January 5, 2012, Kwon Soon-hwal, journalist

포스텍에 새겨진 미래 세대와의 약속
A Promise to Future Generations Carved on POSTECH

신념의 나침반
The Compass of Belief

포스텍에 새겨진 미래 세대와의 약속

"유치원 건물을 지을 때도 일반 건물과 같이 교육적, 예술적 감각이 전혀 없게 지을 것이 아니라, 안데르센 동화 세계와 같이 어린이들에게 꿈을 심어 줄 수 있는 훌륭한 집을 지어야 한다." 1971년 7월 9일

"우리 회사 고등학교에서 교육받은 학생들은 일류 대학 입학률에 있어서나 모든 면에서 서울에서 공부한 학생들보다 더 우수한 학생으로 교육시켜내고야 말겠다." 1977년 9월 20일

"교육한 천하(天下)의 공업(公業)이며 만인의 정성으로 이루어지는 것이라고 믿는다." 1978년 9월 1일

"이번에 회사의 사운을 걸고 시작한 포항공과대학교 설립에 관해 당장 눈앞에 닥친 문제만 생각한다면 고생 끝에 얻은 성과가 우리에게 돌아오는 것이 아니라 다른 데에 쓰이는 것이 아닌가 하는 의구심이 발생할 수 있다. 그러나 포항공과대학교는 지금 당장의 이윤 추구가 아니라 먼 훗날을 위해서, 국가 장래를 위해서 큰 힘이 된다고 하는 확신을 우리 스스로 가져야 한다." 1986년 8월 27일

"포항공과대학교는 '다음 세대의 행복과 다음 세기의 번영'을 기업 이념으로 하는 우리 포스코가 지난 19년 동안 열과 성을 다 바쳐 이룩한 정신적, 물질적 노력의 정화(精華)이다." 1987년 3월 5일

"포항공과대학교가 세계 최고 수준의 명문 대학으로 성장하는 것은 거역할 수 없는 운명이다. 민족 기업 포스코가 낳은 포항공과대학교는 이 나라 이공 분야를 선도해야 하는 숭엄한 사명을 타고났기 때문이다." 2003년 9월 4일

"20년 전 오늘, 나는 포항의 이 언덕에 칼텍과 같은 대학을 세우려는 원대한 포부와 이상을 품고 있었다. 그것이 제철보국에 의한 교육보국의 길이며, 기업의 사회적 공헌을 가장 훌륭하게 실천하는 길이라고 확신했다."

2006년 12월 1일

위의 인용은 모두 '교육보국 의지와 사상'을 드러내는 청암 박태준의 어록이다. 그의 말은 수사(修辭)가 아니고 관념이 아니었다. 그의 말은 늘 약속이고 실천이었다. 그는 생전에 14개 유치원·초·중·고교를 세워 세금의 도움 없이 한국 최고 수준으로, 포스텍을 세워 역시 세금의 도움 없이 세계적 명문 대학으로 육성했다. 이것은 한국사를 통틀어 가장 위대한 교육 공적의 반열에 올리지 않을 수 없는 사실이다.

2011년 가을, 여든네 살의 황혼을 거니는 그가 폐 질환의 기침에 시달리고 있던 계절, 마침 포스텍 개교 25주년(2011년 12월 3일)을 앞둔 시기에 포스텍 총장을 비롯한 보직 교수들과 포항 시민단체 대표들이 '청암 박태준 선생의 교육 공적'을 영구히 기념할 수 있는 조각상을 '성의를 모아 건립하자'는 뜻을 세웠다. 이에 따라 성의 모으기는 11월 3일부터 3주간에 걸쳐 진행되었으며, 포항시민·포스텍 가족·포스코 퇴직자 등 21,982명이 성의를

모아 12월 2일 포스텍 노벨 동산에서 '청암 박태준 조각상' 제막식을 열게 되었다.

　청암 박태준 조각상은 중국 조소원·난징대학 미술연구원 원장이며 세계적 작가로 꼽히는 우웨이산(吳爲山)의 작품이다. 그는 박태준의 정신세계를 깊이 이해하고 있었다. 이대환이 쓴 『박태준』 평전의 중국어 완역본을 읽은 뒤 작품의 주인공과 여러 차례 만나서 정신적 교감을 나눴던 것이다. 그는 박태준의 전신상과 흉상(포스텍 청암학술정보관 소재)을 창작했다. "태연자약하고 기백과 도량이 넘치는 전신 조각상의 모습은 박태준 선생에 대한 우러러봄을 나타냈다."며 "특히 젊은이들이 선생의 정신을 본받게 되기를 염원한다."는 우웨이산, 그는 뛰어난 서예가의 친필로 전신상 받침돌에 '鋼鐵巨人 敎育偉人'을 바쳤다. 강철거인과 교육위인, 이것은 박태준에게 필생의 두 축이었던 제철보국과 교육보국이 최후에 남겨 놓은 결실로, 그의 일생에서 고갱이 중의 고갱이를 추출해낸 두 단어이며, 그의 타계 소식을 접한 국내외 언론들이 일제히 '한국의 영웅이 떠나다'라고 보도한 근거이기도 했다.

"When we design a building for a kindergarten, we shouldn't design it like any ordinary building without educational and aesthetic considerations. We should build a wonderful house that can inspire children with dreams like the world of Andersen's folktales." July 9, 1971

"We will educate our high school students to surpass students who study in Seoul in every respect including their entrance to first-rate colleges."

September 20, 1977

"I believe that education is the manufacturing industry of our world and that it requires sincere devotion from everyone."

September 1, 1978

"If we look at the immediate return from POSTECH, which we established betting on the fortunes of our company, we might wonder whether we would simply be draining our resources. However, we should firmly believe that POSTECH will contribute to our future, the future of our country and that it is not for immediate profit." August 27, 1986

"POSTECH is the flower of spiritual and material efforts that we at POSCO have made for the past nineteen years with all our hearts and might, as POSCO's mission is to achieve 'the happiness of generations to come and the prosperity of the next century." March 5, 1987

"It is inevitable for POSTECH to grow to be a distinguished world-class university. POSTECH, born of POSCO, a national enterprise, has a solemn mission to lead the field of science in our country." September 4, 2003

"Twenty years ago I had a great dream to build a university like CALTECH on this hill in Pohang. I believed that building a school like that is a way to connect "patriotism by steel manufacturing" with "patriotism by education" and the best way for a business to contribute to society." December 1, 2006

The above quotations from Park Tae-joon all reveal his idea of, and will to achieve, "patriotism by education." His words were neither rhetorical nor ideological. They were always concrete promises put into practice. He founded and developed fourteen schools from kindergarten to high school into the best schools in the country without using tax money. He also founded POSTECH and developed it into a world-renowned university also without the help of tax money. These accomplishments belong to the best educational achievements in the history of Korean education.

In the fall of 2011, a little before the 25th anniversary of POSTECH (December 3, 2011), there was a gathering of the president and administrative professors of POSTECH and leaders of civic organizations in Pohang. At this time, when Park Tae-joon, age eighty-four, was in the twilight of his life and suffering from a lung disease, they decided to erect a statue to forever commemorate his achievement in education. Accordingly people collected donations for three weeks from November 3. Altogether 21,982 citizens of Pohang, families of POSTECH, and retirees of POSCO contributed to the making of the statue. They held an unveiling ceremony for the "statue of T.J. Park" on Nobel Hill on December 2.

The statue was made by Wu Weishan, world-renowned sculptor as well as founder and president of the Chinese Academy of Sculpture and director of the Academy of Fine Arts at Nanjing University. He had a deep understanding of the subject of his sculpture, as he met and talked with Park Tae-joon many times after he read the Chinese translation of Park Tae-joon's biography written by Lee Dae-hwan. He created full-body and bust sculptures of Park Tae-joon and the latter is displayed at the TJ Park Library. Wu Weishan said about the full-body statue, "I tried to express my admiration for him through embodying in the piece his composure, high spirit, and generosity." He also added, "I especially hope that young people follow his example." He also had a renowned calligrapher inscribe "Great Man of Steel and Education" in the stand under the statue. "Great Man of Steel and Education" captures the achievements and the very essence of Park Tae-joon's life devoted to "Patriotism by Steel Manufacturing" and "Patriotism by Education." It is because he was the "great man of steel and education" that media all over Korea and the world carried the headlines, "Korea's Hero Passes Away."

신념의 나침반

짧은 인생을 영원 조국에, 이 신념의 나침반을 따라 헤쳐 나아간 청암 박태준 선생의 일생은 제철보국 교육보국 사상을 실현하는 길이었으니, 제철보국은 철강 불모지에 포스코를 세워 세계 일류 철강기업으로 성장시킴으로써 조국 근대화의 견인차가 되고, 교육보국은 14개 유·초·중·고교를 세워 수많은 인재를 양성하고 마침내 한국 최초 연구중심대학 포스텍을 세워 세계적 명문대학으로 육성함으로써 이 나라 교육의 새 지평을 여는 횃불이 되었다. 이에 포스텍 개교 25주년을 맞아 포스텍 가족과 포항 시민이 선생의 그 숭고한 정신과 탁월한 위업을 길이 기리고 받들기 위하여 여기 노벨 동산에 삼가 전신상을 모신다.

2011년 12월 2일
청암 박태준 설립자 조각상 건립위원회

The Compass of Belief

Tae Joon Park devoted his short life to his eternal fatherland, following his deepest convictions in serving his country's steel manufacturing industry and education. For the nation's steel manufacturing he founded POSCO and developed it to be the best steel manufacturing company in the world, making it the engine of economic development. For education, he founded and nurtured not only 14 schools ranging from kindergarten to high schools, but also POSTECH, the first research university in Korea, which became a world-renowned university and a torch illuminating a new horizon in Korean education. On this day, the 25th anniversary of the founding of POSTECH, the POSTECH family and citizens of Pohang dedicate this life-size statue of T. J. Park here on Nobel Hill in order to forever commemorate his noble spirit and outstanding accomplishments.

December 2nd, 2011
Committee for the Commemorative Statue of T. J. Park, the Founder of POSTECH

마지막 연설 | 우리의 추억이 역사에 별처럼 반짝입니다
The Last Address | Our Beautiful Memories Are
Sparkling Like Stars in History

마지막 연설

　2011년 9월 19일 오후 7시부터 포항 '포스코 한마당 체육관'에서 포스코 초기부터 현장 근무를 했던 퇴직사원 370여 명과 박태준 포스코 명예회장이 19년 만에 재회하는 〈보고 싶었소! 뵙고 싶었습니다!〉 잔치가 열렸다. 박 명예회장이 짧은 연설을 하는 동안 체육관은 눈물의 호수를 이루었다. 세계의 기업 역사상 유례를 찾아볼 수 없는 '창업 최고경영자와 퇴직 현장 사원'의 재회. 인간의 이름으로 만들 수 있는 가장 따뜻한 만남의 하나였던 그날 저녁의 감동적인 연설은, 누구도 알 수 없고 오직 하느님만이 알았을 테지만, 그의 생애에 대미를 장식하는 마지막 연설이 되었다. 박태준은 도저히 피할 수 없는 '숙명의 포스코 사나이'라는 사실을 최후로 증명해 준, 앞으로 영상물과 함께 그의 기념관에 되살아와서 '아름다운 문화유산'으로 길이 전승될 그 연설의 전문을 싣는다.

우리의 추억이 역사에 별처럼 반짝입니다

정말 오랜만입니다.

정말 보고 싶었소!

오늘 이 자리에서는 여러분을 그냥 '직원'이라 부르겠습니다. 그 앞에 '퇴직'이란 말을 달고 싶지 않습니다. 여러분도 저를 그냥 '회장님'이라 부르기 바랍니다.

보고 싶었던 직원 여러분.

이렇게 우리가 다시 만날 수 있도록 건강을 허락해주신 조물주에게 감사를 드려야 하겠습니다. 우리가 얼마만입니까? 제가 회장 자리에서 스스로 물러난 때가 1992년 10월이었으니 어느덧 19년이라는 세월이 흘러갔습니다. 19년만의 재회입니다. 지금 저는, 만감이 교차하고 감정이 북받쳐 오릅니다.

친애하는 직원 여러분.

오늘 저녁에 우리는 추억 속으로 걸어가게 됩니다. 우리가 영일만 모래벌판에서 청춘을 불태웠던 시절을 돌이켜보면, 여러분에게 미안한 마음을 금할 수 없습니다. 그때 저는 이렇게 외쳤습니다. "우리는 희생하는 세대다." "우리의 희생과 헌신으로 조국 번영과 후세 행복을 이룰 수 있다." 여러분은 그 외침에 공감하고 기꺼이 동참했으며, 저는 솔선수범으로 앞장섰노라고 자부합니다.

오늘의 대한민국은 그때의 대한민국과 비교할 수 없을 정도로 눈부신 성장을 이루었습니다. 그 바탕, 그 동력은 바로 여러분의 피땀이었습니다. 현재 여러분의 후배들은 한국 최고 수준의 연봉을 받습니다. 그러나 저는 여러분에게 당시의 한국에서 중간 수준을 유지할 수밖에 없었습니다. 여러분의 후배들은 근무조건이 4조 2교대지만, 여러분은 맞교대나 3조 3교대였고 비상시에는 밤잠마저 반납했습니다.

우리 임직원들에게 희생과 헌신을 요구한 저에게 위안이 있었다면, 자녀 교육과 주택 문제, 후생 복지와 문화 혜택을 당시의 한국에서 최고 수준으로 보장하는 가운데, 어려운 시대에 안정된 직장을 제공하고 있다는 것이었습니다.

그런데 우리는 남들이 갖지 않은 특별한 것을 공유하고 있었습니다. 연봉이나 복지보다 더 소중한 정신적 가치, 그것은 제철보국이었습니다. 기필코 회사를 성공시켜서 조국 근대화의 견인차가 되자는 투철한 사명의식을 가슴에 품고, 실패하면 영일만에 빠져 죽자는 "우향우" 정신으로 무장하고 있었던 것입니다. 우리의 그 열정, 우리의 그 헌신, 우리의 그 단결이 마침내 '영일만의 기적'을 창출하고 '영일만의 신화'를 쓰게 되었습니다.

그러나 우리의 힘만으로는 그 기적, 그 신화를 이룰 수 없었을 것입니다. 저는 언제나 잊지 못하는 사람들이 있습니다. 여러분도 그분들을 기억하고 있을 것입니다.

가장 먼저 기억할 것은, 회사의 종자돈이 조상들의 피의 대가였다는 사실입니다. 대일청구권자금, 그 식민지 배상금의 일부로써 포항 1기 건설을 시작할 수 있었습니다. 그래서 우리가 외친 제철보국과 우향우는 한층 더 우리의 가슴을 적시고 영혼을 울렸을 것입니다.

고(故) 박정희 대통령을 잊을 수 없습니다. 제철소가 있어야 근대화에 성공할 수 있다는 그분의 일념과 기획과 의지에 의해 포항제철이 탄생했고, 그분은 저를 믿고 완전히 맡겼을 뿐만 아니라, 온갖 정치적 외풍을 막아주는 울타리 역할도 해주셨습니다. 이 사실을 우리는 망각하지 말아야 합니다.

지역사회의 이해와 협력도 기억해야 합니다. 포항제철을 위해 수많은 주민들이 정든 고향을 떠나야 했고, 신부님과 수녀님들은 귀중한 시설을 포기했으며, 포항시민은 인내와 협조를 보내주었습니다. 그래서 지역사회와 포항제철은 공생공영의 공동체로 거듭날 수 있었습니다.

해병사단은 포항제철의 듬직한 이웃이었습니다. 오늘 이 자리에도 해병 의장대가 우정 출연을 하고 있습니다만, 국가 안보가 요즘보다 훨씬 더 불안했던 그 시절부터 해병사단은 우리 회사를 잘 지켜주었습니다.

일본에도 포스코를 위해 진심으로 협력해준 사람들이 있었습니다. 특히 두 분을 잊을 수 없습니다. 이미 오래 전에 고인이 되신 신일본제철의 이나야마 회장과 양명학의 대가 야스오카 선생입니다.

그리고 우리 모두가 간직해야 할 이름들이 있습니다. 여러분의 현장에는 위험이 상존했고, 크고 작은 안전사고가 발생했습니다. 조금 전에도 그분들을 위한 묵념이 있었습니다만, 조업과 건설 중에 유명을 달리하신 분들은 우리의 마음과 포스코의 역사 속에 영원히 살아 있어야 합니다.

친애하는 직원 여러분.

인생의 황혼에 들어선 사람은 누구를 막론하고 '인생은 짧다'는 생각을 해보기 마련입니다. 저도 그런 생각에 잠길 때가 있습니다. 그러나 인생은 사람이 세운 큰뜻을 이루지 못할 정도로 짧은 것은 아닙니다. 이 자리에 모인 우리는 제철보국이라는 큰뜻을 함께 이룬 동료들입니다. 현재까지 84년에 걸친 저의 인생에서 여러분과 함께 그 큰뜻에 도전했던 세월이 가장 보람차고 가장 아름다운 날들이었습니다.

여러분은 저의 인생에 가장 보람차고 가장 아름다운 선물을 안겨준 사람들입니다. 여러분에게 진심으로 감사를 드리고, 여러분과 함께 청춘을 바쳤던 그날들에 대하여 하느님께도 감사를 드립니다.

사랑하는 직원 여러분.
우리의 추억이 포스코의 역사 속에, 조국의 현대사 속에 별처럼 반짝이고 있다는 사실을 잊지 맙시다. 그것을 우리 인생의 자부심과 긍지로 간직합시다.

여러분, 부디 건강해야 합니다. 부디 행복해야 합니다. 여러분 모두의 건승과 모든 가정의 행복을 빌면서, 포스코의 무궁한 발전을 기원합니다. 감사합니다.

2011년 9월 19일 포스코 명예회장 박 태 준

The Last Address

At 7 p.m. on September 19, 2011, a banquet entitled "I Missed You, We Missed You, Too!" took place at the POSCO Hanmadang Gymnasium in Pohang. This banquet occurred at a meeting between 370 retired founding workers of POSCO and its honorary chairman Park Tae-joon nineteen years after he retired. During Chairman Park's short address, the gymnasium turned into a lake of tears. His moving address that evening during one of the warmest of human gatherings, an unprecedented reunion between retired workers and the founding CEO, became his last address, the grand finale of his life. Only God could have known that fact at the time. We are publishing the address in its entirety here. This address that proved being 'a POSCO man' was Park Tae-joon's unavoidable destiny will live on forever as our beautiful cultural heritage in his Memorial Hall where his words will rejoin his image in the video version.

Our Beautiful Memories Are Sparkling Like Stars in History

It has really been awhile.

I have really missed you!

Today I'll simply call you fellow workers. I don't want to add "retired" in front of those words. Please also call me simply "Mr. Chairman."

Dearest fellow workers,

I would first like to thank God who granted us our health so that we can meet like this again. How long ago was it? It has already been nineteen years since I resigned from the post of chairman in October 1992. We're reunited after nineteen years! A thousand emotions are crowding in my mind and my heart is full.

Dearest fellow workers,

This evening we are walking into our memories. Looking back at those days during which we devoted ourselves to our work with youthful enthusiasm in the sandy field of Young-il Bay, I cannot help feeling sorry for you. I cried at that time, "We belong to the generation that should sacrifice itself" and "We can contribute to the prosperity of our country and the happiness of future generations through our sacrifices and dedication." You sympathized with me and willingly participated in our work, and I am proud to say that I took the initiative and set an example.

Korea today has achieved brilliantly successful development, and is incomparable to Korea back then. The foundation and motive force for such development were none other than your blood and sweat. The salaries of your successors are now on the highest level in Korea. At the time, however, I had to fix your salaries at the mid-level. Your successors are now working four units-double shift, while you had to work simple double shift or three units-triple shift. In times of emergency, you even had to forgo sleep.

I found consolation in the fact that I offered you a secure workplace during a difficult time while simultaneously securing the highest level of benefits for your children's education, and for housing, welfare, and cultural opportunities.

We shared something special, something unique to

us. It was a spiritual value, more precious than salaries or benefits, i.e. "Patriotism by Steel Manufacturing." Cherishing a sense of mission that we would become the driving force for our country's modernization by succeeding in our enterprise, we were also armed with the spirit of "Right Face!"—we would drown ourselves in Young-il Bay if we failed. That passion, that dedication, and that solidarity of ours created "the Miracle of Young-il Bay" and wrote "the Saga of Young-il Bay."

However, we could not have achieved that miracle and saga on our own. There are people I can never forget. I am sure you're remembering them, too.

The first thing I remember is the fact that the seed money for our company came from "the compensation for the blood of our ancestors." We could begin the first stage of the Pohang plant construction only thanks to the Funds from Property Claims Against Japan, part of those indemnities for Japanese colonial rule. That was why our cry of "Patriotism by Steel Manufacturing" and "Right Face!" moved our hearts and rang in our souls.

I cannot forget the late President Park Chung-hee. POSCO could be born only thanks to his plan and will, based on his belief that we could succeed in modernization only when we had our own steel manufacturing company. He not only trusted me completely in this enterprise, but also protected our company from political pressures. We should not forget this.

We should also remember the understanding and cooperation by our neighboring communities. Many residents had to leave their beloved home village because of POSCO. Catholic fathers and nuns also gave up their precious facilities. Citizens of Pohang were patient and collaborative. Thanks to them, our neighbors and POSCO could be reborn in a relationship of co-existence and co-prosperity.

The Marine Corps was our reliable neighbor. Even now, the honor guard of the Marine Corps is making a friendly gesture by attending our celebration. The Marine Corps has protected us carefully since the time when our national security was far less strong than it is these days.

There were people in Japan as well who sincerely helped POSCO. I especially cannot forget two people, the late chairman Inayama of Nippon Steel Company and Mr. Yasuoka, the master scholar of the teachings of Wang Yang-ming.

There are also other names that we all have to remember. You all worked in a workplace where dangers to your safety lurked in every corner. Big and small accidents were inevitable. We have just paid a silent tribute to workers who passed away during those accidents. They will forever live in our hearts and in the history of POSCO.

Dearest fellow workers,

Those in the dusk of life tend to think that 'life is short' regardless of who they are. I sometimes ponder about that, too. However, life isn't as short as not to grant those who conceived an ambitious goal its achievement. We who gathered here are fellow workers who together achieved our goal of "Patriotism by Steel Manufacturing." Those days during which I tried to meet the challenges of our big goal together with you were the most rewarding and beautiful days of my life.

You are the ones who gave me the most rewarding and beautiful gifts of my life. I sincerely thank you for your gifts and I thank God for the days that enabled me to dedicate my youth to our work with you.

My beloved fellow workers,

Let's not forget that our memories are sparkling like stars in the history of POSCO and modern history of our country. Let's take pride in it and treasure them.

Please be healthy! And please be happy! I wish you health, all your families happiness, and POSCO everlasting development and success! Thank you!

Honorary chairman of POSCO September 19, 2011
Park Tae-joon

조사 | 근대화가 기억하는 가장 아름다운 이름
emorial Address | The Most Beautiful Name Remembered from Korea's
Period of Modernization

추모사 | 참된 인간의 길을 보여 준 우리의 사표
Eulogy | An Upright Man and the Light of Our Times

추모사 | 보국과 위민의 선각자
Eulogy | A Pioneer of Patriotism and True Populism

근대화가 기억하는 가장 아름다운 이름

정준양

한국 근대화 역사가 가장 아름다운 이름으로 영원히 기억할 박태준 명예회장님. 존경하고 사랑하고 벌써 그리워지는 우리 회장님. 북받치는 슬픔을 억누르며 다시 당신의 존함을 불러봅니다. 우리의 박태준 회장님!

당신께서 영면하실 여기는 국립 서울 현충원입니다. 당신께서 몽매에도 잊지 못하신 박정희 대통령의 이웃으로 오셨습니다. 두 분의 인연은 갈라놓을 수 없는 숙명이었다는 사실을 새삼 깨닫습니다. 어쩌면 당신께서는 지금쯤 그분과 해후할 준비를 하실 것 같습니다. 응접실에도 사무실에도 그분의 사진을 걸어놓고 그토록 그리워하신 박정희 대통령 곁으로 모시게 되어 그나마 저희에게는 조그만 위안입니다. 오늘 저녁이든 내일 저녁이든 저승 가시는 여독이 풀리시거든, 마치 부산 군수사령부 시절의 어느 저녁과 같이, 두 분께서 다정하게 주막에 앉아 막걸리 잔을 나누시기를 두 손 모아 빌겠습니다. 32년 만에 재회하시니 쌓은 회포가 얼마나 크고 무겁겠습니까?

지난 1992년 개천절이었지요. 4반세기에 걸쳐 포항제철소, 광양제철소 2,100만 톤 조강생산 체제를 완공한 바로 다음이었던 그날, 당신께서는 세계 최고 '철(鐵)의 용상(龍床)'에서 스스로 물러나겠다는 결심을 세우시고 여기 박정희 대통령의 영전에 서서 임무완수를 보고하셨습니다. 그때의 순정하고 비장했던 장면을 어찌 잊을 수 있겠습니까?

"나는 임자를 알아. 제철소는 아무나 할 수 있는 게 아니야. 어떤 고통을 당해도 국가와 민족을 위해 자기 한 몸 희생할 수 있는 인물만이 할 수 있어. 아무 소리 말고 맡아. 임자 뒤에는 내가 있어. 소신껏 밀어붙여봐." 이 한마디 말씀으로 조국 근대화의 제단으로 불러주신 각하의 절대적인 신뢰와 격려를 생각하면서 머리 숙여 감사드릴 따름이라고, 당신께서는 뜨거운 눈물로 회고하셨습니다.

그렇습니다. 당신은 인생을 조국에 바치셨습니다. 6·25전쟁에서 구사일생 살아남은 청년 장교의 푸른 영혼에 조각칼로 파듯이 '짧은 인생을 영원 조국에' 라는 좌우명을 새기시더니, 그 숭고한 애국정신을 필생의 나침반으로 삼으시고 한 치도 벗어나지 않는 길을 완주하셨습니다.

그 길은 '우향우' 와 같이 목숨을 거는 형극의 길이었지만, 황무지를 옥토로 개간하고, 마침내 무에서 유를 창조하는 길이었습니다. 제철보국과 교육보국으로 일류 국가의 밑거름이 되겠다는 신념과 실천은 당신의 삶 그 자체였습니다. 식민지, 해방, 분단, 전쟁, 폐허, 절대 빈곤, 부정부패, 산업화와 민주화, 수평적 정권 교체, 외환 위기 극복 등으로 이어진 20세기 조국의 시련과 고난을 온몸으로 뚫고 나아간 당신의 삶은 늘 우리 시대의 구심점이었습니다.

국내외 많은 언론이 당신의 임종 소식을 '한국의 영웅이 떠났다' 고 보도했습니다. 왜 당신은 우리 시대의 영웅이었을까요?

철(鐵)은 국가다. 당신의 이 정신이 포스코를 조국 근대화의 견인차로 성장시켰습니다. 교육은 천하(天下)의 공업(公業)이다. 당신의 이 신조가 포스텍을 세계적인 명문 대학으로 육성시켰습니다. 당신의 리더십은 강력했습니다. 그러나 그 근본은 통합과 사랑, 청렴과 헌신, 완벽과 합리였습니다. 그것은 '직원 사랑' 의 가장 훌륭한 복지 제도로 구체화되었습니다. '사회공헌의 선구적 모범' 인 포스코의 학교들, 포항산업과학연구원(RIST), 포스코청암재단으로 실현되었습니다. 고희(古稀)의 정치인으로서 '산업화 세력과 민주화 세력의 화해와 통합'이라는 우리 시대의 절실한 메시아를 불러냈습니다. 통합과 사랑, 청렴과 헌신, 완벽과 합리가 당신을 영웅으로 만든 삶의 뿌리였습니다.

국가의 장래를 위해 마지막 일을 하시는 것처럼, 혼란한 우리 사회에 그 정신적 가치들에 대한 통찰의 계기를 마련해준 당신은 이제 홀연히 떠나셨습니다. 탁월한 위업을 당신의 실존처럼 남겨놓으시고, 그것을 끊임없이 발전시켜야 하는 과제를 후배들에게 맡겨놓으셨습니다. 부족하고 미숙한 저희로서는 두려운 마음이 없지 않습니다. 그러나 그 과제를 제대로 풀어나가는 것이야말로 진정 당신의 유지를 받드는 것임을 명백히 알고 있습니다. 또한 저희는 당신께 배운 정신과 지혜와 용기를 간직하고 있습니다. 언제나 한결같은 자세로, 사심 없이, 심혈을 기울여 최선을 다하겠습니다.

당신에 대한 공부와 연구도 더욱 열심히 하겠습니다. 흔히 사람들은 인물의 업적만을 기억하는 습관이 있습니다. 잘못된 습관입니다. 저희가 바로잡겠습니다. '당신의 무엇이 탁월한 위업을 성취하게 했는가?' 이 질문을 통해 당신의 정신세계를 체계적으로 밝혀내서 우리 사회와 후세를 위한 무형의 공적 자산으로 환원할 것이며, 그 가운데 저희가 맞을 난제의 해법을 구할 것입니다.

그런데 어쩐 일입니까? 추모와 다짐을 아무리 되뇌어도 저희의 마음에 넘쳐흐르는 슬픔을 가눌 수 없습니다. "우리 세대는 다음 세대의 행복과 번영을 위해 희생하는 세대다!" 그 카랑카랑한 육성이 여전히 귓전에 생생한데, 어찌 저희가 당신을 떠나보낼 수 있겠습니까? 아니, 그 원대한 소망을 이루셨지만 어찌 당신께서 저희를 떠나실 수 있겠습니까? 어느 누구든 회자정리(會者定離)의 자연법칙을 거스를 수 없다고 해도, 당신과 저희 사이에서 그것은 육신에 한정할 뿐입니다.

존경하고 사랑하는 박태준 명예회장님. 고인이라 부르고 싶지 않은, 포스코의 영원한 우리 회장님. 역경으로 점철된 한국 근대화 역사에 길이 남을 거인이시여. 그래도 저희는 당신을 보내드려야 합니다. 고생만 하신 당신을 편안히 쉬게 해드려야 합니다. 슬픔은 영일만과 광양만의 파도처럼 밀려드는데, 이 냉정한 회자정리의 강요 앞에서 저희의 심정을 형언할 수 없기에 만해 한용운 시인의 시를 삼가 당신의 혼백에 바치오니, 우리 회장님, 부디 편안히 쉬소서.

우리는 만날 때에 떠날 것을 염려하는 것과 같이
떠날 때에 다시 만날 것을 믿습니다.

아아 님은 갔지만,
나는 님을 보내지 아니하였습니다.

2011년 12월 17일 국립 서울 현충원 영결식장에서

정준양 포스코 대표이사 회장, 포스코청암재단 이사장, 한국철강협회 회장, 한국공학한림원 회장

포스코 기술연구소 부소장(1998.12~2002.3)
포스코 상무대우(EU 사무소장, 2002.3~2003.3)
포스코 광양제철소 선강담당 부소장(상무, 2003.3~2004.3)
포스코 광양제철소장(전무이사, 2004.3~2006.2)
포스코 생산기술부문장(대표이사 부사장, 2006.2~2007.2)
포스코 생산기술부문장(대표이사 사장, 2007.2~2008.11)
포스코건설 대표이사 사장(2007.12~2009.2)

The Most Beautiful Name Remembered from Korea's Period of Modernization

Chung Joon-yang

Chairman Emeritus Park Tae-joon: the unmatched beauty of your name and your reputation is destined to live on forever in modern Korean history. Our chairman, who we love and admire and already miss. We suppress our sobs of sorrow and call your revered name once more. Oh Chairman, our Chairman Park Tae-joon!

Here is your place of eternal rest: Seoul's Hyunchoong National Cemetery. You have arrived now to rest by the side of President Pak Chung-hee—he whom you could never forget in life. In this we see again the hand of destiny which tied your two fortunes together. Perhaps you are even now somewhere preparing for your long awaited reunion with him. You longed for him; you placed his photograph in your office and in your parlor. It provides us with some small comfort, then, that we have been able to bring you to his side. I pray with clasped hands that tonight or tomorrow evening, after you have recovered from the hardships of your journey to the otherworld, you will be sitting with him in some little tavern, sharing a loving cup of makgulli, as on one of those evenings long ago, in your Busan Logistical Command Center days. How great must be your joy in your reunion, how heavy the weight of thirty-two years of separation.

It was on Foundation Day, 1992. ("개천절"; October 3rd. Literally, the "day the Heavens opened"—the day the legendary founder of the Korean nation, Dangoon, is supposed to have begun his reign.) The very next day after finishing construction—a task that had lasted a quarter of a century—on the Pohang and Gwangyang steel plants, with a combined manufacturing capacity of 21 million tons, you determined to abdicate your throne, that place from which you reigned as the world greatest steelmaker, and you came here. You came to the funereal image of President Pak Chung-hee, and you stood here, and you reported to him that his orders had been fulfilled. How could we ever forget that moment of pure devotion, that grim and magnificent determination?

"I know you well, my friend. Steelmaking's not for everyone. He who would make steel must be one great enough of heart that he is willing to sacrifice his one body—to endure any suffering for the sake of his country and his people. So don't say a word. Just take on the task. I will be there to support you, my friend. Push on through to the best of your abilities." And with those few words of absolute trust and support, you recalled—the hot tears running down your face—the great man called you to the sacred task of modernizing our nation.

And that was what you did. You devoted your life to your country. You were a young officer, a survivor of the decimation brought by the Korean War, when you adopted your motto: "Life is short; the fatherland is forever." You chiseled it into your green soul. Ever after, that holy spirit of patriotism was the pole star of your life. From that course you never wavered, until your course was run.

The path you trod was one where you had to risk your life at the drop of a hat. But you made fertile jade plains of yellow dust wasteland; in the end, you created *ex nihilo*. Your entire life was based on your faith—and actions rooted in that faith—that you could strengthen your country through steelmaking, through education, that these would provide the foundation for Korea to become a first rate nation. Our nation has endured, over the course of the twentieth century, colonization and liberation, division, civil war, ruin, absolute poverty, corruption and injustice, industrialization and democratization, movements for fair regime change, the overcoming of the foreign currency crisis. Through all of these trials and sufferings, your life often seemed the center of gravity for the life of our nation as a whole.

Media—both domestic and international—have reported the news of your death as "the passing of a true Korean hero." Just what made you a hero of the age?

Your awareness that steel makes a nation is what grew POSCO into what it has become today—a engine driving the modernization of our nation. Your belief that education is the paramount industry is what allowed POSTECH to grow into what it is today—one of the great universities of the world. Your leadership skills were strong. They were founded on the principles of harmony and love, austerity and devotion, perfection and rationality. These principles were actualized in the form of your "Employee Love"—an unmatched system of employee benefits. They were fulfilled in the form of the POSCO schools that "lead the way as model contributors to society"; in the form of the Research Institute of Industrial Science and Technology, and in the form of the Pohang Chungam Foundation. As a septuagenarian politician, you brought into being the doctrine of harmony and reconciliation between the powers of industry and the powers of democratic reform. This doctrine was the messiah our age demanded. Harmony and love, austerity and devotion, perfection and rationality were the roots from which grew your hero's life.

Now, as if to provide us with one last act in service to our nation's future, giving us an occasion to consider those spiritual values in a chaotic era in our society, you have gone. As your legacy—as, indeed, the true meaning of your existence—you have left us with your towering accomplishments. You have bequeathed to us, who follow in your footsteps, the endless task of preserving and developing that legacy. We approach this task with some measure of fear, as befits those aware of their unworthiness, their limitations. But we know, as well, with crystal clarity, that carrying out that task is the true path towards honoring your wishes. And we cherish the spirit and wisdom and courage that we have learned from you. We will do our heartfelt utmost, without wavering, singlemindedly.

We will, as well, study and research your life. Most people are in the habit of only remembering the accomplishments of historical figures. This is an evil custom. We will correct it. We will ask what exactly it was about you, as a person, that made you capable of such great things. We will systematically bring to light the hidden worlds of your mind, your intellect. It will become one of the great abstract resources of our society, of our descendants, freely available to all. In it we will find the solutions to dilemmas we have yet to face.

But no matter how we repeat and reconfirm our resolves, and no matter how earnestly we celebrate your life, we cannot assuage the sorrow overflowing in our hearts. "Our generation is the generation that sacrifices for the prosperity and happiness of the next!" Your ringing tones still echo lively in our ears. So how are we to let you go? How are you to leave, though you have seen your great wishes fulfilled? No one can go against the laws of nature that dictate that those who come together must eventually part. But when it comes to us, that is a law that applies only to matters that concern bodily things.

Beloved and admired Chairman Emeritus Park Tae-joon. Our eternal chairman of POSCO. You, whom we do not wish to call departed. Titan who will be remembered forever in the pages of our hardship-strewn twentieth century history. We must now surrender you. We must deliver you to the rest you never knew in life. Our sorrow swells like the waves of Gwangyang and Yungil Bay. We are speechless in the face of that law that forces farewell. Without words of our own to express what is in our hearts, we dedicate these words from the poet Han Yong-un to your spirit. Our Chairman: rest now, in peace.

Just as we are afraid of parting when we meet,
We believe we will meet again when we part.

Ah, even though you are gone
I have never sent you away.

Chung Joon-yang CEO of POSCO and Chairman of POSCO TJ Park Foundation; Chairman, Korea Iron and Steel Association; President, The National Academy of Engineering of Korea

Deputy director, POSCO Research and Development Institute (December 1998-March 2002)

Associate Managing Director, POSCO (Director of EU Liaison Office, March 2002-March 2003)

Vice Director (in charge of Steel Manufacturing), POSCO Gwangyang Works (Managing Director, March 2003-March 2004)

Director, POSCO Gwangyang Works (Executive Director, March 2004-February 2006)

CEO and Vice president, POSCO (in charge of research and development, February 2006-February 2007)

CEO and President, POSCO (in charge of research and development, February 2007-November 2008)

Chairman and CEO, POSCO Engineering and Construction (December 2007-February 2009)

참된 인간의 길을 보여 준 우리의 사표

조정래

"사람의 몸에서 왜 이런 규사(硅沙)가 나오는지 모르겠다."

10년 전, 포스코 박태준 명예회장님의 폐 아래 물혹 수술을 한 미국 의사들의 의문이었습니다.

"10년이 지났는데도 또 규사가 나왔습니다. 그 이유를 알았습니다."

한 달 전, 옛날 그 부위를 다시 수술한 우리나라 의사들이 한 말입니다.

흔하게 쓰이지 않는 말 '규사'는 잘디잔 모래알이라는 뜻입니다.

왜 박태준 명예회장님의 폐에서는 그리도 오랜 세월에 걸쳐서 잔 모래알들이 나오는 것일까요. 그 수수께끼 풀기는 어렵지 않습니다.

포항제철이 들어서 있는 포항 영일만은 거센 바닷바람 휘몰아치는 모래벌판이었습니다.

또한 광양제철이 세워진 광양만도 세찬 바닷바람 타는 허허벌판 모래밭이기는 마찬가지였습니다. 그 모래 먼지 자욱하게 일어나는 속에서 박태준 명예회장님은 25년 동안 공사를 직접 지휘하며 포항제철과 광양제철을 세우신 것입니다.

사장이면서도 뒤로 물러나 있지 않고 공사 현장에 직접 나선 25년 세월 동안 자잘한 모래알들은 거침없이 그분의 폐로 침투해 들어갔던 것입니다.

오늘의 포스코가 없었다면 이 나라의 가전산업·자동차산업·조선산업이 이렇게 융성할 도리가 없었고, 세계 9위의 경제 대국이 될 수 없었다는 사실을 대다수 국민은 다 알고 있습니다.

그분은 조국의 오늘의 경제 번영을 이룩해내기 위해서 앞이 안 보이도록 진한 모래 먼지를 뒤집어쓰는 것을 피하지 않았고, 모래알들이 몸 안으로 파고드는 것을 두려워하지 않았습니다. 아아. 그분은 결국 그 모래가 일으킨 병으로 이 세상을 떠나갔습니다.

탄광의 막장에서 오래 일한 광부들은 모두 진폐증으로 목숨을 잃게 됩니다. 그분은 민족경제라는 탄광의 막장에서 쉼 없이 곡괭이질을 하시다가 폐를 망쳐 돌아가신 산재(産災) 노동자였습니다. 그것도 퇴직금도, 산재보상도 전혀 받지 못한 외로운 노동자였다는 사실을 아는 사람들은 별로 없습니다.

적지 않은 사람들이 오늘의 포스코가 그분의 것인 줄 알고 있습니다. 또는 그분이 엄청난 재산을 가진 부자인 줄 아는 사람도 많습니다. 20여 년 전 광양제철을 준공시킨 다음 몇 개월 후에 어이없는 정치 보복을 당해 포스코를 떠나 망명길에 오를 때 그분은 퇴직금을 전혀 받지 않았을 뿐만 아니라, 명예회장으로 복귀하신 다음에도 주식을 한 주도 갖지 않았고, 당연히 받는 것처럼 되어 있는 스톡옵션이라는 것도 전혀 탐하지 않았다는 사실은 세상에 별로 알려져 있지 않습니다.

그 정직과 청렴은 포스코를 세워 조국의 경제를 일으킨 업적에 못지않은 참된 인간의 길을 보여준 우리의 영원한 사표입니다. 더구나 집 판 돈 14억 원 중에서 10억 원을 아름다운재단에 기부하시고 집 없는 신세로 돌아가신 사실 앞에서는 전율마저 느낍니다.

"우리의 레닌 동지가 이루고자 했던 이상향이 여기 있다!" 1990년 포스코 공장을 견학한 모스크바 대학 총장이 한 말입니다. 포항과 광양 공장을 빼닮은 중국 장가항의 포스코 전원공장은 중국 모든 철강 회사들의 벤치마킹 대상입니다.

그분은 전 사원들에게 주택을 제공하고, 자식들에게 대학까지 장학금을 지원한 최초이자 마지막 기업인이었습니다. 그 어느 대통령이 이분보다 큰 업적을 세웠습니까. 그분은 대통령보다 더 대통령다운 조국의 일꾼, 민족의 위인이었습니다.

우리는 100년 지나도 얻지 못할 크나큰 별을 잃었습니다. 고인이 떠나신 빈자리가 겨울 하늘처럼 넓고 적막합니다.

고생스러우셨지만 값지게 사신 이여, 우리 모두의 존경과 사랑을 바치옵나니, 먼 길 편안히 가시옵소서.

《중앙일보》 2011년 12월 15일

조정래 소설가

《월간문학》 편집장(1973)
월간문예지 《소설문예》 발행인(1975)
도서출판 민예사 설립, 대표(1978)
《한국문학》 주간(1985-1989)
동국대학교 문과대학 국어국문학과 석좌교수(1997-현재)
제2의건국범국민추진위원회 위원 (1998-2003)
민족문학작가회의 자문위원 (2000)

주요 저서
대하소설 3부작 『태백산맥 1~ 10』(1983~1989) 『아리랑 1~ 12』 (1990~1995) 『한강 1~10』(1998~2000)
중단편집 『어떤 전설 』(1972) 『20년을 비가 내리는 땅』(1976) 『불놀이 』(1983) 외 다수.
장편소설 『인간연습 』(2006) 『사람의 탈』(2009) 『허수아비 춤』(2010)

An Upright Man and the Light of Our Times

Jo Jung-rae

"We found this *gyoosa* in his body. How is this humanly possible?"

This was the question that American doctors asked ten years ago, after they'd performed an operation on Chairman Emeritus Park Tae-joon of POSCO, in order to remove a fluid-filled cyst from the lower part of his lungs.

"It's been a decade, but we've found *gyoosa* in his body again. And now we know why."

This was what our Korean doctors said a month ago, after operating on his lungs again—the same place where he'd been operated on before, so long ago.

Gyoosa's a word you don't hear used much. It's a term for a kind of very fine sand.

Why did we keep finding *gyoosa* in the chairman emeritus's lungs? Why was it there one both of those occasions, separated by such a long expanse of time? That's a mystery easily solved.

Youngil Bay, in the city of Pohang—the site of the Pohang Steel Plant—is a sandy plain buffeted by strong ocean winds.

Gwangyang Bay—the site of the Gwangyang Steel Plant—is also a wide open barren plain of sand.

Chairman Pak spent twenty-five years in that haze of sand

and silt. He directed the construction of both steel plants himself.

He was the head of the company, so he didn't need to be on the construction sites. But he led from the front. And so—over the course of twenty-five years—the tiny grains of sand found their way straight into his lungs.

Korea's consumer electronics, car manufacturing, and shipbuilding industries flourish. Korea's an economic titan, with the ninth largest economy in the world. And, as the majority of Koreans undoubtedly know, none of this would be possible without today's POSCO.

He worked for this. He worked for the prosperity of his homeland. Through blinding clouds of sand he worked, never hiding from them. Sandgrains burrowed into his body but he did not fear. Sorrow for him. In the end the sickness caused in him by that same sand proved to be his death.

Miners who toil long in their tunnels eventually lose their lives to emphysema and black lung. The chairman's mine—the site of his toils—was the prosperity of his people. There he hewed tirelessly with his pick, until with ruined lungs he passed away. He was a casualty of industry. And—this is what few people know—he worked alone, unsupported, without severance, without worker's compensation.

Many of you may believe that he was the owner of POSCO, as it is today. Many of you may believe that he was rich, the possessor of incredible wealth. But twenty years ago, when—due to a senseless act of political revenge—he was forced to leave POSCO scant months after construction on the

Gwangyang Steel Plant had ended, and he began a life of exile, he didn't get any severance pay at all. Not only that, but even after he was recalled from exile, and was appointed Chairman Emeritus, he wasn't given a single share's worth of stock in the company. Stock options are often taken for granted, but he never even asked for them. That's what the world doesn't know about him.

He founded POSCO and so led his nation to prosperity. But his honesty and austere purity of spirit teach us how to be truly human. His spirit sets the bar for us, just as much as his accomplishments do. And when I consider that he donated a billion of the 1.4 billion won earned from the sale of his house to the Beautiful Foundation, and died without a home to call his own, it's enough to give me chills.

"The utopia that our Comrade Lenin tried to establish exists, and it is here!" Those were the words of the president of the University of Moscow, who toured the POSCO plants in 1990. The POSCO power plant in China's Janga Bay, closely modeled after the Pohang and Gwangyang plants, serves as a benchmark for every steel company in China.

He was the first—and remains the only—businessman to provide housing for all of his workers, as well as scholarships through college for their children. What president has matched his accomplishments? He was more presidential than any president. He was a man worthy of the reverence and emulation of his entire people.

We have lost a great light, the kind of star that might shine once in a hundred years. The space left empty by his passing stretches wide and silent as the winter sky.

You led a hard life, but one of great price. You go with all our admiration and love. May you fare well on that long road.

JOONGANG DAILY, December 15, 2001.

Jo Jung-rae Novelist

Editor-in-chief, *Monthly Literature* (1973)
Publisher, *Soseol Munye*, a monthly literature magazine (1975)
Founding CEO, *Minye Publishing Company* (1978)
Editor-in-chief, *Hanguk Munhak* (1985-1989)
University professor of Korean Literature, Dongguk University (1997-present)
Member, Nationwide Campaign Committee for the Second Founding of Our Nation (1998-2003)
Member, Advisory Committee, Association of Writers for National Literature (2000)

Major Publications
Sagas | *Taebaek Mountain Range* 1-10 (1983-1989); *Arirang* 1-12 (1990-1995); *Han River* 1-10 (1998-2000)
Short Story and Novella Collections: *A Legend* (1972), *Land that Has Been Rained on for Twenty Years* (1976), *Fireworks* (1983)
Novels | *Human Practice* (2006), *Human Mask* (2009), *Scarecrow Dance* (2010)

보국과 위민의 선각자

전상인

청암 박태준 선생은 20세기 한국 현대사가 배출한 걸출한 영웅이었다. 무엇
보다 그는 행동과 실천을 통해 우리 민족 앞에 구체적인 업적을 남겼다. 그리
고 그가 이룩한 것들은 아무나 쉽게 흉내 낼 수 없는 문자 그대로 위업(偉業)
이기에 우리는 그를 위인(偉人)이라 불러 당연하고 마땅하다.

 말만 화려하고 겉만 번지러운 스타들만 난무하는 이 시대에 우리는 명실상
부한 역사적 영웅 한 분을 잃었다. 청암의 서거를 애도하는 마당에 모처럼 우
리 사회가 한마음이 된 것도 이 때문일 것이다.

 박태준 포항제철 명예회장을 '철강 왕'으로만 평가하는 것은 단견의 소치
다. 물론 그는 세계적인, 어쩌면 카네기를 능가하는 철강 왕임이 틀림없다.
하지만 그는 성공한 직업군인이었고, 유능한 기업가였다. 세계 굴지의 명문
포항공대를 건립한 교육자였고, 포항산업과학기술원을 설립한 과학기술인이
기도 했다. 또한 그는 이념을 초월하여 나랏일에 매진한 정치인이자 행정가
였다. 여기에 덧붙여 그는 포항과 광양이라는 기업도시를 통해 지방발(發) 국
가발전과 지역 간 균형 발전을 모색한 지방인이기도 했다.

 이와 같은 다양한 경력을 관통하는 핵심적 정신은 국가와 국민에 대한 봉
사였다. 제철이든, 교육이든, 도시든 그는 항상 보국(報國)의 신념으로 임했
다. 그리고 그의 보국 정신은 항상 위민(爲民)사상과 결합되었다. 그가 사원
용 주택단지를 전원도시처럼 꾸민 것이나 사원들을 위한 자녀교육에 거의 완
벽을 기한 것은 다 이런 맥락에서다. 국가와 국민을 위하는 박태준 명예회장
의 태도는 그가 누구보다도 미래를 멀리 내다보는 혜안을 갖추었기 때문에
가능한 것이었다. 동시대인이 미처 생각하지 못하는 것을 예견하고 예상했다

는 점에서 그는 선각자이자 선지자였다.

　오직 국가와 국민, 그리고 미래를 위해 정성을 모으고 정열을 불살랐기에 그는 자기를 버리고 자신을 던졌다. 박 명예회장의 지병으로 알려진 '흉막 섬유종'은 그가 포항제철을 건설할 때 마셨던 바닷모래 먼지가 원인이었다. 그가 지난 2001년에 모래가 주성분인 규사로 가득 찬 물혹 덩어리 제거 수술을 받은 것은 널리 알려진 일이다. 그렇다면 박 명예회장은 한국의 철강업, 한국의 산업화, 그리고 궁극적으로는 한국의 국가발전을 위해 '순국(殉國)' 하신 것으로 생각해야 옳을 것이다.

　박태준 포항제철 명예회장은 희생과 봉사의 가치가 무엇이고, 애국의 의미가 어떤 것인지를 말이 아닌 행동과 업적으로 우리에게 보여주고 떠난 분이다. 그렇기에 이제는 고인에 대한 추모 열기를 진정한 사회 통합과 국가 발전을 위한 에너지로 바꿀 때가 아닌가 싶다.

　그가 떠난 빈자리가 유난히 크게 느껴지는 것이 바로 2011년 세모의 대한민국이다. 삼가 고인의 음성과 행적이 그립다. 모쪼록 고인의 명복을 빌 뿐이다.

《경향신문》2011년 12월 15일

전상인 서울대학교 환경대학원 교수, 한국미래학회 학술이사

민족통일연구원 북한연구실 연구위원(1992.03~1995.02)
한림대학교 사회학과 교수(1995.03~2005.08)
한국사회사학회 회원, 부회장 (1996.03~현재)
미국 워싱턴주립대학교 사회학과 방문교수 (2001.07~2002.08)

주요 저서
『아파트에 미치다 』(2009)
『우리 시대의 지식인을 말한다 』(2006)
『고개 숙인 수정주의 』(2001)

Jun Sang-in

Chungam Park Tae-joon was one of the great heroes of
twentieth century Korean history. His legacy—of actions, of
promises kept—has touched his entire people. And because his
works are monumental, great in the most literal sense of the
word, are not easily to be imitated, it is only right that we
remember him as a great man.

The stars of our age proliferate, their words gaudy and their
appearance slick. And now we have lost a historic hero, a hero
in name and a hero in deed. Perhaps this is why our entire
nation is joined in mourning for the passing of Chungam.

It would be shortsighted to evaluate Chairman Emeritus Park
Tae-joon of Pohang Steel simply as the "King of Steel.' That he
was: one with few peers in the annals of the world; one who
perhaps surpassed Carnegie himself. But he was a successful
career soldier and a brilliant businessman. He was an educator
who founded Pohang University of Science and Technology,
one of the great educational institutions of the world. He was a
man of science and technology who founded the Pohang
Research Institute of Industrial Science and Technology. And he
was a politician and administrator who poured his heart into
working for his country, transcending ideology. And on top of

that, he was a local man who, by making Pohang and Gwangyang into regional urban centers of industry, contributed to locally powered national development and geographically balanced economic development.

The spirit that runs through his varied career is that of service: service to his country, service to his people. Whether in steelmaking, in education, or in urban development, he labored always with the interests of his nation at heart. And the interests of the nation, for him, were always tied up with the welfare of the people. It was in the context of these beliefs that he built garden cities as housing for his employees; that he ensured near perfection when it came to the education of their children. His care for his country and its people was powered by his insight. He saw further into the future than anybody else. He predicted and foresaw things that none of his contemporaries had even thought to look for. In that sense he was enlightened; prophetic.

He worked with focused dedication and passionate fervor for his country, his people, and their future. There was nothing left for himself. He sacrificed himself. He became, as we have come to know, chronically ill with cystic fibrosis, caused by the ocean sand he inhaled while building Pohang Steel. It is widely known that he received surgery in 2001, in order to eliminate a cyst filled with silica particles mostly composed of sand. We must, then, think of him as a martyr—to Korea's steel industry, to Korea's industrialization, and ultimately to Korea's progress as a nation.

Chairman Emeritus Park Tae-joon of Pohang Steel taught us

the value of sacrifice and service. He taught us what it means to be a patriot. He taught us these things, not through words, but through his actions and his accomplishments. He taught us, and now he has left. It is now time, I think, to channel our admiration for the departed into energy to be used towards true social harmony and the advancement of our nation.

The empty space he leaves feels bigger than ever, in these waning days of 2011 in Korea. We long for the voice of the departed, his deeds. We pray for the well being of his spirit.

The Kyunghyang Shinmun, December 15, 2011.

Jun Sang-in Director of Scholarly Research, Korea Future Studies Association

Research Fellow, Center for North Korean Studies, Korea Institute for National Unification (March 1992-February 1995)
Assistant, Associate, and full Professor, Department of Sociology, Hallym University (March 1995-August 2005)
Member and Vice President, Korean Social History Association (March 1996-present)
Visiting scholar, Department of Sociology, University of Washington, USA (July 2001-August 2002)

Major Publications
Crazy about Apartments (2009)
Talk about Intellectuals of Our Times (2006)
Revisionism Bowing (2001)

시론 | 박태준의 길, 젊은이의 길
Essay | Park Tae-joon's Road, a Young Man's Road

박태준의 길, 젊은이의 길

하노이에서 길을 가리키다

2010년 1월 하순, 박태준은 3박4일 계획으로 베트남 하노이를 방문했다. 마침 하노이 시가지에는 '수도 천 년'의 경축 현수막들이 축제 분위기를 자아내고 있었다. 1010년 리타이또 황제 시절에 처음 수도로 지정된 이래 천 년째 베트남의 중심을 지켜내느라 오욕과 영광을 간직한 하노이. 오욕은 중국, 프랑스, 미국이 남긴 침략의 상처이고, 영광은 그들을 차례로 극복한 자부심이다. 하노이의 기억에 남은 가장 끔찍한 제국주의적 야만의 언어는 무엇일까? "하노이를 석기시대로 돌려주겠다"는 미국 장군 커티스 르메이의 호언장담일 것이다. 항미전쟁 동안 저주와 다름없는 미군의 무자비한 폭격에 거의 석기시대로 돌려졌던 베트남의 수도, 그 중심가에 1996년 현대식 특급호텔이 들어섰다. '하노이 대우 호텔'이다. 여든세 살의 박태준은 한국 경제계의 후배 김우중이 세운 호텔에 여장을 풀었다. 하노이 대우 호텔의 문을 열던 때만 해도 "세계는 넓고 할 일은 많다"며 글로벌경영의 기세를 펼치는 김우중에게 그 입지를 추천한 이가 바로 박태준이었다. 왜 그는 후배에게 하노이의 요지를 추천할 수 있었을까?

박태준이 생애 처음 하노이(베트남)를 방문한 때는 1992년 11월 하순이었다. 그의 인생으로는 홀가분하고도 쓸쓸한 계절이었다. 1968년 4월 1일에서 1992년 10월 1일까지, 포항제철소와 광양제철소를 완공하여 연산 2천100만 톤 조강체제를 갖춤으로써 장장 사반세기에 걸친 제철의 대역사를 성공리에 마치고 스스로 세계 최고 철의 용상(龍床)을 물러나 포스코 명예회장으로서

Park Tae-joon: A Memorial Issue **67**

중국과 동남아 진출을 적극 모색하는 그의 기분은 매우 홀가분했을 것이며, 머지않아 한국 최고 권력자로 등극할 김영삼이 몸소 광양까지 찾아와 12월 대선의 '선거대책위원장'을 맡아달라고 간청했으나 끝내 거절하고 말았으니 서서히 다가오는 정치적 보복을 예견하는 그의 기분은 자못 씁쓸했을 것이다. 한국 정부와 베트남 정부의 수교 합의(1992년 12월 22일)가 한창 무르익고 있던 그때, 박태준은 정장 차림으로 하노이 바딘광장부터 찾았다.

끝 모를 줄을 이루며 광장을 에워싼 인민들, 호찌민(胡志明) 영묘의 좌우를 지키는 붉은 바탕의 흰 글씨들. 그의 궁금증을 통역이 풀어줬다. "매일 저렇게 많은 참배객들이 찾아옵니다. 먼 시골에 사는 베트남 인민들도 호 아저씨 영묘 참배를 평생의 소원으로 삼는답니다." 이미 박태준은 '호 아저씨'란 호칭에 익숙해져서 '아저씨'에 담긴 탈권위적 친화감을 느끼고 있었다. 통역이 손가락으로 정면의 선명한 두 문장을 가리켰다. "호 아저씨는 우리 사업 속에 영원히 살아 있다. 베트남 공산당이여 영원하라."

박태준은 묵묵히 호찌민을 추모했다. 청렴하며 지혜롭고, 유연하며 단호했던 지도자. '자유와 독립보다 더 중요한 것은 없다.' 그는 기억했다. 호찌민의 그 말을, 그 절대적 가치를 위해 항불전쟁과 항미전쟁에 승리한 베트남 인민의 위대한 사투를, 그리고 한국이 냉전체제의 최전선을 통과하며 산업화에 몰두한 시절에 '월남 파병'을 감행했던 뼈저린 과거의 불행을. 그래서 베트남 땅에 첫발을 디딘 그의 마음은 경건하면서 착잡했다.

1945년 9월 호찌민이 주석단 한가운데 서서 베트남 독립을 선포한 그 자리에 마련된 영묘. 평안히 잠든 노인처럼 누운 고인에게 명복을 빌어준 박태준은 가장 청렴했던 지도자의 시신을 영원히 부패하지 않게 모셔둔 성역을 나서며 문득 묘한 생각에 잠겼다. 한국에 돌아가서 가장 부패한 정치지도자의 시신을 영원히 부패하지 않게 안치한다면, 그것이 한국 정치인들의 부패 예방에 어느 정도 효과를 낼 수 있을까?

바딘광장을 떠난 박태준은 베트남 최고지도자와 만났다. '도이 모이'라는 개방정책을 이끄는 두 모이 당서기. 박태준은 그의 인품과 영혼에서 호찌민의 제자다운 냄새를 맡을 수 있었다. 그것은 인민에 대한 사랑과 국가경제 발전에 대한 순수한 염원이었다. 박태준은 생각하고 있었다. 경제발전에 먼저 성공한 한국이 베트남에 투자하는 것은 베트남에 대한 한국의 엄청난 빚을 갚아나가는 길이며 한국의 도덕성을 높이는 길이라고. 주인은 경제개발 방향에 대해 묻고, 손님은 한국 경험의 장단점을 간추렸다. 손님이 보반 키엣 총리와 만나기로 약속한 시각에는 주인이 환히 여유를 부렸다. "내가 미리 말해 뒀어요. 늦어도 좋으니 우리 이야기를 계속합시다." "결례가 안 되게 해놓으셨다면 안심하겠습니다." "내가 왜 이리 늦게 당신을 만나게 되었는지 원망스럽군요." 그리고 구체적 현안을 다뤘다. 연산 20만 톤 규모의 전기로 공장, 파이프공장, 하노이-하이퐁 고속도로 건설 등이 화제에 올랐다. 베트남으로 진출하려는 박태준의 선구적 구상. 문제는 한국의 정치권력이었다. 과연 그것이 그에게 포스코 경영의 권한을 언제까지 보장할 것인가?

박태준과 두 모이의 만남은 그의 하노이 대우 호텔 입지 추천으로 이어졌지만, 정작 두 사람의 재회는 이뤄지지 못했다. 그의 베트남 구상도 무산되어야 했다. 이듬해 3월 그가 정치적 박해를 받아 기약 없는 해외 유랑에 올랐던 것이다.

다시 박태준의 베트남 방문이 이뤄진 것은 첫 방문으로부터 꼬박 12년이 지난 2004년 11월이었다. 사이공(호치민)을 찾은 일흔일곱 살의 포스코 명예회장은 1993년 3월부터 1997년 5월까지 이어진 자신의 해외 유랑과 더불어 물거품처럼 사라진 '베트남 구상'을 회상했다. '그때 그런 일만 없었더라면 이 땅에 많은 일들을 하고 우리의 역사적 부채도 갚고 도덕성도 높이는 일거삼득을…….' 12년 전 베트남 지도자들과 공유했던 희망과 약속이 희수(喜壽)의 영혼에 회한을 일으켰다. 그는 그들과 재회하고 싶었다. 두 모이 전 서기장은 너무 늙어서 거동이 불편하다며 "진정 그리웠다"는 인사만 전해왔다. 박태준은 예를 차렸다. "너무 늦어서 미안합니다. 저에게 사연이 있었습니다." 다행히 보반 키엣 전 총리는 만날 수 있었다. 어느덧 여든 고개를 넘어선 혁명과 개혁의 노인이 말했다. "왜 이제야 왔소?" 늙은 손님이 답했다. "미안합니다." 두 노인의 포옹과 악수는 길어졌다.

박태준은 젊은 지도자들도 만났다. 매년 7퍼센트 경제성장을 거듭하여 연간 철강소비량이 500만 톤에 이르는 베트남. 그가 오앙 트렁 하이(47세) 공업부 장관에게 충고했다. "이제 제철소를 세우시오. 조선, 자동차 같은 철강 연관 산업이 일어서야 중진국에 들 수 있소." 그의 생각은 포스코 후배 경영진에 의해 '포스코의 베트남 냉연공장 건설과 일관제철소 건설 프로젝트'로 구체화되었다. 붕따우의 냉연공장은 2009년 10월에 준공되었으나, 아쉽게도 일관제철소 프로젝트는 베트남 당국과 포스코의 의견 차이로 중단되고 말았다.

2007년 6월 박태준은 세 번째로 베트남을 찾았다. 몇몇 동지들과 보름 일정으로 돌아볼 동남아, 홍콩, 중국 여행의 첫 기착지가 호치민이었다. 이번에는 특별한 목적이 없었다. 베트남의 변화와 발전 양상에 대한 궁금증을 직접 풀어보려는 방문이었다. 식사 때마다 그는 베트남의 독한 소주를 반주로 곁들였다. "아주 좋은 술"이라며 기분 좋게 여러 잔을 거푸 마시는 그의 모습은 아직 천진한 청년 같았다.

생애 네 번째로 베트남을 방문한 박태준이 하노이 대우 호텔에 묵는 목적은 베트남 쩨 출판사가 번역 출간한 자신의 평전 『철의 사나이 박태준』 출판 기념회 참석과 국립하노이대학 특별 강연이었다. 출판기념회는 1월 28일 저녁 하노이 대우 호텔에서 열렸다. 베트남의 고위 관료들과 대학 교수들과 철강업계 인사들, 베트남 주재 한국 대사를 비롯해 현지 한국 기업인들이 식장을 가득 메웠다. 나는 저자(著者)로서 인사를 했다.

"저는 한국에서 제법 유명한 '58개띠'입니다. 한국전쟁 후 베이비붐 세대지요. 고향 마을은 바로 포스코의 포항제철소가 들어선 곳입니다. 그 마을을 열 살 때 떠나야 했습니다. 포스코 때문이었지요. 그때 어른들은 스스로를 '철거민'이라 불렀습니다. 그 말은 고향을 상실하는 쓸쓸함과 뿔뿔이 흩어지는 서러움을 담았습니다. 원망과 저항의 감정도 묻었을 겁니다. 마을에는 세계에서 제일 큰 규모였을 고아원이 있었습니다. 벽안의 프랑스 신부가 이끄는 예수성심회의 백오십여 수녀들이 전쟁의 폐허와 절대적 빈곤이 양산한 고아들 오백여 명을 돌보았던 겁니다. 암수 두 그루 커다란 은행나무가 정문을 지켜주는 아담한 성당에서는 일요일마다 청아한 성가가 울려 나왔지만, 마을 분교(分校)에는 교실이 두 칸밖에 없어서 1, 2, 3, 4학년을 이부제로 쪼개야 했습니다. 저의 짝꿍도 고아였습니다. 헤어진 뒤로 다시는 만나지 못했습니다.

어른들이 낡은 트럭에 남루한 이삿짐을 싣는 즈음, 마을에는 '제선공장', '제강공장', '열연공장'이라는 깃발들이 나부끼고 있었습니다. 저게 뭐지? 저는 그저 시큰둥하게 허공의 그것들을 노려보았습니다. 그런데 아주 나중에 듣게 됐지만, 제가 태어난 이듬해 12월 24일, 그러니까 1959년 크리스마스이브, 런던 거리에는 크리스마스트리들이 찬란히 반짝이고 구세주 찬미의 노래들이 넘쳐났을 그날, 영국 BBC가 〈a far Cry〉라는 40분짜리 다큐멘터리를 방영했다고 합니다. 런던에서는 머나먼 한국, 그 〈머나먼 울음〉은 굶주리고 헐벗은 한국 아이들의 비참한 실상을 보여주는 것이었지요. 그 아이들이 바로 저와 친구들이었다고 해도 틀리지 않습니다. 인간이라면 눈물 없이는 보지 못했을 다큐멘터리의 마지막 말이 무엇인지 아십니까? '이 아이들에게 희망은 있는가?', 이것이었습니다. 그 절망적이었던 질문에 대한 답변의 하나로서, 쉰 살을 넘어선 제가 보시다시피 조금 살진 얼굴에 점잖은 신사복을 입고 여기에 서 있다는 사실을 말씀드리고 싶습니다.

제가 고향을 떠날 무렵에 나부끼고 있었던 포스코의 깃발들이 한국의 희망이요 저희 세대의 희망이었다는 사실을 깨달은 것은 그로부터 이십 년쯤 지난 뒤였습니다. 그리고 저는 서른아홉 살에 박태준 선생과 처음 만나게 되었고, 2004년 12월에 한국어판 『박태준』 평전을 펴냈습니다. 그 책은 2005년에 중국어로 번역 출판되었고, 오늘 이렇게 베트남어판이 나왔습니다. 작가가 왜 전기문학을 써야 하는가? 전기문학은 왜 있어야 하는가?

고난의 시대는 영웅을 창조하고, 영웅은 역사의 지평을 개척합니다. 그러나 인간의 얼굴과 체온을 상실한 영웅은 청동이나 대리석으로 빚은 우상처럼 공적(功績)의 표상으로 전락하게 됩니다. 이 쓸쓸한 그의 운명을 막아내려는 길목을 지키는 일, 그를 인간의 이름으로 불러내서 인간으로 읽어내고 드디어 그가 인간의 이름으로 살아가게 하는 일, 이것이 전기문학의 중요한 존재 이유의 하나라고, 저는 생각합니다.

베트남에 여러 종류의 『호찌민』 전기가 출간된 사정도 다르지 않을 것입니다. 저는 아무리 긴 세월이 흐르더라도 저의 주인공이 어떤 탁월한 위업을 남긴 인물로만 기억되는 것을 강력히 거부합니다. 그의 고뇌, 그의 정신, 그의 투쟁이 반드시 함께 기억되어야 한다는 것입니다. 이것이 국가, 민족, 시대라는 거대한 짐을 짊어지고 필생을 완주한 인물에 대한 동시대인과 후세의 기본예의라고 확신합니다.”

이튿날 오전 11시, 국립하노이대학 강당에는 총장과 보직 교수들, 오백여 명의 대학생들이 앉아 있었다. 순차 통역으로 한 시간 넘게 진행된 박태준의 연설은 여든세 살의 노인이 아니라 현역 지도자처럼 패기와 열정이 넘쳐났으며, 베트남과 한국, 아니 세계의 청년을 향해 던지는 그의 사상이 응축돼 있었다. 그래서였을까. 젊은 청중은 강연을 마친 노인을 향해 환호성을 지르고 열렬한 기립박수를 보냈다. 통역을 맡았던 여성(교수)이 젖은 눈빛으로 조심스레 고백했다. “빌 클린턴 전 미국 대통령, 장쩌민 전 중국 주석, 그리고 얼마 전에는 이명박 한국 대통령이 하노이대학에서 강연을 했고, 저는 그분들의 말씀을 경청했습니다. 그러나 박태준 선생의 강연처럼 저의 가슴을 울려주진 못했습니다.”

과연 박태준의 어떤 말들이 베트남 젊은 엘리트들의 영혼에 잔잔한 파문을 일으키고 푸른 가슴을 일렁이게 했을까?

“인간의 큰 미덕은 인생과 공동체의 행복에 대해 사색하고 고뇌하며, 실천의 길을 모색하는 것입니다. 내가 이 자리에 선 이유는, 한국의 경제개발 경험을 말하려는 것이 아닙니다. 파란만장한 격동을 헤치고 나온 경험을 바탕으로, 젊은 엘리트 여러분과 더불어 다시 한 번 인생과 역사를 성찰해 보자는 것입니다. 역사에는 특정한 세대가 감당하는 시대적 고난이 있습니다. 그것은 개개인의 인생에 심대한 영향을 끼치고, 그 세대의 운명이 되기도 합니다."

이렇게 시작한 그의 연설은 한국과 베트남의 20세기에 대한 비교와 특정한 세대의 운명에 대한 생각으로 나아갔다.

"나는 1927년에 태어났습니다. 한국에서 나의 세대는 일본 식민지에서 유년 시절과 학창 시절을 보내고, 청년 시절에 해방을 맞았습니다. 그러나 한반도는 불행했습니다. 세계적 냉전체제의 희생양으로 남북분단이 확정된 것이었습니다. 분단은 곧 처절한 전쟁으로 이어지고, 그 전쟁이 다시 휴전선이라는, 지구상에서 가장 살벌한 대결의 철책을 만들었습니다. 그때 한반도에 남은 것은 민족 간의 적개심과 국토의 폐허, 국가의 빈곤과 인민의 굶주림, 그리고 부패의 창궐이었습니다.

한국전쟁에 청년 장교로 참전하여 '우연히, 운이 좋아서' 살아남은 나는 인생과 조국의 미래에 대해 숙고하지 않을 수 없었습니다. 폐허의 국토를 어떻게 재건할 것인가? 우리 민족을 천형(天刑)처럼 억눌러온 절대빈곤을 어떻게 극복할 것인가? 미국과 서구가 자랑하는 근대화를 어떻게 이룩할 것인가? 이 시대를 나는 어떻게 살아야 하는가? 엄중하게 좌우명부터 영혼에 새겼습니다. '짧은 인생을 영원 조국에!' '절대적 절망은 없다.' 돌이켜보면, 좌우명은 필생의 나침반이었습니다. 지금 이 순간에도 그것은 흔들리지 않습니다. 그것을 따라 걸어온 내 삶의 여정(旅程)에 대해 어떤 후회도 없습니다.

한국정부가 경제개발의 깃발을 올린 1961년, 한국은 1인당 국민소득 70달러로 세계에서 가장 빈곤한 국가였습니다. 당시 경제개발계획에 참여했던 나는 1968년부터 종합제철소 건설과 경영의 책임을 맡았습니다. 자본과 자원이 없고, 경험과 기술이 없는 전무(全無)의 상태에서 포스코라는 종합제철소를 시작하여, 7년쯤 지나서 어느 정도 기반을 잡은 다음, 나는 동지들에게 이렇게 말했습니다. '우리 세대는 순교자처럼 희생하는 세대다. 우리 세대는 다음 세대의 행복과 21세기 조국의 번영을 위해 순교자적으로 희생하는 세대다.' 우리에게 지상과제는 '조국 근대화'였습니다. 그것은 나의 세대가 짊어진 폐허와 빈곤, 부패와 혼란을 극복하기 위한 시대적 좌표였고, 마침내 우리는 근대화에 성공했습니다. 시련의 시대를 영광의 시대로 창조한 것이었다고 자부합니다. 그러나 나의 세대는 후세에 엄청난 과제도 넘겨야 했습니다. 바로 남북분단입니다. 남북화해와 평화통일, 이 짐을 다음 세대에 넘겨주게 되어 참으로 가슴 아픕니다.

지난 백여 년 동안, 베트남에도 각 세대가 감당한 시대적 고난이 있었습니다. 편의상 여러분의 할아버지와 할머니 세대, 아버지와 어머니 세대, 그리고 여러분 세대, 이렇게 삼대로 나누어 봅시다.

여러분의 할아버지와 할머니 세대는 '자유와 독립보다 더 중요한 것은 없다'는 호찌민 선생의 말씀을 실현한 세대입니다. 헤아릴 수 없는 희생과 고통을 넘어서야 했지만, 당신들의 숙명적인 비원이었던 자유와 독립을 쟁취했습니다. 그러나 1954년 7월에 베트남은 북위 17도선에서 분단되었습니다. 그때 어린 아이였을 여러분의 아버지들과 어머니들은, 통일로 가는 기나긴 전쟁이 자기 세대의 운명이 될 줄은 몰랐을 것입니다. 그분들은 자기 세대의 참혹한 운명을 감당했으며, 드디어 1975년 4월에 종전과 통일을 선언할 수 있었습니다. 그분들 세대는 휴식을 누릴 여가도 없었습니다. 전쟁에서 살아남은 사람들에게는 조국재건의 새로운 책무가 기다리고 있었기 때문입니다. 등소평의 중국이 개방의 길을 선도하고, 베트남은 1986년에 개방의 문을 열었습니다. 그것은 일대 혁신이었습니다. 모든 혁신은 다소간 혼란과 시행착오를 초래하기 마련이지만, 나는 베트남 지도부가 현명한 선택을 했다고 판단합니다. 이 자리에서 언급하자니 슬픈 일입니다만, 개방을 거부한 북한의 오늘이 그것을 반증해 줍니다.

베트남은 한국보다 종전이 늦어진 그만큼 경제개발의 출발이 늦어졌습니다. 그러나 베트남은 통일국가고, 한국은 분단국가입니다. 이 자리의 '여러분 세대'는 선배 세대로부터 '자유와 독립의 통일국가'라는 위대한 기반을 물려받았습니다. 그 기반 위에서 '여러분 세대'의 시대적 좌표가 설정되어야 합니다. 현재 한국의 젊은 세대에게 '평화통일과 일류국가 완성'이라는 피할 수 없는 운명이 주어져 있다면, 베트남의 젊은 세대에게는 '경제부흥과 일류국가 완성'이라는 피할 수 없는 운명이 주어져 있습니다. 통일 문제를 고려할 경우에는, 한국의 젊은 세대가 베트남의 젊은 세대보다 더 무거운 운명을 짊어졌다고 하겠습니다."

두 나라 젊은 세대의 시대적 좌표를 제시한 그가 더 목청을 높여서 역설한 것은 부패척결과 자신감이었다.

"세계 어느 나라를 막론하고, 한 나라가 일어서는 과정에서 무엇보다 중요한 전제조건은 지도층과 엘리트 계층이 부패하지 않고 자신감을 바탕으로 분명한 비전을 제시하는 것입니다. 물질적 유혹에 약한 것이 인간입니다. 인간은 강철처럼 강인하기도 하지만, 땡볕에 내놓은 생선처럼 부패하기도 쉽습니다. 부패는 인간 정신의 문제입니다. 지도층이나 엘리트 계층에 속한 인간이 부패하지 않는 것은 자기 정신과의 부단한 투쟁의 결실입니다. 역사 속의 모든 위인들은 끊임없이 자기 정신과 투쟁했습니다. 여러분이 훌륭한 지도자로 성장할 꿈을 간직하고 있다면, 지금부터 자기 정신과의 투쟁을 시작해야 합니다.

나는 지도층과 엘리트 계층이 자신감을 바탕으로 당대의 비전을 제시해야 한다는 주문도 했습니다. 그러나 자기 인생의 미래를 설계하지 않은 사람은 지도자가 될 수 없을 뿐만 아니라, 우연한 기회에 지도자가 된다고 해도 당대의 비전을 제시할 수 없습니다. 먼저, 개개인이 10년 뒤의 자기 모습을 그려보라는 충고를 하고 싶습니다. 여러분은 10년 뒤의 자기 모습을 그려놓고 있습니까? 만약 그려놓았다면, 치밀하고도 정열적으로 그 길을 가야 합니다. 만약 그려놓지 않았다면, 몇날 며칠을 지새우더라도 10년 뒤의 자기 모습부터 그려야 합니다. 개개인의 비전이 모여서 국가와 시대의 새 지평을 열게 된다는 사실을 명심하기 바랍니다.

거듭 강조하지만, 개발도상국이 경제발전을 추진하는 과정에서 가장 중요한 힘은 지도층이 부패하지 않는 것과 인민의 자신감입니다. 베트남에는 20세기의 세계 지도자 중에 가장 청렴했던 호찌민 선생이 국부로 계시고, 프랑스와 미국을 물리친 자부심과 자신감이 있습니다. 문제는 그 위대한 정신적 유산을, 국가의 부강과 인민의 행복을 성취하기 위한 저력으로 활용하는 일입니다. 모든 역사에는 기복이 있지만, 지도층과 인민이 위대한 정신적 유산을 공유하고 그 바탕 위에서 손잡고 나아간다면, 반드시 일류국가를 만들 것이라고 확신합니다."

일류주의, 그 고투의 길

평전 『박태준』을 쓴 작가로서 내가 지켜본 박태준의 최고 매력은 무엇인가? 지장, 덕장, 용장의 리더십을 두루 갖춘 그의 탁월한 능력인가? 흔히들 그것을 꼽는다. 나도 흔쾌히 인정한다. 그러나 그것을 최고 매력으로 꼽진 않는다. 내 시선이 포착한 그의 최고 매력은 '정신적 가치'를 가치의 최상에 두는 삶의 태도였다. 그의 삶은 늘 통속을 거부했다. 통속적 계산을 경멸하는 작가 만큼 치열하게 자기 신념의 정신적 자계(磁界)에서 벗어나지 않았다. 주인공의 요청이나 부탁이 아니었건만 작가 스스로 평전을 쓰게 만드는 그 매력을, 그는 나에게 연인의 향기처럼 풍겼다. 내가 그를 처음 만난 것은 1997년 초여름이었다. 그로부터 15년쯤 지나서 프랑스 《르몽드》가 "한국의 영웅이 떠나다"라고 박태준의 부음을 알린 2011년 12월 13일까지, 나는 그와 숱한 시간을 함께 보내며 그의 생애와 사상과 추억에 대한 온갖 대화를 나누는 '복된 기쁨'을 누렸다. 내가 그의 평전을 쓰는 작업은 인생의 황혼에 접어든 노인이 젊은이에게 제시하는 삶의 새로운 길을 따라 걸어가며 사색에 잠기는 것과 비슷한 일이었다.

나는 포항제철소가 들어선 영일만 갯마을에서 태어나 자랐다고 밝혔지만, 작가의식으로 박태준이란 이름에 깊은 관심을 기울인 때는 서른 살을 훨씬 넘긴 1990년대 초반의 어느 날부터였다. 그때까지 나는 그와 한 번쯤 악수를 나누기는커녕 먼발치에서나마 얼굴을 본 적도 없었다. 나에게 그는 신문이나

텔레비전이 알려주는 존재였다. 그런데 어쩌다 내가 그를 주목했을까. 물론 포스코에 의한 '철거민'이요 '실향민'이라는, 포스코를 바라보는 삐딱했던 시각이 엔간히 철들었다고 할 이립(而立)을 넘어선 뒤로는 오히려 남다르게 포스코를 들여다보는 태생적 인연으로 바뀌었던 것이라는 점을 빼놓을 수 없을 테지만, 무엇보다 중요한 것은 내 세계관의 조정이었다.

내가 이립한 즈음엔 고르바초프가 지각변동의 구심점 역할을 하는 시절이었다. 동서독 분단의 장벽을 무너뜨린 독일시민이 베를린 브란덴부르크 문에 운집해 축제를 여는 밤, 그는 미모의 아내와 나란히 나타나서, "역사는 늦게 오는 자를 처벌한다"고 선언했다. 그때 나의 내면에도 무엇인가 꿍음이 일어났다. 그것은 '한국적 1980년대'를 지탱해온 사회주의적 전망과 이상이 무너지는 소리였다. 그 뒤 현존 사회주의체제의 좌절을 주제로 삼은 사회과학 논문들이 제출되었다. 그러나 나는 작가이기에 인간에서 답을 구했고, 드디어 이렇게 정리했다.

〈인간은 사회주의를 실현할 수 있는 천부적 윤리의 자질이 형편없이 부족한 존재이다. 이데올로기가 인간조건을 생산하는 것이 아니라, 인간조건이 이데올로기를 창조한다. 인민이 체제를 위해 복무하는 것이 아니라, 체제가 인민을 위해 복무해야 한다.〉

우연한 계기였다. 내 안에 고이는 억울함을 분출하듯 박태준 옹호의 칼럼을 쓰게 되었다. 1996년 여름으로, 그와의 첫 악수보다 일 년쯤 앞선 무렵이었는데, 그것은 해외 유랑중인 박태준에 대한 정치적 사면을 만지작거리는 청와대 주인을 향한 고언(苦言)이었다.

〈설령 박태준의 정치적 과오가 63빌딩에 들어간 철근의 무게와 맞먹는다 하더라도 그가 포스코를 통해 한국 현대사에 이바지한 공적은 63빌딩을 63개나 건설할 철근의 무게와 맞먹는다.〉

아직은 박태준을 제대로 공부하지 않은 상태의 주장이었지만 뒷날에 그의 평전을 쓰는 동안 내가 틀리지 않았다는 점을 확인할 수 있었다. 대체 내가 본 박태준은 어떤 인간이었는가? 그의 최고 매력으로 나는 정신적 가치를 최상 가치로 받드는 삶의 태도를 꼽았지만, 실제로 그의 영혼은 강철같은 정신(신념)의 덩어리였다. 모든 공사(公事)를 철저히 그것으로 관장하고 처리했으며, 그것으로 물질적 유혹을 제압하고 배격했다. 그의 솔선수범이란 그것에 당연히 따르는 일종의 부수적 현상에 불과해 보였다. 2010년 1월 그가 국립하노이대학에서 '부패척결의 청렴한 리더십'을 역설한 것은 필생에 걸친 그 실천궁행의 당당한 웅변이었다.

포스코 착공의 장면에서 그가 일으킨 감동적인 일화는 저 유명한 '제철보국'과 '우향우'이다. 어려운 단어가 아니다. 제철보국이란 포항제철을 성공시켜 나라에 보답하자는 것이며, 우향우란 오른쪽으로 돌아 나가자는 군대 제식훈련의 용어이다. 그러나 둘은 박태준의 정신 속에서 짝꿍으로 맺어지자 어마어마한 정신적 무장으로 거듭나서 포스코를 '성공의 고지'로 밀어 올리는 원동력이 되었다.

포항제철 1기 연산 103만 톤 조강체제 완공의 종잣돈은 대일청구권자금(일제식민지 배상금)의 일부였다. 박태준은 그 돈의 성격을 '조상의 혈세(피의 대가)'라 규정했다. 조상의 피의 대가로 세우는 국가적 민족적 숙원사업인 포항제철을 어떻게 실패할 수 있는가? 실패하면 조상과 국가와 민족에 죄를 짓는 것이니 죽는다고 해서 용서받을 수 있는 것도 아니지만, 그래도 실패하면 우리는 목숨을 버려야 한다. 그때는 우향우 하자. 영일만 모래벌판에서 우향우 하면 시퍼런 바다, 그 바다에 빠져 죽자. 이것이 '우향우'다. 이렇게 강렬한 정신운동에 감히 부패가 파고들 틈이 생기겠는가. 그래서 나는 평전에 썼다.

〈박태준은 비장했고 사원들은 뭉클했다. 그의 외침은 가슴과 가슴을 타고 번져나갔다. '조상의 혈세'는 민족주의를 자극했다. '우향우'는 애국주의를 고양했다. 그것은 '제철보국' 이념에 자양분이 되었다.〉

박태준의 강철 같은 정신의 덩어리, 그 핵은 무엇인가? 그의 좌우명이 일러 준다. '짧은 인생을 영원 조국에', 이것이다. 그는 늘 일류를 희원했다. 포항제철이 첫 쇳물을 생산하기 전인 1969년에 발간한 사보(社報) 《쇳물》 창간호에 '무엇이든지 첫째가 됩시다!' 라는 휘호를 만년필로 힘차게 써준 사람, 쇳물이 나올지 안 나올지 모르는 때에 구성원들을 향하여 세계 일등을 꿈꾸자고 외친 박태준이었다. 그리고 그는 25년 동안 불철주야의 노심초사를 바쳐 마침내 초심의 맹세대로 포스코를 세계 최고 철강기업으로 성장시켰다. 그의 일류란 포스코가 보여주는 총체적 일류이며, 그의 일류국가도 포스코가 보여주는 것과 같은 총체적 일류국가였다.

왜 박태준은 일류 또는 최고수준을 고집하며 추구하고 일류국가를 희원했는가? 왜 그는 일류주의와 일류국가주의를 잠시도 놓지 못했는가? 이것은 그가 관통해온 시대적 고난과 분리할 수 없는 문제이다. 그의 일생은 우리 현대사의 한복판을 꿰뚫은 여정이었다.

1927년 부산 기장의 조그만 갯마을에서 태어난 박태준. 어머니의 손을 잡고 아버지를 찾아가는 유년의 도일(渡日) 뱃길에 생애 최초로 부관연락선이라는 철로 만든 근대적 괴물(문명)에게 실존을 의탁한다. 영특하고 달리기와 수영을 잘하는 아이의 귀에는 자주 "센징"이라는 말이 들려왔다. 그러나 모욕은 의식의 씨앗이 되었다. 이것은 일등을 해야만 차별을 덜 받는다는 방어의식과 저항의식으로 돋아나 시나브로 일류의식으로 진화하며 자라났다. 해방이 되어 와세다 대학 기계공학과를 중퇴한 그는 귀향하여 '건국에는 건군이 중요하다'며 육사를 택하고, 거기서 10년 연상의 박정희를 은사로 만난다. 그리고 청년 장교로서 6·25전쟁을 맞아 철원에서 서울까지 밀려나는 사흘 만에 자기 연대의 중대장 12명 중 10명이 전사한 가운데 구사일생 멀쩡히 생존한 중대장으로서 포항까지 후퇴했다가 거꾸로 청진까지 북진하지만 야전병원에서 급성맹장염 수술을 받은 몸으로 1·4후퇴의 일원이 된다. 휴전 후 육군대학을 수석으로 졸업한 그는 당시의 부패한 우리 군대에서 지독한 '딸깍발이'로 손꼽히는 대령이었다. 일절 부정부패와 타협하지 않았다. 결코 용납하지도 않았다. 그 소문이 박정희의 고막을 건드렸다. 이것은 거사를 획책하는 박정희가 1960년 부산군수기지사령부 사령관으로 내려갈 때 그를 인사참모로 발탁하는 인연으로 맺어지고, 5·16정부에서 국가재건최고회의 의장 비서실장과 상공담당 최고위원을 역임한 그는 박정희의 정치참여 제안을 거절한 결과로 대한중석 사장을 거쳐 마치 오래 기다린 어떤 필연이 성사되는 것처럼 한국산업화의 견인차가 되는 포스코를 맡는다. 무에서 유를 창조한 포스코, 절명의 위기는 요람에 들이닥쳤다. 1969년 2월 미국, 영국, 프랑스 등 서방 5개국 철강사들이 포스코에 대한 자금과 기술을 책임지마고 했던 약속을 세계은행(IBRD)의 '한국 종합제철 프로젝트는 시기상조'라는 예견에 따라 헌신짝처럼 팽개친 것이었다. 자본주의의 비즈니스 시스템은 가혹하며 비정했고, 갓 태어난 포스코는 죽어야 했다. 그의 오른팔 황경로(제2대 포스코 회장 역임)가 사장의 비밀지시를 받들어 '회사 청산 계획'을 세워야 하는 상황이었다. 그러나 그는 비상한 돌파구를 찾아냈다. 대일청구권자금 일부 전용의 아이디어, 이에 대한 박정희의 동의와 지원. 박태준은 일본 각료들과 철강업계 지도자들을 설득해서 기어이 협력을 받아낸다. 영일만 모래벌판에 아기무덤으로 남을 뻔했던 갓난아기 포스코가 기적처럼 회생한 것이었다.

포스코를 세계 일류기업으로 성장시킨 명성은 주인공에게 정치참여의 문을 세 번 열어줬다.

첫 번째, 1980년. 박정희의 죽음은 포스코라는 한 기업의 처지에서는 정치적 외풍을 막아주던 튼튼한 울타리가 사라진 대사건이었다. 포스코의 성공요인에는 박태준의 리더십을 맨 먼저 꼽는다. 하버드 대학교, 스탠포드 대학교, 서울대학교, 미쓰비시 종합연구소 등이 학문적으로 규명한 사실이다. 그러나 혼자의 힘으로 리더십을 맘껏 발휘할 수 있었을까. 나는 이렇게 보았다. 〈박정희는 박태준의 순수하고 뜨거운 애국적 사명감만은 '범할 수 없는 처녀성'처럼 옹호했다. 정치권력의 방면으로 기웃거리지 않고 당겨도 단호히 뿌리친 그의 기개를 높이 보았다. 여기엔 한 인간과 한 인간으로서, 한 사내와 한 사내로서 오직 두 사람만이 온전히 알아차릴 수 있는 서로의 빛깔과 향기가 있었을 것이다. 이러한 박정희와 박태준의 독특한 인간관계는 박태준이 자신의 리더십과 사명감을 신명나게 발현할 수 있는 '양호한 정치적 환경'을 조성해 주었다.〉 십여 년에 걸쳐 한결같이 듬직했던 포스코의 울타리가 느닷없이 사라진 암담한 시기에 새 정치권력이 박태준을 불렀고, 그는 자신이 권력에 들어가서 포스코의 울타리가 되겠다는 각오를 앞세워 정치에 발을 들였다.

두 번째, 1990년. 김영삼, 김종필까지 하나로 엮으려는 기획을 마친 노태우가 포스코에 거의 전념하고 있는 전국구 국회의원 박태준을 여당 대표로 끌어들였다. 그는 사양했으나 노태우는 포스코 회장의 인사권자였다. '차출 당하여' 올라간 무대는 1992년 10월 차출 당했던 이가 스스로 정계를 떠나는 것으로 막을 내린다.

세 번째, 1997년. 정치적 박해의 해외 유랑을 끝낸 박태준이 포항 국회의원 보궐선거에 무소속 출마했다. 이번에는 순전히 자기의지였다. 그의 선택은 김대중·김종필과 연대해 헌정사상 초유의 수평적 정권교체를 이룩하고, 6·25전쟁 후 최대 국란이라 불린 외환위기 극복을 진두지휘하게 된다.

과연 박태준의 '정치적 인생'에 대해 부정적으로 여기는 선입견이 정당한 것인가? 동시대인의 부정적 통념은 크게 두 가지이다. 하나는 '훌륭한 사람이 괜히 정치에 들어가서 몸을 더럽혔다'는 것이다. 이 세평(世評)은 박태준의 '첫 번째 정치참여'를 겨냥한 것으로, 대중의 한국정치에 대한 일반적인 혐오증과 전두환 정권에 대한 거부감을 반영하고 있다. 그러나 그때 상황에서 그가 '차출'을 거부했다면 광양제철소는 성공을 보장할 수 없었을 것이며 포항공과대학교(포스텍)는 탄생할 수도 없었을 것이다. 그러니까 그의 첫 번째 정치참여는 한국산업화의 완성에 결정적으로 기여하고 한국 대학 교육의 신기원을 개척하는 '좋은 권력'으로 재창조되었다. 다른 하나는 '훌륭한 사람이 괜히 정치에 들어가서 고생만 하고 실패 기록을 남겼다'는 것이다. 이 세평은 박태준의 '두 번째 정치참여'를 겨냥한 것으로, 그가 해외 유랑을 떠나야 했던 그 이미지를 반영하고 있다. 그러나 이미지일 뿐이다. 그는 말했다. "나는 YS를 구국의 지도자로 보지 않았다. 내 양심에 따라 그의 제안을 거절했다." 만약 박태준이 속류 정치인이었다면 확실시되는 '권력 2인자'를 노리는 정치적 야합을 택했을 것이다. 정말 바람직한 것은, 박태준을 파트너로 삼겠다는 권력자가 그의 눈에 '일류'로 보여야 했다. 이도저도 아닌 조건 속에서 그는 억압을 예견하며 권력의 유혹을 뿌리쳤다. 경우도 다르고 수준도 다르지만 이 장면은 '박정희와 박태준'의 관계와 '김영삼과 박태준'의 관계가 전혀 다른 차원이라는 증거이기도 하다. 박정희는 자신의 정치적 제안을 거절한 그를 경제 방면으로 불러들인 반면, 김영삼은 그것을 거절한 그에게 보복의 칼을 들이댔다. 묘한 노릇이지만, 그를 붙잡은 경우에 한국은 계량하기 어려운 어마어마한 경제적 이득을 챙겼고, 그를 내쫓은 경우에 한국은 계량하기 어려운 어마어마한 경제적 외교적 손실을 입었다. 박태준의 해외 유랑은 그의 중국 구상, 베트남 구상, 미얀마 구상, IT사업 구상(일본 소프트뱅크 손정의와 손잡고 연간 1조원씩 10년간 투자 계획) 등을 파도에 쓸린 모래성처럼 사라지게 했다. 아마도 역사는 그 국부(國富) 손실의 계산서를 완전히 망각할 것이다. 그리고 박태준의 '세 번째 정치참여', 그가 처음 자발적 의지로 선택한 그것은 한국 민주주의의 성장에 합리적 보수 세력의 힘을 보태고 외환위기 수습의 최고 일꾼으로서 생애 마지막으로 국난극복에 이바지했다.

박태준은 일류국가의 밑거름이 되려는 신념을 '포스텍' 설립에도 눈부시게 발휘했다. 1985년이었다. 새로 시작한 광양제철소 건설에 들어갈 자금도 엄청난 규모였지만 그는 과감하고 단호하게 한국 최초 연구중심대학 설립을 밀어붙인다. 그때 포스코는 국정감사 대상이었다. 정치권부터 반대의견이 높았다. 내부도 마찬가지였다. 그러나 그는 흔들리지 않았다. 이미 유·초·중·고 14개교를 세워 세금의 도움 없이 최고 수준으로 육성한 교육의 신개척자는 오히려 포스텍 설립의 당위성을 알리는 전도사를 자임한다. 과학기술이 일류가 아닌 나라는 일류국가가 될 수 없다. 과학기술은 경제와 국방과 국력의 근본이다. 사람을 통솔하는 것은 곧 사람을 키워내는 일이다. 교육은 천하의 공업(公業)이다. 이들은 박태준 사상의 두 축에서 제철보국과 짝을 이루는 교육보국의 뼈대였다. 2010년 영국《더타임스》가 세계 대학 평가에서 28위로 매긴 포스텍, 그 개교를 앞둔 1986년 8월 27일 그는 포스코 내부에 웅성대는 불만의 소리를 듣고만 있지 않았다.

"회사의 사운을 걸고 시작한 포항공과대학교 설립에 대해 당장 눈앞의 것만 생각한다면, 고생 끝에 얻은 성과가 우리에게 돌아오는 것이 아니라 다른 데에 쓰이는 것이 아닌가 하는 의구심이 발생할 소지가 있다. 그러나 포항공대는 회사 백년대계를 좌우하는 구심점이 되고 국가산업 발전에 기여하며 과학영재를 길러내는 대학이 되어야 한다. 지금 당장의 이윤추구가 아니라 국가 장래를 위해서 큰 힘이 된다고 하는 확신을 우리 스스로 가져야 하며, 특히 간부들이 이에 대한 소신을 가져야 한다."

포스코, 포스텍과 포스코의 학교들을 통해 박태준은 제철보국·교육보국 사상을 실현했다. 일류주의도 실현했다. 또한 그것은 일류국가의 토대구축에 지대한 공헌이 되었다. 과연 그의 인생을 한 문장에 담을 수 있을 것인가? 그의 인생에서 가장 중요한 공적이 포스코이고, 포스코가 한국 산업화의 견인차 역할을 했으며, 산업화의 물적 토대 위에 억세고 질기게 민주화 투쟁이 전개되면서 민주주의가 성장했다는 시대적 진실을 통찰할 경우, 요람의 포스코가 절명의 위기를 극복한 장면은 한국의 운명을 밝은 쪽으로 돌려준 큰 행운이었다. 아무리 축복해도 지나치지 않다. 그 주인공이 박태준이다. 무엇이 그것을 이루었을까? 물론 조국 근대화를 향한 그의 절박한 염원부터 떠올리지만, 아이러니하게도 만약 그가 일본에서 식민지 아이와 청년으로 성장하지 않았더라면, 다시 말해 그가 일본의 실력자들과 상대하는 자리에 통역을 데려가는 처지였다면, 그의 설득은 실패했을 가능성이 높았다. 이러한 전후사정을 나는 평전에서 한 문장에 담아 보았다.

〈생존의 길을 찾아 일본으로 들어간 아버지의 뒤를 좇아 현해탄을 건너갔던 수많은 식민지 아이들 가운데, 사춘기를 벗어난 무렵에 해방된 고향으로 돌아와 빈곤에 허덕이는 신생독립국의 어른으로 성장한 다음, 유소년기에 어쩔 수 없이 익혔던 일본어와 일본문화로써 가장 훌륭하고 가장 탁월하게 조국에 이바지한 인물은 박태준일 것이다.〉

이 문장에다 '신문명과 신학문을 배우기 위해 현해탄을 건너갔던 수많은 청년학도'를 집어넣어도 결론은 달라지지 않을 것이라고, 나는 판단한다.

진정한 극일파(克日派), 그 영혼에 맺힌 말들

일본에 친구들이 많고 일본을 잘 아는 지일파(知日派) 박태준, 그의 일본에 대한 궁극적 목표는 극일이었다. 그는 진정한 극일파(克日派)였다. 그의 시대에서 한국은 어느 분야든 일본을 넘어서야 세계 정상을 바라볼 수 있었다. 극일하지 않으면 그의 일류주의는 성취할 수 없는 허상에 불과한 것이었다. 이에 대한 대표적 사례가 포스코와 신일본제철의 관계이다.

'포항제철소 1기 연산 조강 103만 톤 건설'의 첫 장면에 등장하는 가장 중요한 일본인은 신일본제철 이나야마 요시히로 회장이다. 1969년 여름에 박태준은 도쿄로 날아가 그를 찾아가야만 했고 그의 마음을 열어야만 했다. 대일청구권자금의 일부를 포항제철 건설에 전용하는 과정에는 농업 분야에 배정해둔 그것의 전용에 관한 한일(韓日) 양국 정부의 재합의가 있어야 했고, 그 재합의의 전제 조건으로 일본철강업계 대표들의 포항제철에 대한 기술지원 약속이 이뤄져야 했는데, 이나야마 요시히로는 당시 일본철강업계의 리더였던 것이다.

그해 여름 두 사람의 만남은 이른바 '역사적 회담'으로 남았다. 이나야마 요시히로는 서방 5개국의 KISA(Korea International Steel Associates)에게서 버림받은 포스코의 절명적 위기에 관한 전후사정을 경청했다. 포항제철을 성공시키겠다는 '젊은 사장'의 뜨거운 의지와 순수한 사명감과 비즈니스의 비전에 감동했다. 그는 첫 만남에서 일본철강업계의 전폭적 지원을 약속했다. 이것이 포항제철 건설을 지원하는 일본기술단으로 구체화되고, 그들이 허허벌판 영일만에 들어와 '경험도 기술도 전무한' 한국인들의 제철소 건설현장에서 감독 역할을 맡는 전환점이 되었다. 포스코가 태어난 것은 1968년 4월 1일이었지만 그로부터 꼬박 이태가 지난 1970년 4월 1일에야 박정희 대통령, 김학렬 부총리, 박태준 사장이 영일만에서 착공의 발파 버튼을 누를 수 있었다. 바로 그 2년 동안은 요람의 포스코가 아기무덤으로 남을 뻔했던 위기를 극복해가는 긴박한 드라마의 시간대였다.

신일본제철을 비롯한 일본 엔지니어들로 구성된 일본기술단이 영일만 건설 현장의 감독을 맡은 상황에서 박태준의 기술력 확보에 대한 단기적 목표는 '완공과 동시에 공장을 완전히 우리 손으로 돌리는 것'이었으며, 중기적 목표는 '기술식민지에서 완전히 벗어나 기술자립을 이룩하는 것'이었고, 장기적 목표는 '세계 최고 기술력을 보유하는 것'이었다.

　단기적 목표 달성을 위해 박태준은 어려운 살림살이에도 직원들의 해외연수 비용을 아끼지 않았다. 하나의 기술도 놓치지 말라고 연수생들에게 보내는 그의 당부와 격려는 간곡했다. 이때도 이나야마 요시히로는 깊은 배려를 보여주었다. 박태준의 부탁을 받아 홋가이도 무로랑제철소 전체를 포스코 연수생이 직접 돌려보게 하는 '대담한 선물'을 선사한 것이었다. 실제로 포스코는 톤당 생산단가 경쟁에서 압도적 세계 1위를 달성하며 포항제철소 1기를 완공했을 때(1973년 7월 3일), 포스코 직원들의 손으로 공장 전체를 직접 돌리는 기록을 세웠다. '영일만의 신화'를 쓰기 시작한 것이었다.

　일본기술단이 영일만에서 완전히 철수한 때는 1978년 12월 포항제철소 3기를 완공(연산 조강 550만 톤 체제)한 직후였다. 그들은 글을 남겼다. 〈모든 역경을 딛고 포항제철은 단기간에 일본의 제철소에 버금가는 대규모 선진제철소를 건설하는 데 성공했다. 이 회사가 4기 확장을 마칠 때면 아마도 생산능력과 시설 면에서 세계 최고가 될 것이다. 고급인력과 최고경영자의 탁월한 능력이 합쳐져 포항제철은 머지않아 세계 최고가 될 것이다.〉 포스코가 기술자립을 확신하고 일본기술단이 그것을 인정한 무렵, 중국 덩샤오핑이 신일본제철을 방문해 이나야마 요시히로와 환담을 나누었다. 그 자리에서 중국에 포항제철과 같은 제철소를 지어달라는 덩샤오핑의 요청을 받은 이나야마 회장이, "제철소는 돈으로 짓는 것이 아니라 사람이 짓는데 중국에는 박태준 같은 인물이 없어서 포항제철 같은 제철소를 지을 수 없다"고 답하자, 덩샤오핑은 잠시 생각에 잠겼다가, "그럼 박태준을 수입하면 되겠다"고 말했다. 이것이 유명한 덩샤오핑의 '박태준 수입' 일화이며, 그로부터 십여 년 뒤에 포스코가 중국으로 진출하는 초기에 든든한 힘으로 작용한다.

일본철강업계가 '부메랑 이론'을 들고 나와 포스코를 공격한 것은 1981년 여름이었다. 논리는 간단했다. 한마디로 일본철강업계가 포스코라는 호랑이 새끼를 키웠다는 것이었다. 세계적 불황이 철강업계를 억누르고 있는 상황에서 포항체철소 4기를 완공하고 광양제철소 건설을 추진하는 포스코와 박태준을 향하여 이나야마의 후배들은 '지원 중단'을 결의했다. 그러나 포스코는 이미 기술자립에 들어서 있었다. 그렇다고 '스승'과의 불편한 관계를 지속하는 것은 피차 이로울 것이 없었다. 박태준은 어려운 상황을 전방위적 수단으로 치밀하고 과감하게 돌파해나갔다. 영일만에서 축적한 기술과 경험을 광양만에서 꽃피워 세계 최고 제철소로 설계해 나가는 한편, '선진국이 먼저 가고, 그 뒤를 중진국이 가고, 후진국은 또 그 뒤를 따라가는 것'이라는 순환론으로 신일본제철 사이토 사장을 몰아세우고, 일선에서 은퇴한 이나야마 회장을 움직여 후배들을 타이르게 하고, 광양제철소 설비구매에 대해 유럽 철강업계와 먼저 협의하는 '사업적 방법'으로 일본철강업계를 자극하여 자중지란이 일어나게 만들었다. 광양제철소 설비계약이 진행될 즈음, 일본철강업계는 스스로 부메랑을 거둬들였다.

　　세계 최고 기술력 확보라는 장기적 목표를 광양제철소 완공과 더불어 성취하고 있을 때, 박태준은 그 '순환론'을 유감없이 실천한다. 1980년대 후반 들어 현대적 제철소 건설에 후발주자로 뛰어든 중국 철강업계에 업무 매뉴얼까지 제공한 것이었다. 그는 걱정하는 후배들에게 말했다. "피할 수 없는 도리다. 우리는 더 좋은 기술로 더 앞으로 나가야지." 이를 실천하는 것처럼 포스코가 보여준 '세계 최고 기술력'의 하나는 1992년 박태준의 지시로 시작한 '파이넥스 공법에 의한 쇳물 생산 상용화 연구'를 15년 만인 2007년에 세계 최초로 성공한 쾌거이다. 세계 철강사에 새 지평을 개척한 파이넥스 공법, 이것은 기존의 고로 공법에서 가장 많은 공해를 생산하는 공정인 코크스공장과 소결공장을 짓지 않아도 되는, 그야말로 획기적인 친환경 쇳물생산 방식이다. 경제적으로도 고로에 비해 투자비와 생산원가가 각각 15퍼센트씩 절감된다. 현재 포스코에는 신일본제철에서 나온 연수생들이 적지 않다. 세월이 흘러 바야흐로 '스승'의 나라에서 '제자'의 나라로 배우러온 가운데, 여러 부문에 세계 최고 수준인 포스코는 '유소년기의 스승' 신일본제철과 전략적 동반관계를 맺고 있다.

아마도 박태준이 공식 연설에서 일본을 가장 따끔하게 나무란 것은 2005년에 열린 한일국교정상화 40주년 기념 학술대회의 기조연설자로 나선 때였는지 모른다. 그날, 그는 한일관계의 과제를 한국인의 시각에서 알아듣기 쉽게 제시했다.

"일본은 한국을 가리켜 '일의대수(一衣帶水)'라 부르곤 합니다. 현해탄을 한 줄기 띠에 비유한 말입니다. 한국은 일본을 가리켜 흔히 '가깝고도 먼 나라'로 부릅니다. 가깝다는 것은 지리적 거리이고, 멀다는 것은 민족감정을 반영합니다. 한국, 일본, 중국이 쓰는 말에 '친(親)'자가 있습니다. 친교, 친숙, 친구 등 한국인은 '친'을 '사이좋다'는 뜻으로 씁니다. 매우 기분 좋은 말입니다. 그러나 '친'을 매우 기분 나쁜 뜻으로 알아듣는 경우가 있습니다. 바로 '친일'이란 말입니다. '친일'의 '친'은 묘하게도 '반민족적으로 부역하다'라고 변해 버립니다. 이것은 국교정상화 40주년 한일관계에 내재된 문제의 본질에 대한 상징입니다. 한국인의 언어정서에서 '친일'의 '친'이 '사이좋다'는 본디의 뜻을 회복할 때, 비로소 한일수교는 절친한 친구관계로 완성될 것입니다."

이어서 그는 작심한 것처럼 신랄한 어조로 한반도 분단에 대한 일본의 책임을 추궁하고 반성을 촉구했다.

"한국전쟁의 기원은 분단입니다. 분단의 기원은 식민지지배입니다. 미소 양극 냉전체제가 타협의 산물로 한반도 분단을 강요했지만, 식민지지배라는 일본의 책임이 분단의 근원에 깔려 있습니다. 아무리 패전국이었더라도 일본은 한반도 분단의 고통을 망각하지 말아야 합니다. 해방을 맞았으나 분단에 이은 전쟁이 빈곤의 한국을 비참한 나락(奈落)으로 밀어넣은 3년 동안, 과연 일본은 한국을 위해 무엇을 했습니까? 이 질문 앞에서 일본 지도층은 엄숙해지길 바랍니다. 한국전쟁에서 일본은 한국의 동맹국이 아니었습니다. 그때 일본은 미군의 군수기지 역할을 담당했습니다. 그것은 패전의 무기력과 잿더미 위에서 일본경제를 일으키는 절호의 기회로 활용되었습니다. 일본 노인들은 1950년대 '진무경기(神武景氣)'라는 호황시절을 잘 기억할 것입니다. '진무'는 일본국 첫 번째 임금의 원호(元號) 아닙니까? 진무경기란 말은 '유사 이래 최고 경기'라는 민심을 반영했던 것입니다. 실제로 진무경기는 막강한 일본경제 성장의 기반이 되었습니다. 한국전쟁이란 특수경기가 일본경제 회생에 신묘한 보약으로 쓰였던 것입니다. 오죽했으면 한국 지식인들이 '한국전쟁은 일본경제를 위해 일어났다'는 자탄을 했겠습니까? 그 쓰라린 목소리는 전쟁 도발자를 향한 용서 못할 원망도 담았지만, 분단의 근원에 대한 일본의 책임의식과 한국경제를 도와야할 일본의 도덕의식을 촉구하고 있었습니다."

식민지, 분단, 전쟁, 폐허, 절대빈곤, 부정부패, 산업화와 민주화의 투쟁, 외환위기……. 박태준은 자신이 감당해낸 시대를 어떻게 기억했을까. 그것을 알아낼 실마리를 나는 두 개쯤 잡을 수 있었다.

첫째는 박태준의 책임과 무관했으나 그의 운명에 심대한 영향을 끼쳤던 식민지의 원인에 대한 그의 생각이다. 경술국치, 이 통곡할 비극에 대하여 그는 '조선이 일본에 일방적으로 얻어터지고 한 입에 먹혔다'고 곧잘 표현했다. 왜 조선은 일본을 때리진 못할망정 방어조차 못했는가? 이 문제를 거론하는 요새 한국인이 을사오적과 친일파의 멱살부터 잡아채는 것에 대하여 그는 몹시 못마땅해 했다. 반론은 이랬다. "을사오적이 없었으면 조선이 일본에 안 먹혔나? 친일파가 없었으면 안 먹혔나? 물론 을사오적과 친일파 반민족자들을 역사적으로 엄히 처벌해야 하지만, 그들의 죄보다 우선 따져야 할 것이 있어. 그게 뭐냐? 조선 집권층, 지도층, 사대부, 소중화(小中華)를 우주라고 착각했던 지식인들, 그들 전체의 책임부터 엄히 묻고, 백성들의 책임도 엄히 물어야 돼. 나라 전체의 책임을 엄히 묻고, 그 다음에 을사오적이다 뭐다 하는 것들의 죄를 물어야 하는 거지. 을사오적이니 친일파니 그자들을, 집권층과 지도층과 지식인들 전체의 책임과 죄업에 대한 면죄부로 둔갑시켜서는 안 된다는 거야."

둘째는 박정희 통치시대를 염두에 둔 박태준의 근대화에 대한 기억의 방식이다. 그는 '독재의 사슬도 기억케 하고 빈곤의 사슬도 기억케 하라'고 했다. 산업화와 민주화가 마치 동일한 역사의 무대에 공존할 수 없는 것처럼 격렬한 대립과 갈등을 보여줬지만, 겉보기 양상과는 달리 본질적으로 둘은 모순관계가 아니라 상보관계라는 것이 그의 판단이었다. '다음 세대의 행복을 위해 순교자적으로 희생하는 세대'가 자기 세대라 외치며 그 길에 앞장섰던 박태준은 정치의 억압과 빈곤의 억압으로부터 해방된 젊은이들을 향하여, 우리 역사상 최초로 출현한, 공공적 거대억압으로부터 해방된 젊은이들을 향하여 대놓고 물으려 했던 것이다. 산업화와 민주화가 원수지간처럼 으르렁거렸지만 그 기간 동안에 어느 한쪽이라도 진정성을 상실했더라면 우리가 산업화와 민주화의 성공토대를 동시에 마련할 수 있었겠는가? 너희들은 박정희에 대해 정치적 억압의 사례만 기억하려는 모양인데 그 시대가 오천 년 대물림되어온 절대빈곤의 시대가 아니었다면 현명한 국민 대다수가 영남 호남 구분없이 그러한 리더십을 용인했겠는가? 또 그 시대의 조건 속에서 그러한 리더십이 아니었다면 경제개발을 성공할 수 있었겠는가? 경제개발에 성공하지 못한 나라에서 민주주의와 복지제도가 얼마나 성장할 수 있었겠는가? 그러니 근대화 시대라는 과거에 대한, 박정희 통치시대에 대한, 나도 모든 물욕과 사심을 버리고 일류국가의 밑거름이 되겠다는 사명감 하나에 미쳐서 헌신했던 그 시대에 대한 너희의 기억방식이 공평해야지 않겠는가? 너희의 기억이 공평하지 못하다면 나만 해도 얼마나 억울하겠는가?

박태준은 일류주의의 길을 개척했다. 그것은 고독한 투쟁으로 공동체의 영광을 창조하는 길이었다. 그가 완주를 눈앞에 바라보는 즈음부터 비로소 동시대인들이 마치 이심전심 뒤늦게 어떤 덮혀 있던 진실을 깨달은 것처럼 그를 '영웅'이라 부르고 있었다. 늙은 영웅은 영혼에 맺힌 말들을 미처 세상에 다 공개하지 못하고 눈을 감았다. 그것은 지금 내 기억에 고스란히 저장돼 있다. 이슬처럼 맺혔던 그의 말들이 내 안에는 구슬처럼 남을 것이다.

만약 포스코의 성공에 기여한 박태준의 공로가 아무리 적어도 1퍼센트는 될 것이라 인정한 국가가 그에게 포스코 주식에서 공로주로 1퍼센트만 줬더라면, 그는 수천억 원을 소유한 재벌급 대부호로 살았을 것이다. 그러나 그는 포스코 주식을 한 주도 받지 않았다. 인생의 황혼에 가진 재물이래야 그저 평범한 서울 중산층에 불과했던 그가 생전에 풀지 못한 개인적 소망은 둘이었다.

하나는 북한의 원산이나 함흥 어디쯤에 포스코와 같은 제철소를 포스코의 자금과 기술로 세우는 것. "평양이 문을 열기만 한다면 내가 늙은 몸을 끌고 가서라도 제철소를 지어서 근대화의 기반을 놓아줄 텐데. 기술자들은 인민군 중에 우선 천 명쯤 골라서 포항이나 광양 데려다가 훈련시키면 되는 건데 말이야. 자금? 걱정 없어. 포스코의 신인도면 빌려줄 은행이 줄을 서 있어." 어린아이처럼 흥분한 그의 육성이 지금도 내 귓전에는 쟁쟁하다.

또 하나는 한국인의 노벨과학상 수상. 이 소식을 그는 학수고대했다. 수상자에게 맛있는 밥을 사주려 했다. 2010년에는 포스코청암재단에 일러 노벨과학상을 많이 받은 나라의 교육 시스템에 대한 조사연구도 실시했다. "일본과 축구해서 우리 대표팀이 1:0으로만 져도 난리를 치는 우리가 왜 노벨과학상에서는 17:0이 되어도 무신경한 거야? 뭔가 크게 잘못됐어. 교육부터 바로돼야 해. 교육의 비교우위가 중요해. 교육이 일본에 앞서야 일본을 앞서는 거고 극일도 하게 되는 거야." 확신에 찬 그의 육성이 지금도 내 귓전에는 쟁쟁하다.

무엇을 어떻게 기억할 것인가?

포스코 회장 정준양은 고 박태준 명예회장 영결식 조사에서, "당신의 정신세계를 체계적으로 밝혀내서 우리 사회와 후세를 위한 공적 자산으로 환원할 것이며 앞으로 맞을 난제에 대한 해법을 구할 것"이라 다짐했다. 남은 것은 실천이다. 포스코가 훌륭한 뜻과 방향을 세워야 하고, '먹물'들은 연구와 공부를 맡아야 한다. 물론 명민한 촉각을 곤두세워 정치적 풍향 탐지에 골몰한 나머지 약삭빠르게 눈치나 살피는 '비겁한 먹물'에게는 어울리지 않는 일이다. 박태준은 무엇보다 부패를 경멸하고 혐오했기 때문인데, 비겁함이야말로 지식인의 '상(上)부패' 아닌가. 2008년 7월 20일 여든 살을 넘은 노인임에도 그는 한 신문과 인터뷰에서 이렇게 말한 사람이었다. "나는 군에서도 그랬지만 바른 일 해서 모가지 잘리는 것이라면 언제든지 좋다고 생각했다."

박태준은 이병철·정주영과 동시대를 감당하며 탁월한 위업을 성취했다. 그들은 하나같이 대성취를 이루었다. 그러나 박태준에게는 이병철·정주영에게 없는 매우 독특한 무엇이 있다. 그것은 '나'를 위해 일하지 않았다는 점이다. 나의 사업을 하지 않았으며, 나의 대성취를 결코 나의 재산이나 가족의 재산으로 여기지도 않고 만들지도 않았다는 점이다. 국가의 일을 맡아 자기 소유의 일보다 더 성실하게 더 치열하게, 세계적 유일사례로 기록될 만큼 가장 탁월하게 가장 모범적으로 성취했다는 점이다. 이 지점에서 박태준은 이병철·정주영과 갈라지게 된다. 이 지점에서 송복은 박태준의 사상과 대성취를 '태준이즘(Taejoonism)'이라 명명했다. 이제 태준이즘은 지식인의 '상부패'를 진실로 경계하는 이 나라 먹물들의 학식과 양심의 조명을 기다리고 있다.

대한민국의 큰 일꾼 박태준, 그에게 대한민국이 차린 '아주 지각한 예의'이자 '마지막 예의'는 서울 동작동 국립 현충원에 두어 평짜리 무덤을 마련해준 일이었다. 영하 10도의 차디찬 동토 속에 눕는 고인에게 바친, 고인의 제자같은 후배 정준양의 조사는 만해 한용운의 「님의 침묵」 결련(結聯)으로 마무리 되었다.

　　　우리는 만날 때에 떠날 것을 염려하는 것과 같이
　　　떠날 때에 다시 만날 것을 믿습니다.

아아 님은 갔지만

나는 님을 보내지 아니하였습니다.

　후세가 님을 보내지 아니하는 것은 당연히 님의 공적만 쳐다보고 기억하는 일이 아니다. 그의 고뇌, 그의 정신, 그의 투쟁을 체계적으로 연구하고 공부하여 사회적 자산으로 환원하고 활용하는 일이다. 다산 정약용의 실체적 공적은 크지 않은 개혁 성과와 저술들이며, 그것이 다산의 텍스트로 끊임없이 연구되고 공부되고 활용된다. 청암 박태준이 20세기 한국사에 끼친 실체적 공적은 지대하다. 다산 정약용의 삶과 저술들이 당대에 끼쳤던 그것을 압도한다. 서로 견줄 형편도 못될 것이다. 다만 그는 다산과 같이 학구적 저술들을 남기지 않았다. 그러나 저술은 결국 언어의 체계이고, 언어의 체계는 신념의 집이며 사상이다. 청암 박태준은 저술 대신 수많은 현장의 말을 남겼다. 그의 어록을 국판 크기로 편집하면 일만 쪽을 넘길 것이다. 청암 박태준 연구와 공부에 대한 텍스트는 넉넉히 준비돼 있다. 포스코, 포스텍, 포스코의 학교들, 포스코청암재단, 한국 현대사에 끼친 지대한 공로, 그리고 그의 신념의 집이며 사상인 방대한 어록……

이대환 소설가, 《ASIA》 발행인

국제 펜클럽 한국 본부 주관 장편소설 공모 당선(1980)
《현대문학》 지령 400호 기념 장편소설 공모 당선(1989)
포스코청암재단 이사
(사)한국작가회의 이사
(사)포항지역사회연구소 소장
포스코경영연구소 자문위원

주요 저서
장편소설 『새벽, 동틀 녘』(1991) 『겨울의 집』(1999) 『슬로우 불릿』(2001) 『붉은 고래』(2004) 『큰돈과 콘돔』(2008)
소설집 『조그만 깃발 하나』(1995) 『생선 창자 속으로 들어간 詩』(1997)
평전 『박태준』(2004) 『쇳물에 흐르는 푸른 청춘-포스코 창업시대 열전』(2006)

Lee Dae-hwan

Pointing to a Road in Hanoi

Towards the end of January 2010 Park Tae-joon visited Hanoi, Vietnam for a four-day three-night trip. It so happened that there were placards all over the city celebrating "the millennial anniversary of Hanoi" as the capital of Vietnam. Hanoi is a city of both disgrace and honor, and has sustained the core of Vietnam for a thousand years ever since it was designated the capital by Emperor Ly Thai To in 1010. Its disgrace is the wound inflicted on it during the invasions by China, France, and America, while its honor is the pride that Vietnamese feel from vanquishing those invaders one by one. What were the most horrifyingly imperialistic words of savagery inscribed deep in the memories of Hanoi? They would probably be American General Curtis LeMay's boastful, "We're going to bomb them back to the Stone Age." At the downtown center of this capital of Vietnam, the city that ruthless bombings by the American military indeed almost sent back to the Stone Age, is a five-star modern hotel, the Hanoi Daewoo Hotel, constructed in 1996. At the age of eighty-three, Park Tae-joon stopped at this hotel, built by Kim Woo-choong, his younger business colleague from Korea. It was Park Tae-joon who had recommended that Kim Woo-choong build a hotel on this site. At the time Kim Woo-choong, at the height of his career, was known for his catchphrase, "The world is large and there are a lot of things to be done." How did Park come to recommend that Kim build a hotel at this location of such great importance in Hanoi?

Park Tae-joon first visited Vietnam and Hanoi in 1992 towards the end of November. This was a time of both lightheartedness and bitterness for Park. He was lighthearted, for he had just successfully completed his great quarter-century project, from April 1, 1968 to October 1, 1992, of building a steel manufacturing company. After building both the Pohang and Gwangyang Iron and Steel Plants that had a combined annual production capacity of 21 million tons of crude steel, Park Tae-joon voluntarily left the world's highest royal throne of iron and went off to explore the overseas market in China and Southeast Asia as honorary chairman of POSCO. However, he also must have been somewhat unhappy, for he had just firmly declined the position of chief of campaign headquarters for Kim Young-sam for the upcoming December presidential election, a position offered to him by soon-to-be president Kim himself. Kim Young-sam came all the way to Gwangyang to visit him, and Park could easily predict that political retribution was slowly but surely approaching. When Park Tae-joon visited Ba Dinh Square in Hanoi in suit and tie, negotiations between Korean and Vietnamese governments to establish diplomatic relations were advancing. These negotiations bore fruit on

December 22, 1992.

There were endless lines of people surrounding the square and red placards with white letters hung both left and right of the Ho Chi Minh Mausoleum as if guarding it. Park Tae-joon's interpreter satisfied his curiosity: "Everyday we have so many visitors who come to pay their respects. A visit to Uncle Ho's mausoleum is a lifetime wish even for people living in the distant countryside." Park Tae-joon had already gotten used to the name Uncle Ho, appreciating the anti-authoritarian nickname "uncle." His interpreter pointed to two vividly colored sentences written on the placards right in front of them: "Uncle Ho Lives Forever in Our Cause" and "Long Live the Communist Party of Vietnam!"

Park Tae-joon paid silent tribute to Ho Chi Minh, a leader who was virtuous, wise, flexible, and firm. "Nothing is more important than freedom and independence." Park Tae-joon remembered this phrase by Ho Chi Minh and the life-or-death struggles the Vietnamese had to wage against France and America, the wars through which they eventually succeeded in defending those absolute causes. He also remembered the deeply regrettable and unfortunate past, i.e. the fact that Korea had dispatched troops to Vietnam when Korea was at the forefront of the Cold War and devoting itself to its own modernization. Because of this past, on this first trip to Vietnam, Park was solemn and humbled.

The mausoleum was built at the site where Ho Chi Minh stood in the center of a platform and declared the independence of Vietnam in September 1945. After praying for the deceased, who looked like an old man comfortably asleep, Park Tae-joon left the consecrated place where the body of the cleanest leader had been preserved, and was suddenly struck by an idea. If he went back to Korea and preserved the body of the most corrupt political leader from decay, would it serve as a deterrent to other corrupt Korean politicians?

After his visit to Ba Dinh Square, Park Tae-joon met with the highest official in Vietnam, Du Muoi, secretary-general of the Communist Party of Vietnam, who was spearheading the country's open-door policy called "Doi Moi." Park Tae-joon could sense in Du Muoi the kind of character and soul that befitted Ho Chi Minh's student. It was clear that Du was motivated purely by a love of his people and a sincere wish for his country's economic development. Park Tae-joon thought that by investing in Vietnam, Korea, as a country that had already succeeded in developing its own economy, could begin to repay its colossal debt to Vietnam and restore its moral character. The host asked about the best direction for the economic development of his country and the guest summed up the strengths and weaknesses of Korea's experiences. When it came time for the guest to meet Prime Minister Vo Van Kiet, the host told him to take it easy, with a bright smile. "I've already told him. It's ok for you to be late. We can continue our conversation." "I'm fine if you have already made sure that by delaying my meeting with him I won't be acting impolitely." "I wish I had met you earlier." Then they discussed pending questions. They talked about an electric furnace plant with an annual production capacity of 200,000 tons of products, a pipe plant, and the construction of the Hanoi-Haiphong Highway. Unfortunately, there was a stumbling block to Park Tae-joon's groundbreaking plan of investing in Vietnam. Korean political power—how long would it allow him to manage POSCO?

Although Park Tae-joon's meeting with Do Muoi resulted in his recommending the site of the Hanoi Daewoo Hotel to Kim Woo-chung, the two leaders would never meet again. Park's plan was also destined to fall apart, as he had to go into exile from March of the next year, because of anticipated political persecution.

It was not until November 2004, twelve long years later, that Park Tae-joon could visit Vietnam again. The honorary chairman of POSCO, now seventy-seven, visited Saigon (Ho Chi Minh City) and recollected his "Vietnam plan" that had gone up in smoke during his exile from March 1993 to May 1997. "If that hadn't happened, we could have killed three birds with one stone, doing a lot of good things for this country, beginning to repay our historical debts, and recovering our moral character..." The hopes and promises he had shared with Vietnamese leaders twelve years earlier prompted regret in the soul of this old man in his seventies. He hoped to see these leaders again. Do Muoi, the former secretary-general who was too old to travel, sent his regrets and greetings: "I really missed you." Park Tae-joon politely replied: "I apologize for getting back so late. I had unavoidable reasons." Luckily, he was able to meet former Prime Minister Vo Van Kiet. The elder statesman of revolution and reform, already in his eighties, said, "Why did you come so late?" The old guest answered, "My apologies."

The embrace and hand shaking between the two old men went on for a long time.

Park Tae-joon met young leaders as well. Vietnam's economy, boasting an annual 7% growth rate, was consuming 5 million tons of steel every year. Park Tae-joon advised Minister of Industry Hoang Trung Hai: "It's now time for you to build your own steel company. Vietnam can join the developing countries only when you have steel-related industries like shipbuilding and automobile manufacturing." His ideas were concretized as "The POSCO Project: Building a Cold-rolled Steel Mill and an Integrated Steel Mill in Vietnam" by junior management officers of POSCO. Construction of the cold-rolled steel mill in Vung Tau was completed in October 2009, but regrettably, the integrated steel mill project was suspended due to a difference of opinion between Vietnam authorities and POSCO.

Park Tae-joon visited Vietnam for the third time in June 2007. Ho Chi Minh City was his first stopover during his two-week trip to Southeast Asia, Hong Kong, and China with his colleagues. He wanted to find out in person how Vietnam had changed and developed in the mean time. He drank Nep Moi, very strong Vietnamese soju, at every meal. While savoring it and praising it as "very good liquor," he looked like a very innocent young man.

Park Tae-joon visited Hanoi for the fourth time in 2010 and stayed at the Hanoi Daewoo Hotel in order to attend a party celebrating the publication of his biography, *Man of Steel, Park Tae-joon* and to give a special lecture at Vietnam National University, Hanoi. The celebratory party was held at the Hanoi

Daewoo Hotel on the evening of January 28. The room was brimming with Vietnamese high officials, professors, steel industry personages, and many Koreans including people from the Korean Embassy and Korean businessmen in Vietnam. As the author of Park Tae-joon's biography I gave a speech:

"I was born in 1958 in the year of the dog, and belong to the well-known post-Korean War baby-boomer generation. My home village was the site later slated for POSCO to build the steel plant. I had to leave my village when I was ten because of POSCO. Village adults called themselves "torn-down people." That term suggested the dreariness and sadness that came of losing their home village and having to go away. There was probably also a feeling of resentment and protest in that phrase. There used to be an orphanage, probably the largest in the world, in that village. About a hundred and fifty nuns from the Sacred Heart of Jesus Community led by a blue-eyed French Catholic priest took care of about five hundred orphans produced by the disastrous war and the extreme poverty. While elegant hymns flowed out every Sunday from the graceful Catholic church, its front gate guarded by two male and female gingko trees, the branch school in our village had to operate on a double shift, because there were only two classrooms for grades one through four. The student who shared my desk was also an orphan. I never met him again after we parted.

Around the time when adults were loading their shabby household goods onto old moving trucks, in the village placards were flapping on which words like "iron melting plant," "steel manufacturing plant," and "hot-rolled steel plant" were written. *What are they?* I looked up angrily and impertinently at those words in the air. At any rate, according to what I learned much later, on December 24, 1959, i.e. on Christmas Eve, a year after I was born, the BBC in England broadcast a forty-minute documentary entitled *A Far Cry.* This was a documentary about the wretched reality of Korean children, starving and in need of clothes, far from London. It wouldn't be wrong to say that my friends and I were those children. Do you know what the last words were in that documentary that no human being could watch without tears? "Is there any hope for these children?" As a way to answer that rather hopeless question, I would like to point out that I stand here today wearing a nice suit and with a somewhat plump face, as you can see.

It was about twenty years later that I realized that the flags of POSCO flapping in the air when I was leaving my home village were the hope of our generation. I met Mr. Park Tae-joon for the first time when I was thirty-nine and published his biography in Korean in December 2004. This biography was published in China in Chinese translation in 2005, and today we are celebrating its translation and publication in Vietnam. Why should a writer write a biography? Why do we need one?

The age of suffering gives birth to a hero, and the hero opens up a horizon for history. However, a hero without a human face and human warmth becomes a mere symbol of achievement like an idol made of bronze or marble. To make sure that such a lonely fate does not befall such a person, to call him by a human name, to perceive him and make him live as a human being—I think these are some of the most important reasons why there should be a biography.

This must be true of many biographies of Ho Chi Minh that have been published in Vietnam. I strongly object to a future in which my hero will be remembered only as someone who left outstanding achievements. I believe that his anguish, his thoughts, and his struggles should also be remembered. That is the least we can do as his contemporaries for posterities for someone who ran the whole course during his entire life, shouldering the great burden imposed on him by his country, nation, and age."

At 11 A.M. the next morning, the president of the university, deans, and more than five hundred students gathered in the auditorium of Vietnam National University, Hanoi. Park Tae-joon's speech that lasted more than an hour and was delivered through consecutive interpretation was full of youthful aspirations and passions more like those of an active leader than an eighty-three-year-old man. He delivered the essence of his thoughts for young people in Vietnam and Korea, indeed for all the people of the world. Perhaps because of this, the youthful audience in the auditorium cheered and gave a standing ovation to the old man after he finished his speech. The female professor who worked as interpreter cautiously confessed, "Former American President Bill Clinton, former Chinese Chairman Jang Zemin, and recently, current Korean President Lee Myung-bak gave a speech here, and I listened to them all very carefully. Nobody moved me as much as Mr. Park

Tae-joon."

What did Park Tae-joon say that stirred the souls of the young Vietnamese elite and made their youthful hearts flutter?

"The great human virtue is to think deeply about our lives and our community's happiness, and to make an effort to accomplish it. I'm not here to talk about Korean economic development. Based on my experience of overcoming stormy and turbulent historical times, I would like to think about our lives and histories together with you the young elite. In history, there are sufferings that a particular generation has to shoulder willingly. They deeply influence our individual lives and become the destiny of that generation."

After beginning like this, his speech went on to a comparison between Korea and Vietnam during the last century and his thoughts about the fate of a specific generation.

"I was born in 1927. My generation in Korea spent our childhood and adolescence under Japanese colonial rule, and greeted the liberation of our country as young people. But the Korean peninsula was unlucky. Our country was divided. We became a scapegoat of the Cold War system. Division was followed by war, and war gave birth to the truce line, the iron fence of the most hostile confrontation on earth. After the war, the Korean peninsula remained afflicted by internal hostility, ruin, poverty and starvation, and rampant corruption.

As a young officer who 'happened to' survive 'through sheer luck,' I couldn't help think about my future and that of my fatherland. How could I contribute to rebuilding my ruined country? How could I contribute to overcoming the absolute poverty that had been oppressing our people like some sort of divine retribution? How could I contribute to the modernization of my country, the kind of modernization that America and Europe were enjoying? How should I live in these times? I came up with solemn mottos for myself. 'Let me devote my short life to my eternal fatherland!' and 'There is no absolute despair.' Looking back, I think that those mottos became my lifelong compass whose needle hasn't budged even to this moment. I have no regrets whatsoever about my life's journey guided by those mottos.

In 1961, the year the Korean government undertook a campaign to advance the economic development of the nation, Korea was the poorest country in the world with an annual national per capita income of only $70. As a participant in the planning this economic development, I took charge of building and managing an integrated steel mill. Seven years after we started this project with no capital, no resources, no experience, and no technology, we were finally able to lay the foundation, and at that time I told my comrades, 'We belong to a generation of martyrs. Ours is a generation of people that sacrifice themselves for the happiness of the generations to come and the prosperity of our fatherland in the twenty-first century.' Our supreme task was 'modernization of our fatherland.' That was the directive of our time so we could overcome the ruin, poverty, corruption, and disorder that had been thrust upon us. And we finally succeeded. I am proud that we transformed an age of suffering into an age of glory. But our generation is also handing down an enormous task to the next generation. Addressing the division of our country is that task. It pains me to think that we're handing down this burden—the burden of reconciliation between the south and the north and peaceful reunification.

For the past century or so, each generation in Vietnam also had to shoulder its own suffering specific to its times. For convenience's sake, let's divide them into three generations, i.e. the generations of your grandparents, parents, and yourselves.

Your grandparents' generation embodied Ho Chi Minh's motto, 'Nothing is more important than independence and freedom.' Although they had to endure innumerable sacrifices and sufferings, they won independence and freedom, their fateful and earnest wishes. But Vietnam was divided in July 1954 at the 17th parallel. Your parents, then still children, probably didn't know at the time that a long drawn-out war of reunification would be the cruel destiny of their generation. They willingly shouldered this harsh destiny and could finally declare in April 1975 that the war was over and your country was reunited. They didn't have time to rest, though. Survivors of that war had to take upon themselves the task of rebuilding their country. Deng Xiaoping in China initiated an open-door policy and Vietnam adopted the same policy in 1986. That was a sort of revolution. Although some confusion and trial and error inevitably accompanied this revolution, I believe that Vietnamese leaders made a wise decision. It saddens me to say this, but present-day North Korea, which refuses to open its door, proves that.

Because Vietnam emerged from war later than Korea, you

began economic development later than us. But while Vietnam is a unified country, Korea is a divided country. Your generation here received the great foundation of 'a unified country with freedom and independence' from the previous generation. The coordinate axes of your generation should be built upon it. While the inevitable historic task of 'peaceful reunification and the completion of building a first-rate country' has been given to the current generation of Korean youth, the inevitable historic task of 'economic revival and the completion of building a first-rate country' was given to the current generation of Vietnamese youth. Given the momentousness of the task of reunification, one might say that Korean young people have to shoulder an even heavier fate than their Vietnamese counterparts."

After presenting the coordinate axes to the younger generations of both countries, Park Tae-joon emphasized further the importance of both a fight against corruption and self-confidence.

"One of the most important prerequisites for a country's prosperity is for its leaders and elites not to be corrupt but to guide its people with vision and confidence wherever they are in the world. Human beings are by nature susceptible to material temptations. Human beings can sometimes be as strong as steel, but at other times as easily corruptible as fish in the hot sun. Corruption is a matter of the human mind. If a human being who belongs to the class of leaders and the elite does not succumb to corruption, it would be as the result of his ceaseless struggles with himself. Great people in history constantly fought with their own desires. If you have a dream to become an excellent leader, you have to begin to fight with your own desires from now on.

I said that leaders and the elite should guide people with vision and confidence. However, a person who has no plan for his or her future cannot become a leader. Also, even if he or she happens to become a leader, he or she cannot present a vision. I would first like to advise you to picture yourself ten years in the future. Can you imagine it? If you can, then you should be on your way to it passionately and meticulously. If you can't, then you should begin by imagining it, even if that means you have to stay up for many nights. Do remember that the sum total of individual visions can open a new horizon for your country and time.

I emphasize again that the most important motive force for economic development in a developing country comes from uncorrupt leaders and confident people. Vietnam has Master Ho Chi Minh, the cleanest leader in the world in the twentieth century and you also have the pride and confidence that come from vanquishing France and America. Now the question is how to turn such a great moral heritage into the underlying strength to achieve wealth and power for your country and happiness for your people. Although there are always ups and downs in history, I am confident that you will build a first-rate country, if your leaders and people share the same idea of your moral heritage and collaborate with each other based on it."

Tough Road Towards the Best

What was the most attractive aspect of Park Tae-joon's character to me as his biographer? Was it his excellent ability as an intelligent, virtuous, and brave leader? Most would say that. I, too, acknowledge that this trait is an attractive one. But it was not the most attractive aspect of his character for me. Instead I found his attitude towards life that put 'spiritual value' above all else the most attractive. Throughout his life he consistently rejected vulgarity. As passionately as a writer who despises commercial success, he never ventured outside the spiritual magnetic field of his belief. The fragrance emanating from such an attitude reached me as it would a lover, and it was this fragrance that made me offer to write his biography. I first met him in the early summer of 1997. For fifteen years from then until December 13, 2011, the day when the French paper *Le Monde* published his obituary entitled, "A Korean Hero Passes Away," I had the fortunate pleasure of spending much time with him and conversing with him about his life, ideas, and memories. Writing his biography was like walking along with an elderly man in his waning years and thinking with him about the new road he was showing for a young man.

Although I was born and grew up in the seaside village of Young-il Bay, where POSCO built its plant, as a writer I became interested in Park Tae-joon only in my mid-thirties, in the early 1990's. Until then, I had never even seen him from afar, let alone shaken hands with him. To me, he was a personality that I met through newspapers and TV programs. What made me interested in him? There was of course the karma of my birthplace being the future POSCO site, which at first prejudiced me against him, but later made me more interested in him, after I became more mature when I reached the age of thirty, the age that Confucius called the "age of independence." What was more relevant, though, was the fact that I had to adjust my way of looking at the world by then.

Around the time I reached the "age of independence" Gorbachev was at the center of a massive global shift. The night when Germans gathered around the Brandenburg Gate and were celebrating the fall of the Berlin Wall that divided East and West Germany, Gorbachev stood in front of them with his beautiful wife and declared, "History punishes the latecomers." At that very moment, I heard a roaring sound within me as well. It was the sound of the socialist visions and ideals that had sustained Korea in the 1980s collapsing. Afterwards, many social science articles that discussed the failure of the socialist system were written and published. Because I am a writer, however, I looked to human beings for answers to my questions. My answer was something along these lines.

"Human beings are born with morals that are too weak to put socialism into practice. Ideology doesn't produce the human condition. Rather, it is the human condition that creates ideology. People shouldn't serve the system, but the system should serve people."

I happened to write a column that supported Park Tae-joon. It was as if every bit of resentment was leaving me. This was in the summer of 1996, about a year before I shook hands with him for the first time. My column was outspoken advice for the master of the Blue House, who was fumbling with the idea of a political pardon for Park Tae-joon in exile. I wrote, "Even if Park Tae-joon's political mistake weighed as much as the steel that went into building 63 Building, his service to modern Korean history weighs as much as the steel that could build sixty-three 63 Buildings."

I made that argument before I knew Park Tae-joon well, but I could confirm later when I was writing his biography that I wasn't at all off the mark. Who is the Park Tae-joon that I saw? As I mentioned above, his soul was truly a steel-like bastion of spiritual beliefs. He took charge of and managed all public affairs from the depths of his soul, and that was how he was able to suppress and renounce all materialistic temptations. It seems that he could take the initiative and set an example for others very naturally because of the kind of spirit he possessed. No wonder he emphasized "clean leadership that scrapes out corruption" at Vietnam National University, Hanoi in January 2010. That dignified speech was a natural result of his own lifelong practice.

There are a couple of famous phrases—"Patriotism by Steel Manufacturing" and "Right Face!"—that relate to a moving anecdote about Park Tae-joon on the day of the groundbreaking ceremony for POSCO. Both are simple phrases. By "Patriotism by Steel Manufacturing," he meant that people should contribute to their country by building a successful steel manufacturing company. "Right Face!" is a military term used during a close-order drill that means an order to turn to the right." These two very simple phrases partnered within Park Tae-joon's mind were reborn as the enormous mental energy and motive force that pushed POSCO up the hill of success.

The seed money for building the first stage of the crude steel manufacturing system (annual production capacity of one million and thirty thousand tons) of POSCO came from the Funds from Property Claims Against Japan (Indemnities for Japanese Colonial Rule). Park Tae-joon considered this fund "the tax paid by the blood of our ancestors." How could we fail in building POSCO, that long-cherished national enterprise, when we were using "the tax paid by the blood of our ancestors" to do so? If we failed, that would make us guilty of disappointing our ancestors, country and nation. If we died, we couldn't be forgiven, but even so, if we failed, then we deserved to die, so let's "right face!" If we "right face" at the beach of Young-il Bay, there will be the navy blue sea. Let's drown in that sea. That was the meaning of "Right Face!" How could there be a crack for corruption to enter and take hold in such a spiritually strong movement? So I wrote in his biography, "Park Tae-joon was heroic, and his workers were moved. His outcry spread from heart to heart. 'The tax paid by the blood of our ancestors' stirred nationalism in them. 'Right Face!' elevated patriotism, nourishing the idea of 'Patriotism by Steel Manufacturing.'"

Park Tae-joon's steel-like bastion of spiritual beliefs—what is its essence? His motto gives us the answer: "Let me devote my short life to my eternal fatherland!" He always wanted to be the best and the foremost. Park Tae-joon wrote, "Let's be the First in Everything!" in his own handwriting for the inaugural issue of the company newsletter *Melted Iron* in 1969, even before POSCO had begun producing any melted iron. He urged his workers to become the best in the world when they weren't even sure whether they could ever begin producing melted iron. Afterwards, he developed POSCO into the number one steel manufacturing company in the world as he had vowed to do in the very beginning by working day and night for the next twenty-five years. His number one was the collective number one that POSCO embodied, which in turn became an example for the country to become number one.

Why did Park Tae-joon insist upon working towards becoming number one, and push, by pursuing the highest standards, for the country itself to become number one? Why was he unable to relax, even for a second, in this pursuit of number one status for himself, POSCO, and his country? The answer is bound up with the suffering of our country that he experienced growing up, for his life was a journey right through the center of modern Korean history.

Park Tae-joon was born in a small seaside village in Gijang, Busan in 1927. He depended on a Busan-Simonoseki ferryboat, a modern monster of steel, to take him as a child to join his father in Japan with his mother. He, the smart child who was also a talented runner and swimmer, often heard the word "Senjing."[*] This insult planted a seed in his mind, a seed that

* "Senjing" is a pejorative name Japanese used to call a Korean.

would grow into a defensive and resistant awareness that he should be number one in everything so he would not be discriminated against. He returned home after the liberation of Korea, cutting short his studies at Waseda University, where he was studying mechanical engineering. At home, believing that building a strong military force was important in building a strong country, he entered the Military Academy, where he met Park Chung-hee, ten years his senior, as his teacher. During the Korean War, he was one of two surviving members among his regiment's twelve commanders after a three-day retreat from Cheolwon to Seoul. His regiment retreated south to Pohang, advanced north to Cheongjin, and then retreated again during the January 4th retreat, right after he had an emergency appendectomy. After the ceasefire, he graduated from the Army University as a valedictorian and became a colonel, famous for his integrity, for which he acquired the nickname "a penurious scholar" in the military, known for its corruption at the time. He neither compromised with corruption nor accepted it. His reputation reached Park Chung-hee's ears. Park Chung-hee chose him as a member of his human resources staff when he was appointed commander of the Busan Military Supply Complex Headquarters in 1960 and was already planning his coup. After the coup, Park Tae-joon served as chief of staff for the chairman of the Nation Rebuilding Supreme Council and the council member in charge of commerce and industry. After he refused Park Chung-hee's invitation to a political career, he first became the president of Korea Tungsten Manufacturing Company and then took charge of POSCO project that would be the driving force of Korean industrialization. Although POSCO had built something out of nothing, it faced a life-or-death crisis in February 1969, when steel companies from five advanced countries including the US, Britain, and France broke their promise to support POSCO with funding and technology after IBRD predicted that the Korean steel company project was premature. The capitalist business system was cruel and cold, and newborn POSCO had to die. Park Tae-joon was in a position to secretly order Hwang Kyung-ro, his right-hand man, to draw up a "company liquidation plan." Park Tae-joon, however, had found an extraordinary breakthrough. He came up with the idea of diverting a portion of the Funds from Property Claims Against Japan and received Park Chung-hee's approval and support. Park Tae-joon then succeeded in persuading Japanese cabinet members and leaders of the steel industry to offer their support. The infant POSCO that could have ended up in an early grave on the sandy plain of Young-il Bay was miraculously restored to life.

The fame that Park Tae-joon won through his success in developing POSCO into the number one enterprise in the world brought him three opportunities to participate in politics.

The first opportunity came in 1980. Park Chung-hee's death meant a great disaster for POSCO in that it removed a strong defense against political pressure. People point out that Park Tae-joon's leadership was the most important factor in the success of POSCO. Scholarly papers have been written and published about that at Harvard University, Stanford University, Seoul National University, and the Mitsubishi Research Institute.

However, could his leadership alone have been sufficient for the task? The following is my opinion: "Park Chung-hee passionately protected Park Tae-joon's pure and passionate patriotic mission as if it were an 'inviolable virginity.' He greatly appreciated Park Tae-joon's courage in rejecting a political career, which had been offered to him without his asking. There must have been a man-to-man recognition of each other's nature and values. The unique relationship between Park Chung-hee and Park Tae-joon created an environment favorable for Park Tae-joon to fully demonstrate his leadership and mission." In a situation in which the constantly reliable protective fence around POSCO suddenly disappeared, the new political power summoned Park Tae-joon, and Park Tae-joon entered the world of politics in order to become that fence himself.

The second opportunity came in 1990. With a plan to consolidate power with Kim Young-sam and Kim Jong-pil in mind, Roh Tae-woo invited Park Tae-joon, who was devoting himself almost entirely to POSCO as a member of the Assembly elected from the national constituency, to become chairman of the ruling party. Although he refused at first, he ultimately had to accept, as Roh Tae-woo had the power to appoint or fire him as chairman of POSCO. He resigned this post in October 1992.

The third opportunity came after Park Tae-joon returned from exile in 1997. He ran as an independent in the special election for the representative of Pohang. This time, he did it on his own. This choice enabled him to contribute to the horizontal change of regime for the first time in history, in collaboration with Kim Dae-jung and Kim Jong-pil. He also took the lead in overcoming the financial crisis that swept over Korea and other Asian countries, "the biggest national disaster since the Korean War" according to some.

Is there any reason to see Park Tae-joon's participation in politics as a negative act? There are roughly two negative views concerning his political participation. According to the first, "a great man got unnecessarily soiled his name by being involved in politics." People who say this mainly have his first entry into politics in mind, reflecting a general dislike of Korean politics and an objection to the Chun Doo-hwan regime. However, if Park Tae-joon had rejected Chun's invitation, there would have been no guaranteeing the success of the Gwangyang Steel Plant, and POSTECH (Pohang University of Science and Technology) would never have been founded. In other words, by participating in politics, Park Tae-joon made a critical contribution to the completion of Korean industrialization and inaugurated a new epoch for Korean college education. He didn't soil his name, but created "good power." Another negative view goes something along the lines that "a great man had an unnecessarily difficult time and a record of failure by entering politics." This popular judgment mainly has to do with Park Tae-joon's second participation in politics, reflecting the fact that he had to go into exile for a while. That's merely an image, though. He said, "To me, YS (Kim Young-sam) did not come across as the leader who would save our country. I rejected his offer based on my conscience." If Park Tae-joon were a vulgar politician, he would have chosen the collusive agreement with Kim, securing his position as a leader second only to Kim. This would have been desirable if the leader who wanted Park Tae-joon as his second in command looked "first-rate" to him. As that wasn't the case, Park Tae-joon rejected the temptation to power, even while anticipating persecution. This might prove that the relationship between Park Chung-hee and Park Tae-joon must have been fundamentally different from that between Kim Young-sam and Park Tae-joon. In fact, while Park Chung-hee supported Park Tae-joon's economic pursuits even after Park Tae-joon rejected his invitation to a political career, Kim Young-sam stabbed him in the back in retaliation. Interestingly, Park Chung-hee benefited the economy of our country enormously, while Kim Youg-sam harmed our country enormously, both economically and diplomatically. During Park Tae-joon's exile, his China Project, Vietnam Project, Myanmar Project, and his IT Business Project (a project in which he planned to invest one trillion *won* every year for ten years in an information technology business in collaboration with Masa Son's Softbank in Japan) were all swept away like sand castles by a wave. History will probably completely forget these losses in national wealth. Park Tae-joon's third participation in politics, his first voluntary participation, contributed to the growth of Korean democracy by adding to it the power of rational conservatism. He was also able to help our country overcome a national disaster, his last contribution to his nation as a supreme worker with mature experience.

Park Tae-joon's belief in building a first-rate nation

materialized in the founding of POSTECH in 1985. Despite the enormous scale of investment necessary for building the Gwangyang Steel Plant, he bravely and firmly pushed forward his plan to found the first research-oriented college in Korea. At that time, POSCO was subject to annual parliamentary inspection. Objection to this plan was very high within political circles. This was true of Park Tae-joon's inner circle within POSCO as well. He didn't budge, however. As someone who had successfully founded, managed, and developed fourteen schools from preschool to high school to the highest level without governmental tax money, he volunteered to become a missionary for the establishment of POSTECH, educating people about the necessity for this kind of institution. "A country without first-rate science and technology cannot become the most advanced country. Science and technology are the basis of a country's economy, national security, and power. To lead people is to educate them. Education is the manufacturing industry of our world." These were the basic ideas behind two of Park Tae-joon' important slogans, i.e. "Patriotism by Education," and "Patriotism by Steel Manufacturing." On August 27, 1986 on the eve of the inauguration of POSTECH, which *The Times* of London would rate 28th among world's universities in 2010, Park Tae-joon addressed the people inside POSCO who were making disparaging remarks.

"If we look at the immediate return from POSTECH, which we established betting on the fortunes of our company, we might wonder whether we would simply be draining our resources. However, POSTECH will be at the center of our company's century-long future as a university that nurtures talented scientists who will contribute to the development of our country's industries. We, especially the executives, should firmly believe that POSTECH will contribute to the future of our country: this is not a venture that will return an immediate profit."

Park Tae-joon achieved what he believed, i.e. "Patriotism by Steel Manufacturing" and "Patriotism by Education," through POSCO, POSTECH, and other schools built by POSCO. He also achieved the first-rate results that he pursued. His achievements contributed greatly to the construction of a foundation for a first-rate country. Would it be at all possible to describe his entire life in one sentence? When we consider the fact that POSCO is his most important achievement, that POSCO was the engine for Korean industrialization, and that our democracy matured through a strong and persistent movement based on the material advances made possible by industrialization, we might want to remember the moment when POSCO survived a life-or-death crisis in its infancy. That was a very fortunate moment when Korea turned a corner towards the light, a moment one cannot praise too much. The driving force behind that overcoming was Park Tae-joon. What made it possible for him to do it? Of course there was his desperate yearning for the modernization of his country, but ironically, if he hadn't grown up in Japan as a child and young man, i.e. if he had had to depend on interpreters at the negotiation table with Japanese leaders, he might not have been so persuasive. I quote here what I wrote about this in one sentence in his biography.

"Among the many children from the colony who went to Japan across the Straits of Korea, following their fathers who had gone to Japan in search of work, the person who contributed the most dramatically and efficiently to his country, with the Japanese language and culture he had to learn as a child and adolescent after returning home as a young man after liberation and becoming an adult of a newly independent poverty-stricken country, must be Park Tae-joon."

If I inserted the phrase, "and many young students who went to Japan across the Straits of Korea to learn new civilizations and modern sciences," into the above sentence, I believe that the remainder wouldn't change.

Truly Overcoming Japan: Words Smoldering in His Heart

Park Tae-joon has many friends in Japan and he knew Japan very well. However, his goal was to overcome Japan. He belonged to that group of people who truly meant to do this. In his times, Korea had to overcome Japan in order to become the best in the world in any area. Without overcoming Japan, Park Tae-joon's dream of becoming first was merely an illusion. The relationship between POSCO and Nippon Steel Corporation is a good example of this.

Inayama Yoshihiro, a Japanese and chairman of Nippon Steel Corporation, was one of the most important characters involved in the first phase of the building POSCO, a crude steel manufacturing plant with a 1,030,000-ton annual capacity. In the summer of 1969, Park Tae-joon had to fly to Tokyo to meet with him and persuade him to help. In order to redirect part of the Funds from Property Claims Against Japan to the construction of POSCO, both the Korean and Japanese governments had to be on board with this plan, and one of the most crucial prerequisites for this agreement was a promise from the leaders of the Japanese steel industry to provide technical support for POSCO. Inayama Yoshihiro was the leader of the Japanese steel industry at that time.

The meeting between the two leaders that summer was truly "historic." Inayama Yoshihiro attentively listened to Park Tae-joon's explanation of the circumstances surrounding POSCO's life-or-death crisis after being dumped by KISA (Korea International Steel Associates). He was deeply moved by the "young" chairman's passionate enthusiasm, pure sense of mission, and vision for business. He promised Park Tae-joon the Japanese steel industry's full support for POSCO during this first meeting. This promise materialized in the Japanese Technical Support Team, which came to the desolate plain of Young-il Bay and supervised the building of the steel plant by Koreans who had "neither the experience nor the technology." Although POSCO was born on April 1, 1968, it wasn't until April 1, 1970, two full years later, that President Park Chung-hee, Prime Minister Kim Hak-ryul, and Chairman Park Tae-joon were able to press the blast button at the groundbreaking ceremony. Those two years were a time of suspense and drama during which POSCO struggled to survive its life-or-death crisis, escaping the fate of being stillborn.

While the Japanese Technical Support Team, comprised of Japanese engineers from Nippon Steel Corporation and other Japanese companies, was supervising the construction of the POSCO plant in Young-il Bay, Park Tae-joon set a three-step goal for securing steel manufacturing technology for POSCO. The short-term goal was to "operate our plant on our own while the construction of the plant was being completed," the mid-term goal was to "break from the status of technological colony by accomplishing technological independence," and the long-term goal was to "own the highest level of technology in the world."

In order to reach the short-term goal, Park Tae-joon didn't spare any expense in providing study and training abroad for his employees despite POSCO's tight budget. Park Tae-joon earnestly encouraged and sincerely requested that trainees thoroughly learn advanced skills. When Park Tae-joon asked Inayama Yoshihiro for a favor concerning a training abroad program for his employees, Inayama Yoshihiro kindheartedly offered to assist. He did Park Tae-joon a great and "bold favor" by arranging for POSCO trainees to try running the entire system at Muroran Works in Hokkaido. As a result, POSCO employees ran the entire plant on their own on July 3, 1973, the day they completed the first phase of construction of the Pohang plant. At that time, POSCO also achieved the lowest unit cost of production in the world. POSCO had already begun writing "The Saga of Young-il Bay."

The Japanese Technical Support Team withdrew completely in December 1978, when POSCO finished its third phase of construction, attaining a 5,500,000-ton annual crude steel production capacity. Members of the Japanese team wrote, "POSCO overcame various hardships and succeeded in building a large-scale advanced steel company equal to Japanese steel companies in a very short period of time. By the time this company completes its fourth phase construction and expansion, it will be the best in the world in its production capacity and facilities. Due to the combination of excellent manpower and superb leadership of its CEO, it is only a matter of time before POSCO becomes the best steel manufacturing company in the world." About the time when POSCO became confident about its technological independence and the Japanese Technical Support Team acknowledged it, Deng Xiaoping of China visited Nippon Steel Corporation and had a pleasant chat with Inayama Yoshihiro. When Deng Xiaoping requested that Nippon Steel Corporation build a steel company like POSCO in China, Chairman Inayama answered, "It doesn't simply take money but a human being to build a steel company. You cannot build a steel company like POSCO if you don't have a person like Park Tae-joon in China." After thinking a while, Deng Xiaoping responded with "Then, we'll import Park Tae-joon." This is the famous episode of the "Park Tae-joon import," an incident that no doubt helped the early stages of POSCO's entry into China about ten years later.

It was the summer of 1981 when the Japanese steel industry began turning against POSCO, citing "the boomerang theory." Their logic was simple. They argued that by helping POSCO, the Japanese steel industry had raised a tiger cub. Inayama's successors decided to stop their technological support for POSCO altogether when POSCO had already completed its fourth phase of construction and Park Tae-joon was pursuing the building of Gwangyang Works. This didn't hurt POSCO, however, because it had already achieved technological independence. Nevertheless, Park Tae-joon decided that POSCO couldn't continue to have an uncomfortable relationship with its "teacher" and that such a relationship couldn't be helpful to either side. He broke through this difficult situation meticulously and boldly from all directions. While continuing to push forward his plan to build the best steel plant in the world in Gwangyang Bay, applying the skills and experiences accumulated in Young-il Bay, Park Tae-joon countered "the boomerang theory" with "the cycle theory." His theory was that "an advanced country should be followed by a developing country, which should also be followed by an underdeveloped country." After countering Chairman Saito of Nippon Steel Corporation in this way, he also lobbied President Inayama, retired from day-to-day operation, to influence on his successors. He also went first to European steel companies to discuss the possibility of importing facilities for Gwangyang Works, bypassing their Japanese counterparts. In the end,

Japanese steel leaders couldn't agree among themselves and ended their export freeze based on their "boomerang theory."

When POSCO reached its long-term goal of "owning the highest level of technology in the world" together with the completion of Gwangyang Works, Park Tae-joon put his "cycle theory" into practice. He even gave POSCO's operation manuals to the Chinese steel industry that had jumped in as a latecomer and began building a modern steel company only in the late 1980s. When his successors were worried, he said, "This is inevitable. We have to go forward with better technology." As if to prove this idea, POSCO succeeded in the "Study of Commercialized Iron Production through the Finex Process" in 2007 for the first time in the world, fifteen years after it had begun the study in 1992 according to Park Tae-joon's instruction. The Finex process, a technology that broke new ground in the history of the world steel industry, is an innovative, eco-friendly iron-making process that does not require a preparation stage for the iron ores or other source materials including the cokes and sintering processes. In other words, the Finex process bypasses the cokes and sintering processes necessary in the Corex process, the only traditionally used iron-producing process, and the processes that emit the most environmental pollutants. Financially, the Finex process reduces both construction and operating costs by 15%. Currently there are many trainees from Nippon Steel Corporation of the former "teacher" country learning at POSCO in the former "student" country. POSCO, which has achieved the highest status in the world in many areas of steel manufacturing, is now collaborating strategically with Nippon Steel Corporation, its childhood teacher.

Perhaps it was during his keynote speech at the conference commemorating the 40th anniversary of the Korea-Japan Diplomatic Normalization in 2005 that Park Tae-joon criticized Japan most directly. He presented the task for the relationship between Korea and Japan from a Korean point of view in very simple language.

"Japanese often say that only a narrow strip of water lies between Korea and Japan, likening the Korean Strait to that narrow strip. Koreans often say that Japan is a country simultaneously close to and far from Korea, meaning geographically close, but psychologically distant. Koreans, Japanese, and Chinese all use the word *chin* (a Chinese word meaning 'friendly' or 'close'). Koreans usually use this word very positively like in *chingyo* (friendship), *chinsuk* (familiar), and *chingu* (friend). However, there are times when this word *chin* can mean something negative as in the word *chinil* (pro-Japanese). Interestingly, the *chin* in *chinil* means anti-nationalistic betrayal of our country. This symbolizes the problem inherent in the relationship between Korea and Japan even today forty years after the Korea-Japan Diplomatic Normalization. Only when the word *chin* in *chinil* can recover its original meaning of 'friendliness,' can the relationship between Korea and Japan become a close friendship."

He then continued to sharply criticize the Japanese role in the division of the Korean peninsula and urged Japanese to reflect on their responsibility.

"The Korean War originated from the division of our country. That division originated from colonial rule. Although the Cold War system of the US and USSR forced this division, Japanese colonial rule was at the bottom of it. Despite the fact that Japan was defeated in the Second World War, Japan should not forget the painful suffering that came from the division of the Korean peninsula. During those three years when poverty-stricken Korea fell into a hellish state because of the war as a result of the division, what did Japan do for Korea? I hope that Japanese leaders think seriously about this question. During the Korean War, Japan was not our ally. Japan played the role of military supplier for the US. This offered Japan a golden opportunity to rise from helpless ruins after its defeat in WW II and revive its economy. Older generations in Japan must remember well the period of prosperity during the 1950s called "the Jinmu boom." "Jinmu" was the era's name for the first king of Japan, right? So "the Jinmu boom" meant the greatest economic boom in Japanese history. In reality, "the Jinmu boom" became the basis for the strong growth of the Japanese economy. This special boom originating from the Korean War was a marvelous tonic for the revival of the Japanese economy. No wonder Korean intellectuals sighed, 'The Korean War occurred to revive the Japanese economy.' This bitter opinion expresses an unforgiving resentment towards those who incited the war, but it also urges Japan to realize its responsibility for the division of Korea and its moral obligation to help the Korean economy."

Colonization, division, war, ruins, extreme poverty,

corruption, the struggle between industrialization and democratization, and the financial foreign currency crisis... How did Park Tae-joon remember the times he lived through? I discovered a couple of clues to his thoughts.

First, his thoughts about the cause of colonization, for which he had no responsibility but which had influenced his life greatly. He very often expressed the tragic loss of our country in this way: "Chosun was unilaterally beaten and swallowed alive by Japan." Why couldn't Chosun fight back, let alone defend itself? He did not like the way people these days blame the Five Public Enemies of the Year of Eulsa and Japanese sympathizers above all. His counter argument was as follows: "Would Chosun not have been swallowed alive by Japan if it weren't for the Five Public Enemies of the Year of Eulsa, or Japanese sympathizers? Of course, we have to strictly punish the Five Public Enemies of the Year of Eulsa and pro-Japanese traitors, but there are things we have to consider even before their guilt. What, for example? First, we have to inquire about the responsibility of Chosun elites, leaders, high officials, and intellectuals who thought in terms of 'small China,' i.e. Chosun as the center of the universe, and we also have to inquire about the responsibility of our people. We have to first inquire about the responsibility of the entire country and only then that of the Five Public Enemies of the Year of Eulsa, etc. We should not use those Five Public Enemies and Japanese sympathizers to cover up the responsibility of the entire class of officials, leaders, and intellectuals."

The second clue was about Park Tae-joon's way of

remembering Korean modernization, especially during the rule of Park Chung-hee. He argued, "Let's remember both the chains of dictatorship and those of poverty." Although our history showed the fierce opposition and struggle between industrialization and democracy as if they couldn't co-exist, Park Tae-joon thought their relationship should be complementary, not adversarial. Park Tae-Joon, who took the lead in following the road of sacrifice, who claimed that he belonged to "a generation that had to sacrifice itself for the happiness of future generations," wanted to ask young people who were liberated from political oppression and the oppression of poverty, those who were liberated for the first time in history from society-wide oppression this question: "Although industrialization and democracy snarled at each other like enemies, could we have succeeded in securing a basis for the success of both industrialization and democracy if either side had lost its way? It looks as if you guys want to remember Park Chung-hee only as an example of a political oppressor, but would the majority of our wise people throughout the entire country have accepted his kind of leadership if it hadn't been for the absolute poverty we inherited from five thousand years ago? Besides, in our condition at the time, could we have succeeded in economic development without the kind of leadership Park Chung-hee showed? In a country that didn't succeed in developing economically, how much democracy and social welfare could we have achieved? Therefore, don't you have to assess more objectively the period of modernization, the period of Park

Chung-hee's rule during which I, for one, devoted myself with all my heart, without caring for my own material gain, to building the foundation for a first-rate country, motivated only by my sense of mission? If you don't remember that period fairly, shouldn't I be resentful?"

Park Tae-joon opened up the road to a first-rate country, a road that created glory for the community through his lonely struggles. Only when he was nearing the end of his life did his contemporaries begin calling him a "hero." The old hero closed his eyes without expressing to the world all the words pent up in his soul. They are now stored in my memory. His words like dewdrops will remain inside me like precious beads.

If he had received only 1% of POSCO stocks in recognition for his contribution to the success of the company he could have enjoyed a life of luxury like other founders of corporations, owning billions of dollars. But he did not receive a single POSCO stock. Owner of an estate as big as that of the average middle class residents of Seoul, he had only two wishes in the dusk of his life.

One wish was to build a steel company utilizing the funds and technology of POSCO in Wonsan or Hamheung in North Korea. "If only Pyongyang would open its doors, I could drag my old body there and lay the foundation for modernization by building a steel company. We could select about a thousand technicians from the North Korean army and train them in Pohang or Gwangyang. Funding? No problem! Banks will be lining up to lend money, given POSCO's credit rating." His voice with its childlike excitement is still ringing in my ears.

The other wish was for a Korean to win the Nobel Prize in the field of science. He eagerly looked forward to such news. He hoped to buy the winner a nice dinner. In 2010, he had POSCO TJ Park Foundation conduct research on the educational system of countries that had many Nobel Laureates in science. "We make such a fuss if we lose a soccer game against Japan even by a single goal. Why are we so careless when we lose 17:0 to Japan in Nobel Prizes in science? Something's definitely wrong, very seriously wrong. We have to improve our education. We have to educate better than Japan. Only then can we beat and overcome Japan." His voice carrying firm conviction is still ringing in my ears.

What and How to Remember?

Chung Joon-yang, the CEO of POSCO, promised in his memorial address for Park Tae-Joon, honorary chairman of POSCO, that "we will systematically illuminate your ideas and thoughts, share them with our society and descendants as public resources, and seek solutions to our future challenges from them." All we have to do now is to follow through on this promise. POSCO should establish the direction and "intellectuals" should be in charge of study and research. Of course, this is not the kind of task cowardly intellectuals, quick to follow where the political wind is blowing, would take on. Park Tae-joon despised corruption above all. Isn't cowardice the highest form of corruption for intellectuals? On July 20,

2008, Park Tae-joon, an elderly man in his 80's, said in an interview with a newspaper, "Like in the military, I never minded being fired for acting justly."

Park Tae-joon made a great achievement for his times like Lee Byung-chull of Samsung and Chung Ju-yung of Hyundae. However, Park Tae-joon was different from others in one fundamental way, he never worked for himself. His business was not 'his' business, and his great achievement didn't become his or his family's assets. He took care of national business even more sincerely and passionately than his own business. His achievement was most outstanding and exemplary, yet most exceptional in the world of business. This is how Park Tae-joon differs fundamentally from Lee Byung-chull and Chung Ju-yung. Song Bok called the kind of thought Park Tae-joon embodied in his achievement "Taejoonism." Now Taejoonism is waiting for intellectual and conscientious illumination by our intellectuals who are alert for signs of corruption. The Republic of Korea paid a "very belated and last courtesy" by having Park Tae-joon, its great worker, buried in a plot of ten or so square yards in the National Cemetery in Dongjak-dong, Seoul. Chung Jun-yang, his junior and student, ended his memorial address dedicated to the deceased, who was lying in the cold winter earth of minus 10 degrees Celsius with the last lines of Han Yong-un's "Your Silence."

Just as we are afraid of parting when we meet,
We believe we will meet again when we part.

Ah, even though you are gone
I have never sent you away.

Not sending Park Tae-joon away does not mean simply looking up to him and remembering his achievements. It means systematically researching and studying his anguishing thoughts, ideas, and struggles, in order to share them with society and apply them to future situations. Dasan Jeong Yak-yong left small achievements of reform and his writings, which we continue to study and apply to our contemporary situations. Chongam Park Tae-joon's achievements in twentieth-century Korea are enormous, overwhelmingly and incomparably greater than those of Dasan in his times. Unlike Dasan, however, he didn't leave us writings. Yet, writings are in the end a system of language, and a system of language houses thoughts and beliefs. Chongam left many words behind, just not written ones. A collection of his sayings would fill more than ten thousand octavo pages. There are enough texts for the study of Park Tae-joon's ideas: POSCO, POSTECH, schools built by POSCO, the POSCO TJ Park Foundation, his enormous contributions to modern Korean history, and the enormous collection of his sayings which form a home for his beliefs and ideas.

Lee Dae-hwan Novelist; Publisher of *ASIA: Magazine of Asian Literature*

Winner of the 1980 International PEN Korean Center Novel Contest
Winner of the 1989 Novel Contest Commemorating the 400th Issue of *Hyundae Munhak*
Director of POSCO TJ Park Foundation
Member of the Board of Directors, The Association of Writers for National Literature
Director of the Pohang Community Research Institute
Member of the Advisory Committee, POSCO Research Institute

Major Publications
Novels | *Dawn, Just Before Sunrise* (1991), *Winter House* (1999), *The Slow Bullet* (2001), *The Red Whale* (2004), *Kundon* (Big Fortune) *and Condom* (2008)
Short Story Collections | *A Small Flag* (1995), *Poetry That Went Into Fish's Stomach* (1997)
Biographies | *Park Tae-joon* (2004), *Blue Youth on the Stream of Melted Iron: the Lives of Founding Members of POSCO* (2006)

연구논문 | 특수성으로서의 태준이즘 연구
Article | A Study on Taejoonism as a Principle

특수성으로서의 태준이즘 연구

송복

Ⅰ. 왜 태준이즘(Taejoonism)인가

태준이즘은 가능한가. 포항종합제철주식회사(이하 포스코)를 창업한 박태준(朴泰俊) 회장의 이름 뒤에 이즘(ism)을 붙인 '태준이즘'이라는 명명(命名)이 영국의 대처리즘, 미국의 레이거니즘처럼 가능한가. 그처럼 거부 없이 수용되고 저항 없이 소통되는 사상 유형이나 지식 체계 혹은 사고방식이나 실행 모드가 될 수 있는가.

태준이즘 뿐 아니라 지난 100년의 한국사에서 최고의 기업인으로 꼽히는 이병철(李秉喆) 정주영(鄭周永) 구인회(具仁會) 유일한(柳一韓) 회장 등[1], 이 최고 CEO 이름 뒤에도 태준이즘과 꼭 같이 이즘을 갖다 붙일 수 없을까. 태준이즘이 가능하다면 이들 네 사람의 이름 뒤에도 이즘이 붙을 수 있고 그리고 그 '○○이즘'의 창시자가 분명히 될 수 있다. 이들은 모두 그 특유의 사상이나 지식 체계, 사고나 실행 모드가 있고, 그로 해서 무(無)에서 유(有)를 창조해냈다.

그런데 왜 유독 태준이즘인가. 더 말할 것도 없이 유독 태준이즘일 이유는 없다. 이미 본 대로 우리는 그 이름 뒤에 '이즘'을 붙이고도 남을 인물들이 많다. 그들은 모두 그들 특유의 사상과 방식으로 그들 특유의 스타일로 국가 '재조의 운(再造之運)'[2]을 만들어낸 사람들이다. 그럼에도 태준이즘을 내세우

---

1) 한국경영사학회가 지난 100년의 한국사에서 최고 기업인으로 이 네 분을 선정했다《중앙일보》, 2011년 1월 4일, B1.
2) 나라를 다시 세우고 부흥시키는 전통 사회에서 빈번히 기원되고 시도되었던 국가관.

는 이유는 무엇인가. 그것은 위에 사람들이 모두 사기업(私企業)을 일으킨데 비해, 유독 박태준(朴泰俊)만은 공기업(公企業)을 사기업 이상으로 일으켰기 때문이다. 자본주의 시장경제에서 '주인 없는 기업은 반드시 망한다'[3]는 정설(定說)을 깨고, '주인 없는 기업을 주인 있는 기업 이상으로', 그것도 초일류 기업으로 만들어냈기 때문이다. 세계 공기업 사상 그 유례를 찾을 수 없는 유일한 사례를 거기서 또한 찾을 수 있기 때문이다.

'태준이즘'의 명명은 그 같은 대성취의 특수성에서 비롯된다. 확실히 포스코는 한국 산업사에서 가장 '빛나는 성취'일 뿐 아니라 가장 '특별한 성취'다. 삼성과 현대, LG, 유한양행은 빛나는 성취이지만 특별한 성취는 아니다. 그 성취는 자본주의 시장경제가 작동하는 사회에선 어디든 보편적으로 존재하는 보편적 성취다. 그 보편적 성취는 미국에도 있고 서유럽에도 있고 일본에도 있다. 그러나 포스코는 그 어느 나라에도 없다.

오직 한국에만 있는 '특별한 성취'다. 보편성이 아닌 지극히 특수성을 띤 성취다.

무엇이 그렇게 만들어 냈는가. 그 어떤 요인 그 어떤 비결이 그것을 가능케 했는가. 그 성취의 비결은 많은 참여자들의 입을 통해 널리 알려졌고, 그 성공의 요인들은 많은 학자들의 연구를 통해 이미 잘 설명되었다. 그러나 그것은 모두 분리된 개별 사건을 분리된 개별 요인들의 인과론을 통한 설명일 뿐이다. 그것이 태준이즘이라는 주제로, 태준이즘이라는 시각으로, 그리고 태준이즘이라는 사상과 철학 신념으로 종합화해서 설명되지는 못했다. 이론적으로 태준이즘은 그 모든 사건들, 그 모든 요인들을 하나의 맥락으로 만들어 융합하고 종합화하는 설명 체계다.

---

3) 그 대표적 사례는 세계 최고 항공사인 일본 항공 JAL이 망한 것. 1987년 민영화하면서 최대 주주 지분이 3%에도 못미침으로써 사실상 정부가 주인 행세 하는 '주인 없는 민영기업'이 되고, 끝내는 천문학적인 부채를 감당 못해 지난 2010년 1월 법정 관리 기업으로 들어갔다.

1. 이즘의 두 얼굴

자전적(字典的) 의미의 이즘(ism)은 주의(主義)다. 공산주의 사회주의 자본주의처럼 으레 무슨 주의라 하면 모두 영어의 이즘이다. 이 주의와 대동소이한 의미로 쓰이는 교리(敎理), 교의(敎義), 학설(學說)도 모두 이 이즘이다. 특정 유형의 사상 특정 성격의 행위도 이즘이다. 이처럼 이즘은 갖가지로 표현될 만큼 그 외연(外延)이 넓다. 그러나 아무리 그것이 넓고 아무리 다른 표현으로 구사되어도 거기에는 하나의 공통성이 있다. 그것은 일관성이다. 이즘은 이 일관성이 핵심이며 요체다. 일에 대해서든 외부 세계에 대해서든 일관성 있는 인식이며, 일관성 있는 행동 원칙이 이즘의 근간(根幹)이다. 바로 뿌리며 줄기다.

이 일관성 때문에 이론이나 지식도 체계화되고, 자기주장도 오롯한 체계를 갖는다. 이 일관성 때문에 사람들 간에 우의도 생기고 신의도 두터워지고, 사업도 함께 도모할 수 있게 된다. 무엇보다 이 일관성 때문에 인간 사회 유지에 가장 중요한 행위 예측이 가능해진다. 어떤 사업을 할 것인가, 그 사업을 하면 그 결과는 장차 어떻게 될 것인가가 예측된다. 그래서 사람들은 마음 놓고 미래를 계산하며 일을 한다. 거기에 자기 동료나 윗사람의 이즘 – 주의가 분명하고 확실하면 그가 가지고 있는 생각과 행동의 일관성 또한 분명하고 확고해서 성원 간 원활한 소통과 효과적인 작업은 말할 것도 없고, 기대한 것 이상의 성과도 낼 수 있다.

그러나 이 이즘이 갖는 일관성이 반드시 좋은 것만은 아니다. 다른 말로 이즘의 역기능이 그 순기능에 못지않다는 것이다. 부작용도 많고 폐단도 많고 병도 많이 유발하는 것이 이 이즘의 또 다른 측면, 다른 얼굴이다. 가장 단적인 예가 이즘의 도그마성이다. 도그마는 자기가 믿는 바를 부동(不動)의 진리로 생각하는 것이다. 이성으로써 비판하거나 증명하는 것을 인정하지도 않고 용서하지도 않는다. 이러한 도그마성은 이즘이 확고할수록 단단해지는 경향이 있다. 이 모두 이즘이 내포한 일관성 때문이다.

그래서 이 이즘과 이즘이 갖는 일관성 때문에 시의(時宜)를 놓치는 경우가 비일비재하다. 일관성을 고집하다 때를 놓쳐 망하는 조직이 수도 없이 많다. 니체는 이 일관성의 사슬에 묶여 변화를 거부하는 모든 이데올로기, 모든 주의와 사상, 학설, 교리, 교의를 모두 우상이라 했다. 그리고 지식인의 가장 중요한 역할은 이 우상파괴라고 역설했다. 공산주의 국가들이 수십 년간 굳게 지키기만 했던 그들의 이즘이 붕괴되는 것도 변화를 거부한데서 온 이즘의 우상화 때문이라는 것을 생각하면, 이 이즘의 부정성, 이즘이 내포하는 일관성의 역기능성이 얼마나 심각한 것인지 알 수 있다. 그래서 'ㅇㅇ이즘'이라는 이름 뒤에 붙은 이즘이 꼭 좋은 것만은 아니다.

문제는 정상 현상의 이즘이냐 병리 현상의 이즘이냐다. 혹은 순기능하는 이즘이냐 역기능하는 이즘이냐이다. 정상 현상의 순기능하는 이즘만이 이즘으로서의 의미가 있다면, 그 이즘은 어떻게 작동되는 이즘인가. 그것은 이즘 원래 속성인 일관성을 지니면서 '열려 있는 것'이어야 하고, '소통되는 것'이어야 하고, 그리고 '변화를 수용하는 것'이어야 한다. 열림과 소통과 변화 수용, 그러나 이 셋은 모두 열림에서 시작된다. 열리면 소통되고 소통하면 변화한다. 이즘의 도그마성 탈피, 우상파괴도 이에서 비롯된다. 이 때 이즘은 두 얼굴이 아니라 하나의 얼굴이면서, 'ㅇㅇ이즘'으로써 길이 되고 동력이 된다.

2. 이즘 형성의 3요소

정상 현상, 순기능하는 긍정적 의미의 이즘, 길이 되고 동력이 되는 'ㅇㅇ이즘'은 3가지 요소로 구성된다. 그 첫째가 사상이라면, 둘째는 리더십, 셋째로는 업적 혹은 치적(治積)이고, 더 나아가 그 업적, 치적으로 이룬 그 사람의 대성취를 헤아려 볼 수 있다. 물론 그 사람의 독특한 개성, 카리스마도 들 수 있고, 명민한 두뇌와 탁월한 통찰력도 들 수 있다. 그러나 이는 모두 사상과 리더십에서 설명할 수 있다.

(1) 사상(思想)

첫째로 사상. 사상은 사회와 인간에 대한 자기 생각이고 견해다. 하지만 단순한 생각이나 견해가 아니라 좀 더 깊이 사고하고 좀 더 면밀히 추구하고, 그렇게 해서 좀 더 정확히 판단을 내린 생각이며 견해다. 그 같은 사고와 추구 그리고 판단의 과정을 거치면 그 생각, 견해는 반드시 체계가 서고 논리가 따른다. 여기서 말하는 사상은 그 같은 추구 과정과 사고작용을 거친, 사회와 인간에 대한 특정 판단 체계며 인식 체계다. 단순한 생각이나 견해보다는 좀 더 고차원적이다.

이 사상이 'ㅇㅇ이즘'이 되려면 거기에는 반드시 다른 사상과 차별되는 두 가지 특징이 있어야 한다. 그 하나가 그 사상의 특유성(特有性)이라면, 다른 하나는 그 사상의 유연성(柔軟性)이다. 첫째로 특유성은 그 사람 고유의 사상이다. '하늘 아래 새로운 것은 없다'는 말처럼, 사실 그 사람만이 갖는, 유일무이한 사상이란 있을 수 없다. 그러나 동시대인의 다른 사람과 눈에 띄게 차별화되는 그 사람 특유의 사고며 원칙, 그 사람 특유의 정책, 혹은 그 사람 특유의 행태는 있다. 이런 것이 있어 그 사람 특유의 부르짖음 혹은 외침, 특유의 절규가 있다.

그 사람 특유의 사상은 이 모든 것의 종합이다. 이 종합화된 특유의 사상이 있어 그 사람 특유의 길이 창시된다. 남이 걷는 길과는 다른 그 특유의 길, 그 길은 남이 향하는 방향과 다른 방향의 길이며, 남이 향유하는 시각(視覺)과 다른 시각의 길이다. 물론 그 길은 자기 혼자만 가는 길이 아니다. 자기와 더불어 함께 가는 사람, 혹은 함께 일하는 사람과 같이 가는 길이다. 바로 '조직의 길'이다. 으레 자기가 속해 있고 자기가 관리하고 그리고 그 모두가 공유하는 공동의 목적을 다함께 달성하려는 그 '조직의 길'이다. 예컨대 포스코-way 삼성-way 현대-way가 만들어진다면, 그렇게 해서 만들어진다.

'특유하다'는 것, 그것은 범상(凡常)하다는 것과 반대되는 것이다. 범상하다는 것은 어디나 다 있는 것이다. 그것은 누구나 생각할 수 있고 누구나 해 낼 수 있고 누구나 달성할 수 있는 것이다. 누구나 할 수 있는 예사로운 것이다. 범상한 것은 동시에 범용(凡庸)한 것이다. 범용한 것은 보통으로 어디나 통하는 것이다. 중용(中庸)과 같은 것이다. 보통으로 가장 많이 통하고 가장 잘 통하는 것이 중용이라면, 범상한 것, 범용스러운 것은 좋은 것이다. 하지만 그것이 세상을 바꾸지는 못한다. 그것이 침체된 것을 일으킬 수 없고 정체된 것을 변화시킬 수는 없다. 오직 '특유'한 것, 세상의 보통 사람들이 생각하지 못한 것 해내지 못한 것, 그것이 새로운 기업을 일으키고, 나라를 새롭게 부흥시키고, 세상을 다르게 바꿔 놓는다. 그래서 남이 갖지 못한 혹은 남과 차별되는 그 사람 특유의 사상이 'ㅇㅇ이즘'을 만들고, 그 'ㅇㅇ이즘'이 대성취를 가져오는 길이고, 동력이 되는 것이다.

사상의 특유성에서처럼 'ㅇㅇ이즘'이 되려면, 둘째로 그 사상은 반드시 유연성을 떼어야 한다. 유연성은 글자 그대로 부드럽고 무른 것이다. 돌이나 쇠처럼 굳거나 경직(硬直)되어 있는 것이 아니다. 경직은 곧고 꼿꼿한 것이고, 굽거나 휘어짐이 없는 것이다. 유연은 그 반대의 성질을 지닌 것이다. 가장 부드러운 것, 가장 무른 것은 물이다. 물이 유연의 전형(典型)이라 해도 인간이 물처럼 될 수는 없다. 그저 가장 좋은 것, 흔히 말하는 상선(上善)은 상선약수(上善若水)[4]라는 말처럼 물이라고 생각할 뿐이다.

유연의 또 다른 면은 신축성(伸縮性)이다. 아니, 유연하면 신축성이 생겨나는 것이다. 유연은 신축성의 원인 제공자이고 신축성은 유연의 결과인 것이다. 사상의 유연성, 그것은 사고와 행동의 신축성을 불러오고, 신축성은 다시 사고와 행동의 폭을 넓힌다. 신축성은 늘임과 줄임, 굽힘과 폄을 다 아우르는 것이다. 그러나 경직된 돌과 쇠는 그렇게 할 수가 없다. 오로지 곧고 굳기만 하면 부서지지 않으면 깨어질 뿐이다. 거기에는 유연이 갖는 흡수력도 탄력도 발휘될 수 없다. 오로지 이즘의 일관성만 유지해서 새로운 변화를 강구할 수도 시도할 수도 없게 한다.

그러나 사상의 유연성과 그리고 신축성은 이즘의 특성인 일관성, 무엇보다 그 일관성에 내포된 부정성과 역기능성을 제거한다. 그리고 조직에 신선한

---

4) 노자(老子) 8장, 상선(上善)은 최상의 선, 상고(上古)시대의 선 개념. 물이 최고의 선이라는 것.

바람 새로운 바람을 불어 넣어 조직이 응고되는 것을 막는다. 나아가 조직의 관료제화를 막고, 조직 지도자들의 독단주의 권위주위를 막는다. 이렇게 해서 사상의 유연성은 사상의 특유성과 한가지로 '○○이즘'을 만들어 내고, 그리고 그 이즘이 대성취로 나가는 길이 되고 동력이 되게 한다.

(2) 리더십

둘째로 리더십. 리더십 역시 '○○이즘'을 형성하는 한 큰 축이 되려면 그 사람 특유의 리더십 유형, 내지 리더십 스타일이 있어야 한다. 그 유형과 그 스타일은 다른 리더에게서 느끼지 못하는 그 사람 특유의 정신일 수도 있고, 그 지도자만이 내보이는 미래상이며 비전일 수도 있다.

리더십 연구자들이 나누는 리더십 유형은 으레 두 개 아니면 세 개, 드물게는 네 개 정도다. 그 중에서 가장 많이 언급되고 인용되는 리더십 유형은 거래형과 변환형, 또는 민주형, 방임형, 권위형이다.[5] 이런 리더십 유형의 분류는 현실에서 작동되는 가지가지 형태의 리더십 특징들을 추상화해서 이론적으로 나눈 것일 뿐이다. 이런 이론화 과정에선 실제 현실에서 보여지는 그 어떤 특이한 감동적 리더십도 거래형 아니면 변환형, 또는 민주형과 방임형, 아니면 권위주의형으로 추상화되고 만다. 따라서 '○○이즘'을 만드는 리더십 스타일 또는 특징들을 찾아내는 데 이런 유형의 분류는 그다지 효용적 가치를 보여주지 못한다.

그렇다면 리더십의 그 어떤 요소들이 '○○이즘'을 형성하는가. 혹은 아니면 리더십의 그 어떤 특징들이 그것을 만들어내는가. 그것은 세 가지로 나눠볼 수 있다. 첫째로 영감이다. 지도자는 조직 성원들에게 영감을 보여주어야한다. 영감은 종교적 지도자나 카리스마적 지도자가 자기를 따르는 사람들에게 보이는 감응력(感應力)이다. 감응력은 몸과 마음을 함께 움직이는 힘이다. 마치 전류가 흐르듯 마음에 감동이 일고, 영성(靈性)이 생겨나듯 지도자와 행동 의지를 같이 하는 것이다. 이러한 영감은 종교 지도자나 카리스마적

---

5) 이러한 리더십의 분류와 연구는 James M. Burns, *Leadership* (Harper & Row)가 대표적 저서.

지도자가 아닌 일반 리더들에게도 얼마든지 있다. 핵심은 성원들에게 주는 감응력이다. 정신과 마음으로 감응을 주는 리더는 모두 영감의 리더십을 발휘하는 지도자다. 이 영감, 이 감응력이야말로 'ㅇㅇ이즘'을 만들어내는 리더십의 필수 요소다.

둘째로 몰입이다. 몰입(沒入)은 일에 전념케 하는 리더십이다. 전념(專念)은 마음을 오로지 자기가 하는 일, 그 한 가지 일에만 쏟는 것이다. 그러나 몰입을 가져 오는 리더십은 그런 전념 이상의 것이다. 전념하되 자기를 초월하는 희생정신과 자기의 모든 정력을 다 바치는 헌신, 그리고 충성심을 자아내는 리더십이다. 이기적 인간들에게 도시 그러한 것이 가능한가. 영성이 덮인 종교 기관이 아님에도 그러한 몰입은 생겨나는가. 더구나 자기 계산에 관성화된 현대인에게 더 높은 보상이 주어지지 않는데도 그런 몰입과 전념이 가능한가. 'ㅇㅇ이즘'이 형성되려면 리더는 반드시 그런 몰입의 리더십을 발휘해야 한다. 그 리더십 없이는 무엇보다 'ㅇㅇ이즘'이 내는 '대성취'가 일어날 수 없다.

셋째로 사기다. 사기(士氣)는 의기의 충만이다. 의기가 충만해서 사기가 넘쳐나게 하는 리더십, 그 리더십은 영감, 몰입의 리더십 못지않게 리더십의 한 축(軸)을 이루는 핵심 요소다. 말할 것도 없이 이 핵심 요소는 'ㅇㅇ이즘'을 만들어내는 리더십의 절대 요소이다. 흔히 말하는 사기는 물질 보상의 함수이고, 지위 높낮이의 함수다. 보상이 많으면, 지위가 높이 올라가면 사기도 그만큼 진작된다. 하지만 그렇게 해서 사기를 올리는 리더십은 금세 임계점에 도달한다. 물질이든 지위든 그 보상은 한정되어 있기 때문이다. 그런 사기의 리더십을 여기서 재론할 필요는 없다. 오직 'ㅇㅇ이즘' 창출에 직결되는 사기는 물질적 보상이 많든 적든, 지위의 사다리에 쉽게 올라앉든 못 앉든, 그에 관계없이 향상되는 사기다. 항시 사기가 충만해서 혈기 왕성한 작업의 공간, 혹은 도전의 공간을 만들어내는 리더십, 그런 사기 진작의 리더십이 'ㅇㅇ이즘'을 만들어내는 리더십이다.

(3) 업적(業績)

셋째로 업적. 업적은 지도자의 사상과 리더십의 결과다. 더 구체적으로는 성과(成果)다. 성과가 없다면 'ㅇㅇ이즘'도 없다. 대처리즘이 '대처리즘'인 것은 대처 수상의 성과, 높은 업적 때문이다. 레이거니즘이 '레이거니즘'인 것도 같은 이유에서다. 중요한 것은 이 성과 – 업적이 어떤 업적이냐이다. 그 것은 무엇보다 가시적이어야 하고, 그리고 대다수 사람들이 공인하고 지지하는 것이어야 한다. 그것도 그의 생전에, 치적과 동시에 공인되고 지지받는 것이 일반적이다. 먼 훗날 그의 사후에 인정되어 그 지도자 이름 뒤에 붙여진 'ㅇㅇ이즘'의 예는 찾아보기가 그리 쉽지 않다.

문제는 어느 정도의 업적이냐는 것이다. 그것은 한마디로 '대성취'다. 누구에게나 이론의 여지없이 받아들여지는 대성취, 지금까지 추세를 뒤엎는, 혹은 역사의 장을 다시 쓰도록 하는 그런 대성취여야 하는 것이다. 단순히 높은 수준, 혹은 괄목할 만한 수준에서 평가되는 그런 '높은 수준'의 업적, 혹은 '괄목할 만한 수준'의 업적은 언제나 이론(異論)의 여지를 남긴다. 그 높은 평가, 괄목할 만한 평가에 대한 다른 논의의 반대자가 속출한다는 뜻이다. 'ㅇㅇ이즘'을 만드는 대성취는 비록 반대자가 반대를 해도 인정하는 대성취이고, 거부자가 거부를 해도 수용하는 대성취다. 그런 면에서 'ㅇㅇ이즘'과 대성취는 둘이 아니고 하나이다. 또 다른 측면에서 대성취는 'ㅇㅇ이즘'의 시작이며 끝이다.

Ⅲ. 태준이즘 성립의 특성들

앞머리 「왜 태준이즘인가」의 논의에서 태준이즘 성립의 근거며 시작은 '대성취'라 했다. 다른 사기업 창시자들과 달리 공기업을 사기업 이상으로 일으킨 대성취. 그것도 보편성으로서의 대성취가 아닌 특수성으로서의 대성취다. 그 특수성도 선진국에서 보는 '유(有)의 세계'에서의 그것이 아니라 개발 초창기 국가들이 직면한 '무(無)의 세계'에서 나타난 특수성이다. 개발 초창기 국가도 터키나 브라질처럼 세계은행(IBRD)이 가능성을 인정한 나라의 그것이 아니라 그같은 세계적 대기구가 아예 희망도 가능성도 저버린 국가[6]에서 나타난 특수성으로써의 대성취다.

비유컨대, 거대한 강, 시혜 가득한 대하가 대성취라면, 그리고 그 대하를 만든 대자연이 대지(大地)의 작동(作動)이며 기류이고 바람, 바로 대기(大氣)의 작용(作用)이라면, 대성취를 가져온 힘은 자연이 아닌 인간, 한 인간의 사상이며 리더십이다. 한 인간의 특유하고도 확고한 사상 없이 대성취는 존재할 수 없고, 한 인간의 특유하고도 탁월한 리더십 없이 대성취는 실현될 수 없다. 그 사상은 미래상(未來像)으로써 가시적인 것이며, 가치(價値)로써 지금 바로 이 순간 최상의 것이며, 그리고 성취로써 반드시 흔들림 없는 믿음을 제시하는 것이다. 그 리더십은 영(靈)으로 심(心)으로 매료되는 것일 뿐 아니라 내 모든 에너지를 전력투구케하는 리더십이고, 그리고 내 의기(意氣)를 하늘 높이 치솟게 하는 리더십이다.

태준이즘의 형성 그리고 그 성립은 오직 이 같은 사상, 그 같은 리더십이 있음으로해서이다. 오직 사상이며 리더십의 존재여부다. 그렇다면 그 태준이즘을 구성하고, 태준이즘을 'ㅇㅇ이즘'으로 체계화하고 지속적으로 존속, 유지하도록 하는 그 사상은 무엇이며 그 리더십은 어떤 것인가. 그리고 태준이즘이 만들어내는 현실태(現實態) — 태준웨이(Taejoon-way)[7]는 어떻게 이 사상이 리더십으로 만들어지고 실제 '조직의 길'로 어떻게 기능하고 어떻게 정착하는가.[※]

태준이즘을 형성하는 사상은 3가지로 요약할 수 있다. 그것은 박태준 사상의 특징이기도 하고 박태준 사상을 박태준 고유의 사상으로 만드는 요소이

---

6) 1969년 2월 세계은행(IBRD)은 "한국에서의 일관제철소 건립 타당성 없음"으로 결정을 내렸고, 대한국제제철 차관단(KISA)도 차관 공여를 거부했다. 세계은행은 터키와 브라질이 일관제철소 건립이 타당하다고 하여 차관을 해주었으나 이들 두 나라는 그 후 모두 실패했다.

7) 태준웨이는 통상적으로 포스코-웨이(POSCO-way)로 지칭된다.

※ 이글에서는 리더십과 업적은 제외하고 사상 하나만으로 태준이즘을 보기로 한다.

기도 하다. 이 셋은 또한 박태준 사상의 요체이면서 박태준의 진면목이기도 하다. 이것이 있어 태준이즘이 대처리즘이나 레이거니즘과 구별되는 것이다. 그것은 순명(殉命)과 성취(成就) 그리고 가치(價値)이다.

1. 순명(殉命)

첫째로 순명. 순명은 목숨을 걸고 목숨을 바치는 것이다. 목숨을 걸고 목숨을 바치는 것이 어떻게 사상이 될 수 있는가. 순명은 사상이기 전에 정신이다. 이 정신이 있어 세상을 보는 눈과 생각이 달라지고, 일에 임하는 의지와 의식이 새로워지고, 그리고 자세와 행동에 변화가 온다. 사상은 정신의 소산이다. 어떤 정신을 갖느냐가 어떤 사상을 형성하느냐를 결정한다.

목숨을 걸고 목숨을 바치는 순명보다 이 세상에서 더 지극한 것은 없다. 누구나 생명은 하나뿐이다. 그 하나뿐인 생명을 걸고 생명을 바친다는 것, 그것은 지극한 상태에 이른다는 의미다. 극한 상황에 다다른다는 것이다. 그 극한 상황, 아무나 이를 수 없는, 오직 생명을 바쳐야만 이를 수 있는 순명의 상황, 그 상황에 도달하고 그리고 극한을 경험한 사람은 어떤 정신과 어떤 심경, 어떤 영성을 갖게 되는가. 그것을 경험하지 못한 사람과는 어떻게 다른가.

거기에는 사회과학의 영역에서 도저히 과학화해서 설명할 수 없는 '재탄생(再誕生)'의 세계, 오로지 극한 상황에 한 번 올라섰던 사람만이 보여주는 거듭난 부활(復活)의 세계, 지금까지와는 전혀 다른 새로이 재조(再造)되는 그 어떤 영성의 상태를 상정할 수 있다. 흔히 보듯 눈빛이 달라져 형형하고, 얼굴이 생기로 충만해 광채가 이는 카리스마적 지도자나 종교지도자에게서 발견되는 그런 영적 상태가 바로 순명의 극한 상황에 이른 사람들의 그것이라 할 수 있다.

이런 사람들이 보이는 신통력과도 같은 형통하는 능력, 이 형통의 힘이 만들어내는 이른바 대성취는 이같이 순명하는 사람들에게서 빈번히 찾아 볼 수 있는 사례들이다. 역경(易經)에서 말하는 궁즉변(窮則變)이며 변즉통(變則

通)의 상황[8])도 바로 이런 순명을 말하는 것이라 할 수 있다. 극한 상황에 이르면 반드시 변화가 오고 변화가 오면 반드시 형통하는 길이 만들어진다는 것이다. 여기서 말하는 변화는 일반적으로 경험하는 통상의 그 변화가 아니라, 하늘과 땅이 뒤집히고 목숨이 모두 끊어지는 듯한, 완전히 극에 이른 상태의 변화다. 그 끝점에 도달한 상태에서 맞이한 변화가 곧 재탄생이고 부활이며, 그 재탄생이며 부활의 순간, 마침내 형통의 길이 열린다는 것이다.

그렇다면 박태준의 이러한 순명, 극한 상황에 이르러 비로소 형통의 길을 열은, 그래서 절대불가능한 상황에서 대성취를 이룩하는 박태준의 이러한 '순명'은 도대체 어디서 왔는가. 가장 쉽고 가장 간단한 대답은 DNA론이고 그리고 숙명론이고 신의 섭리론이다. 그런 DNA를 가지고 태어났다는 것이고, 숙명적으로 그리 되었다는 것이고, 신의 섭리가 그렇게 만들었다는 것이다. 그러나 이는 종교 지도자나 카리스마적 지도자들을 설명할 때 흔히 하는 말이다. 객관적이지도, 과학적이지도 못하다. 보다 객관적이고 과학적인 분석은 행태론자들이 설명하는 사회 환경론—도대체 어디서 어떻게 살아왔느냐이다. 어떤 인생의 역정이 그로 하여금 초생명(超生命)의 순명정신, 순명의 의지를 갖게 했느냐이다.[9])

미상불 그는 일제 식민지 시대를 살면서 강렬한 민족애의 고뇌, 그 자존의 상처가 폐부를 찌르고 있었을 것이고, 6·25의 처참한 전장(戰場)을 누비며 기약 없는 생명의 무상함 허무감, 분노와 원한, 뼛속 깊이 스며드는 적대감 그리고 치열한 조국애에 불탔을 것이고, 그리고 5·16의 사선을 넘으며 생명을 던지는 또 한번의 절대 상황에 도달했을 것이다. 그의 인생의 전반기는 조국도 민족도 국가도 사회도 최저점에 놓인 처절한 한계 상황을 사는 삶이었고, 그 한계 상황에서 그는 초생명 초현실의 순명을 내재화(內在化)했을지 모른다. 어쨌든 그의 인생 역정에서 순명은 최고의 정신세계가 되었고, 그것

8) 『역경(易經)』 「계사하전(繫辭下傳)」.
9) 포스코에서 흔히 말하는 "실패하면 우측에 있는 영일만으로 모두 들어가야 한다"는 "우향우 정신"도 순명의 한 표현이라 할 수 있지만, 그러나 이는 순명처럼 '지극한 상태'가 아니고 그럴 수도 있는 상황에 대한 경고며 각오의 의미, 치열한 마음 다짐의 의미로 보아야 할 것 같다.

도 그의 '고유의' 사상으로 승화되었을 것이다. 고유하다는 것은 동시대 비슷한 연배의 사람들이 일제시대와 6·25, 5·16을 같이 경험했으면서도 특이하게도 그만이 이 순명 사상에 이르렀다는 의미다.

그런 면에서 행태론자들의 이 사회환경론적 설명도 숙명론이나 생물학적 DNA론과 별 차이 없이 미진하다고 할 수 있다. 왜냐하면 같은 역경, 역정을 겪으면서 다른 사람들은 어째서 그와 같은 순명에 이르지 못했느냐, 아니면 그런 순명의 의지를 가진 사람이 어째서 그렇게도 드물었느냐의 해답은 이 행태론자들의 사회환경 결정론으로는 온전히 설명할 수 없기 때문이다. 그렇다면 그가 어떻게 순명 정신을 갖게 되었느냐에 대한 규명은 여기선 특별한 결과를 얻기 어렵다. 보다 중요한 것은 그의 순명 정신, 순명의 의지가 현실적으로 어떻게 구현되어 태준이즘이며 태준웨이를 만들어 냈느냐이다.

(1) 절대정신(絶對精神)

그의 순명이 절대정신을 갖게 했다는 것이다. 절대정신은 주·객관이 하나가 되어 완전한 자기 인식에 도달한 정신적 상태다. 누구에게나 주관이 있고 객관이 있다. 주관은 자기 위치, 자기 처지, 자기 입장에서 가진 자신의 생각이며 견해이자 관점이다. 이러한 주관은 자기 입장에서 세워진 그만큼 이미 형성된 자기 믿음, 자기 이념, 자기 소망과 굳게 결부되어 있고, 결부되어 있는 그만큼 사실을 사실대로 보기 어렵고, 현실을 현실 그대로 파악하기 힘들다. 자기 처지와 연결되어서 왜곡된 '사실'을 사실로 생각하고, 구부러진 '현실'을 현실로 인식한다. 객관은 자기를 벗어나고 자기를 초월해서 사실을 보고 현실을 보는 것이다. 절대정신은 그 같은 주관이 객관과 완전히 동일화(同一化)하는 것이고, 그것은 오직 자기 초월에서만 가능한 자기 초월의 정신이다.

순명은 이같이 자기 초월이고, 자기 초월에서의 주·객관이 완전히 일치한 절대정신이다. 태준이즘은 이 절대정신이 구현된 것이고, 현실적으로 그것은

「절대적인 절망은 없다」로 드러난다.[10] 전장터에서 죽음의 계곡을 누비고, 전쟁이 끝나고도 생사의 갈림길을 수없이 헤쳐 나온 사람만이 갖는 순명의 의지가 '절망은 없다'로 구체화되고, 그것도 일반적인 절망의 부정이 아니라 '절대적으로 존재하지 않는다'는 절대정신으로서의 절망에 대한 절대적 부정이다. 누구에게나 희망이 보이지 않는 상황은 존재한다. 마침내 희망이 완전히 사라져버리는 절대적 절망의 상황도 겪을 수 있다. 그때 절대적 절망은 절대로 없다는 절대부정이 가능할 수 있겠는가. 가능하다면 무엇이 그것을 가능케 하는가.

포스코의 건립 과정은 시초부터 '절대적 절망'의 연속이고, 그것도 가장 적나라한 상태에서 표출되는 절대절망의 연속 과정이라 해야 할 것이다. IBRD 차관공여에서나, 대일 청구권자금의 전용을 둘러싼 한일 각료 회담에서나 한결 같이 모든 것이 절대 절망의 표출이었다. 그러나 이런 절대 절망도 빙산의 일각처럼 그 많은 절대 절망의 한 부분일 뿐이었다. 그럼에도 절대적 절망의 절대적 부정이 있었다면 그 무엇이 그 절대 부정을 가능케 했는가. 말할 것도 없이 그것은 순명의 의지이고, 그 순명의 의지로 하여 주관과 객관이 완전히 하나가 되는, 그리고 자기 신념과 행동이 완전히 일치하는, 그 절대정신이 형성됨에 의해서다. 「절대적 절망은 없다」는 이 절대 부정의 이 절대정신이야말로 태준이즘의 벼리(대강 大綱)이고 태준웨이의 동력―엔진이다.

(2) 초결단(超決斷)

그의 순명이 초결단을 갖게 했다는 것이다. 태준이즘은 이 초결단이 있어 다른 이즘과 차별되는 태준이즘이 되고 다른 웨이와 다른 길을 가는 태준웨이―포스코웨이가 된다는 의미다. 초결단은 한마디로 운명을 가르는 결단이다. 삶과 죽음을 가르는 결단이고, 유(有)와 무(無)를 가르는 결단이며, 흥(興)과 망(亡), 성(成)과 패(敗)를 가르는 결단이다. 그 한 번의 결단으로 강줄기가 달라지고 산 높이가 달라지고 마침내 역사의 흐름이 달라지는 것이

10) 박태준 문집 6.25회상 글 중 「절대적인 절망은 없다」, 『우리 친구 박태준』 글 중 류찬우(柳贊佑). p.103.

다. 그 역사의 흐름을 바꿔놓는 그 엄청난 결단도 한 번으로 끝나지 않고 연속적으로 계속 새로 내려야만 하는 그런 초결단인 것이다.

일상(日常)에선 누구나 결단하고, 누구나 또 그 결단을 할 수 있는 능력—결단력을 지니고 있다. 그러나 그 결단은 결코 초결단으로 가지는 못한다. 그 결단이 설혹 잘못됐다 해도 운명이 달라지지는 않는다. 물론 운명을 바꾸는 결단도 많이 있다. 하지만 그같은 결단은 대개는 필연이 아니라 우연이다. 인간은 운명이 달라지는 그런 결단 상황에 가지도 않거니와 그런 상황에 이를 만큼 비현실(非現實)에 처하지도 않는다. 그만큼 일상에서 우리의 결단은 평범한 것이다. 그리고 그 평범한 결단도 그것을 보좌해주는 친구가 있고 그것을 상담해주는 선생이 있다. 자기 결단을 위해 자문할 수 있는 멘토는 어디든 있다.

그러나 이 초결단은 다르다. 누구도 그 초결단을 보좌할 수가 없다. 크라우제비츠가 그의 『전쟁론』에서 "어떤 명참모도 지도자의 결단력만큼은 보좌할 수 없다"고 말한 것이나 다름없다.[11] 전쟁은 생사를 가르고 흥망을 가르는 것이다. 그것도 작게는 수만 명 군대의 생사를, 크게는 한나라의 운명을 결단하는 것이다. 그야말로 초결단을 요하는 것이다. 종합제철소의 입지 선정—포항으로 할 것이냐 삼척으로 할 것이냐. 제2제철소를 아산만으로 할 것이냐 광양만으로 할 것이냐. 그것은 단순히 제철소의 건립 지역을 결정하는 것이 아니라 제철소의 운명 생(生)과 사(死)를 결정하는 초결단이다.

대일청구권자금을 전용(轉用)해서 제철자금으로 조기 활용한다는 '하와이 구상'—그 하와이 구상이 없었다면 그 아무것도 없었을, 그 어떤 결단도 의미가 없고 존재조차도 불가능했을, 당시 상황에선 그 누구도 생각할 수도 없고 가능할 수도 없었던, 그 자금전용의 결단이야말로 엄청난 초결단이다. 부실공사를 폭파해버리는 것. "선조들의 피값을 묻겠다" "조국의 백년대계가 여기서 출발한다"며 잘못된 공사를 아예 폭파해버리는 상상을 불허하는 대결

---

11) 『전쟁론』, 독일 프로이센의 장군인 카를 클라우제비츠(Carl Clausewitz, 1780-1831)가 나폴레옹 1세의 전쟁을 정리 분석하여 전쟁 이론을 체계화한 전쟁 전술의 고전. 이 책은 그의 사후인 1832년에 나왔다.

단, 예산과 인력과 공기(工期)에 매달리는 여느 CEO들에겐 그냥 어물쩡 얼마든지 눈감아 갈 수 있는 공사를 아예 '부실'이라는 단어조차 없애버리는 대폭파의 결단—이 모두 산업의 역사 그 어디에도 찾을 수 없는 초결단이다.

이 초결단이 도시 어디서 왔는가. 목숨을 걸고 목숨을 바치는 초생명(超生命)의 순명의 의지 없이는 불가능한 것이다. 그 순명 정신 순명 의지에서 만들어지고 구현되는 이 초결단, 그것이 바로 박태준(朴泰俊) 특유의 정신이며 길이다. 그리고 그것이 곧 태준이즘이며 태준웨이다. 태준이즘 태준웨이는 오로지 이 초결단으로 차 있다.

2. 성취(成就)

성취는 해내는 것이다. 우리말에 '해내는 것'은 첫째로 어려운 일, 감당하기 힘든 일, 누가 봐도 안된다고 생각하는 일을 잘 해낸다는 것이고, 둘째로 그것은 달리 생각할 여지도 없이 잘 당해내고 잘 이겨내서 놀랍도록 높은 성적을 낸다는 의미다. 한자어의 성취는 그렇게 해서 목적한 바를 달성한다는 것이다. 우리말의 '해낸다'는 말이든, 한자어의 성취든, 그 핵심에는 목적(目的)이 있고 그 목적을 가능한 수단을 다 동원해서 이룩한다는 공통적 의미가 있다. 그러나 여기서 말하는 해내는 것, 목적달성하는 것의 그 성취는 흔히 말하는 그런 성취가 아니라 대성취(大成就)다. 도저히 해낼 수도 없고 세울 수 없는 그런 대성취다.

하지만 그 대성취가 사상이 될 수 있는가. 놀랍도록 높은 업적을 이룩한 그 '대성취'는 대성취 일뿐, 결코 사상은 아니다. 목숨을 바치는 순명 정신처럼 '대성취 정신'이라고 표현할 수도 없고 하기도 어렵다. 다만 순명 의지처럼 대성취 의지라는 표현이 가능할 뿐이다. 그러나 의지만으로는 사상이 될 수 없고 'ㅇㅇ이즘'으로 형상화(形象化)할 수도 없다. 아이젠하워는 유럽전쟁에서 승리해서 대성취를 거뒀고, 맥아더는 태평양전쟁에서 승리해서 대성취를 이뤘다. 그러나 누구도 아이젠하워나 맥아더 이름 뒤에 '이즘'을 갖다 붙이지는 않는다. 그 대성취가 사상으로 연결되지 않기 때문이다.

그렇다면 '태준이즘'은 가능한가. 포스코, 포스텍이라는 박태준의 대성취가 사상이 될 수 있는가. 그 이전에 박태준의 대성취를 아이젠하워나 맥아더의 대성취에 비견할 수 있는가. 인류의 역사라는 측면에서, 또 글로벌 대성취라는 면에서 분명히 박태준의 대성취는 아이젠하워나 맥아더의 그것과 비교할 수 없다. 성취의 규모가 너무 다르기 때문이다. 만일 성취의 규모가 아니라면, 박태준의 그것과 아이젠하워—맥아더의 그것은 어떤 차이가 있는가. 결론적으로 한쪽은 사상을 이즘으로 형상화할 수 있는데 반해 다른 한쪽은 그것이 어렵다는 것이다. 왜 그런 다름이 만들어지는가. 이는 2가지로 요약해 설명할 수 있다. 그 하나가 불가능불용(不可能不容)사상이라면, 다른 하나는 조국애승화(祖國愛昇華)사상이다.

(1) 불가능불용(不可能不容)

불가능불용사상은 불가능은 없다, 절대 불가능은 절대로 없다는 사상이다. 나의 사전에 불가능은 없다는 말은 누구나 할 수 있고, 또 한다. 누구나 말할 수 있는 것만큼 실은 아무도 그 말을 믿지 않는다. 삶 자체가 가능보다는 불가능을 경험적으로 더 많이 증명해주기 때문이다. 그 경험의 세계에 살면서 '나의 사전에 불가능은 없다'는 말을 아무리 되뇌어도 거기에는 믿음이 없다. 믿음이 없는 만큼 그것은 허구이고, 허구인 만큼 사상이 될 수 없다. 그것이 사상이 되려면, 그것은 흔들림 없는 신념이 되어야 하고, 종교에서처럼 신앙이 되어야 한다. 이미 말한 것처럼 사상은 일관성이고, 일관된 믿음의 한 유형이다.

1950년대와 1960년대, 한국은 절대 불가능 상황에 처해 있었고, 사람들은 그 불가능 상황이 생활 세계 속에 일상화되고 관념화되어 있었다. 아무 것도 할 수 없다. 우리는 아무 것도 할 수 없는 민족이다라는 체념이 가슴으로 뼈로 농밀(濃密)해 있었다. 이런 상황은 어느 정도의 차이가 있다 해도 1970년대도 계속되었다. 이때 제철보국(製鐵報國)한다는 것, 아니, 그 이전에 제철산업을 시작한다는 것 자체가 불가능한 것이었다. 그 불가능, 그것도 '절대

불가능'이라는 것을 가장 정밀하게 아는 사람들이 일본 기업인이며 일본 정치인들이었다. 일본의 산업화와 전후 일본의 번영기를 만들고 살아온 이들 정·재계의 지도자들이 보는 한국에서의 절대 불가능 상황은, 미국보다 심지어는 세계 최고의 분석 기관이라고 하는 세계은행(IBRD)보다 더 확고했다.

일본도 미국도 세계은행도 대한국제철차관단(KISA)도 하나 같이 제철산업의 불가능, 그것도 '절대 불가능론'을 들고 나왔을 때, 박태준은 말했다. "나는 해냅니다. 기어코 해냅니다. 그것이 내가 이 땅에 태어난 의미입니다." 이 말은 일본 수상 후쿠다 다케오(福田赳夫)에게 정중히 그러나 단호히 한 말이고, 후쿠다 수상은 그의 회상에서 "나는 그의 단호한 태도에 너무 놀랐고, 당신이라면 가능할지도 모른다고 생각했다. 마침내 그는 나의 예측을 비웃기라도 하듯 해냈다. 경이로운 일이 아닐 수 없다"[12]고 말했다. 이런 상황은 포스텍을 만들 때도 많은 시차가 있었음에도 상황의 유사성은 지속되었다.

죽음의 계곡을 수없이 누비며 살아왔듯, 어떤 역경도 넘어설 수 있다, 어떤 불가능도 가능으로 바꿀 수 있다, 절대 불가능은 절대로 존재하지 않는다는, 그 의지가 굳은 신념이 되고 서원(誓願)이 되고 신앙이 되었을 때, 반드시 '해내고야 만다'는 치열한 욕구는 강렬한 성취 의지가 되고 성취 정신이 돼서 마침내 사상이 되고 이즘이 된다. "해 냅니다, 기어코 해냅니다, 그것이 내가 이 땅에 태어난 뜻입니다"—그보다 더 절실한 뜻은 없고 더 지극한 서원은 없다. 서원은 반드시 해내겠다, 맹세코 이루어 내겠다는 신 앞에서의 맹세다. 온몸을 불사르는 맹세며, 힘차게 솟아오르는 아침 태양과도 같은 확신이다. 그래서 절대 불가능은 절대로 존재할 수 없었던 것이다. 그 절대로 존재할 수 없다는 확신, 그것이 내가 태어난 의미와 하나가 되었을 때 그 보다 더한 서원 그보다 더한 신앙은 없다. 그 이상의 서원, 그 이상의 신앙이 없는 것만큼 그의 성취는 사상이 되고 이즘이 된다.

아이젠하워나 맥아더는 그 긴 전쟁 기간 중에도 한번도 절대 불가능이라는

---

12) 후쿠다 타케오, 『우리 친구 박태준』, p150.

상황에 처한 일이 없다. 어려운 상황과 힘든 고비는 수없이 겪었어도 그것이 절대 불가능 상황으로 떨어질 수는 없었다. 무엇보다 제2차세계대전은 영미 측에서 보면 처음부터 가능한 전쟁—이기는 전쟁이었다. 단 하나의 수치가 이를 말해준다. 전쟁 당시 1인당 GNP가 미국은 6천 달러가 넘고 영국은 6천 달러에 육박하는 데 비해 독일은 겨우 5천 달러 수준이고 이탈리아 3천 달러 일본은 2천 달러 수준이었다. 거기에 영미 측은 4천 달러 수준의 프랑스가 있었고, 거기에는 훨씬 못 미치지만 배후를 공격하는 소련이 있었다.[13] 연합국 측의 경제력이 그 적대 세력의 세 배에 달했다. 더구나 무기도 전쟁 인력도 전쟁을 지휘하는 인재도 영미 측이 월등했다. 아이젠하워—맥아더의 대성취 는 오직 대성취 일 뿐, 그 대성취가 신앙으로 이어질 이유도 없고, 사상으로 재무장될 필요도 없었다.

(2) 조국애 승화(祖國愛 昇華)

조국애 승화사상은 자신의 모든 애착과 모든 욕구를 조국이라는 대상으로 승화(昇華)시키는 것이다. 이 승화로 하여 성취가 신념이 되고 신앙이 되고, 마침내 사상이 되고 이즘이 되는 것이다. 승화는 보다 높은 영역, 보다 높은 차원으로 나아가는 것이다. 자신의 욕망 자신의 소망을 자신의 그것보다 더 높은 사회적인 것 국가적인 것 혹은 정신적인 것으로 바꾸어 놓는 것이다. 조 국애 승화는 자신의 모든 것—자기의 몸과 마음 모두를 조국에 바치는 것이 다. 자신은 없고 자신의 자리에 오로지 조국만 있고, 자신의 심장에 흐르는 피는 오로지 조국을 위해서만 뛰는 것이다. 흔히 말하는 사명감(使命感)— 주어진 책무를 각별한 의의와 긍지를 갖고 있는 힘을 다해 수행한다는, 그 같 은 사명감은 이 조국애 승화에 비하면 마음으로나 감정으로나 그 순도와 열 도가 훨씬 낮은 것이다.

문제는 그것이 가능한가이다. 아무리 충성을 가르쳐도 사람들은 나라에 잘 충성하지 않는다. 충성하는 경우에도 겨우 '의무적으로' 충성할 뿐이다. 예나

13) Robert S. Phillips ed., *Funk & Wagnalls New Encyclopedia*, Volume27, "World War Ⅱ", pp420-448.

지금이나 나라에 대한 충성심은 언제나 약하다. 그것은 어느 시대나 마찬가지이고 어느 나라나 마찬가지이다. 전통 사회에서 더러 보는 충성심, 그것은 자기가 모시는 군주에 대한 소위 말하는 불사이군(不事二君)의 충성심이다.[14] 오늘날 말하는 나라에 대한 충성심—로열티(loyalty)는 아니다. 로열티는 개인이 아닌 국가며 제도(制度)에 바치는 충성심이다. 자기 윗자리에 앉은 상관에 대한 충성심이 아니라 그 상관이 앉아 있는 자리—지위(地位)에 대한 충성심이다. 조국애 승화는 자기 나라 자기 조국에 바치는 충성심이다.

어떻게 그것이 가능한가. 어떻게 자신의 모든 애착, 욕구를 자기 나라 자기 조국애로 승화시킬 수 있는가. 어떻게 자신에게서 떼어내어 생명보다 더 소중한 사랑을 조국에 바칠 수 있는가. 그것도 신앙이 되고 마침내 사상으로 체화(體化)하도록 승화시킬 수 있는가. 더구나 조국이 자신에게 아무것도 베푼 것 없이 고통만 주고 절대 절망만 안겨 주었을 때, 그 조국을 향한 애정이 가능하겠는가. 일제 식민지 시대는 차치하고, 해방 후 아니면 1950년대나 1960년대로 되돌아가 보라. 그때 지식인들, 특히 대학생들이 울분을 토하며 버릇처럼 읽고 절규하던 시(詩)가 무엇이었는가를.

> 적을 골탕먹이게 진정 적에게 내주고 싶은 나라
> 이런 나라를 위하여
> 무슨 인과(因果)로 우리는 싸워야 하느냐고
> 언제나 나를 울리는 이 나의 모국이여.
>
> 유치환, 「나의 모국」 (1951)

> 먼 나라로 갈거나 / 가서는 허기져 콧노래나 부를가나
> 이왕 억울한 판에는 / 이 나라보다 더 억울한 일을
> 뼈에 차도록 당하고나 살가나

---

14) 두 임금을 섬기지 않는다는 전통사회 충성심의 전형(典刑).

고향의 뒷골목 돌담 사이 풀잎마냥

남의 손에 뽑힐 듯이 뽑힌 듯이 / 나는 살가나.

박재삼, 「서시」 (1956)

그런 시대에 살고, 그런 나라에 산다고 그렇게 모두 생각했다. '조국(祖國)'은 사전에만 있는 단어일 뿐 현실에는 없었다. 현실에 존재하는 나라는 적에게, 그것도 나의 원수인 적에게 그냥 내주어버리고 싶도록 나에게 고통만 안겨주는 나라, 그래서 너희들 골탕 한번 먹어봐라 여길 만큼 '나에겐' 아무 가치도 소용도 없는 나라, 그런 나라였다. 얼마나 억울하였으면 돌담 사이 풀잎처럼 언제 뽑혀 없어질지 모르는 그러한 나로, 내가 살아야만 하는 나라가 그런 나라이냐고 외치고 있었겠는가. 그 나라에 어찌 충성심이 일어날 수 있으며, 생각이라도 할 수 있겠는가. 그 나라에 내 사랑을 승화시키는 조국애는 차치하고, '조국사랑'이라는 말이라도 할 수 있겠는가.

그런데 박태준은 어떻게 조국애로의 승화가 가능했을까. 그의 모든 것, 몸과 마음을 송두리째 그 조국에 바칠 수 있었을까. 주는 것은 부담과 압박, 고통 밖에 없었던 가장 비참했던 나라, 심연으로부터 차디찬 고뇌만이 솟아 오르는 그 나라에 그는 어떻게 승화된 조국애를 가질 수 있었을까. 그것은 분명 미스테리다. 누구도 풀기 어렵고 누구도 설명하기 힘든 수수께끼 같은 사항이고 이벤트다. 그러나 그것은 명백히 수수께끼도 미스터리도 아니다. 그의 대성취가 눈에 보이는 현실로, 그 누구도 믿지 않을 수 없는 실제로 나타나 있기 때문이다.

"누를 수 없는 용광로 같은 뜨거운 조국애로 그는 대사업을 이룩했다." 야스히로 도스쿠니의 이 한마디가[15] 그의 대성취와 용광로 같은 그의 뜨거운 조국애를 함께 말해준다. 이 감동에 차고 심장을 찌르는 촌철살인(寸鐵殺人)의 그의 말이 그 모든 것에 앞서 그의 조국애 승화를 말해주고, 그로 해서 그

15) 야스히로 도스쿠니(八尋俊邦), 『우리 친구 박태준』, p188. 야스히로 도스쿠니는 일본 재계를 이끌어 온 재계 지도자. 일본 최대 종합상사인 미쓰비시 상사 사장(前).

의 대성취가 이루어졌음을 해명해준다. 그의 성취가 사상이고 이즘이 될 수 있었음은 앞서의 절대불가능 불용이나 다름없이 이 조국애 승화가 신앙처럼 체화(體化)돼서 대성취로 체현(體現)되었기 때문이다.

3. 가치(價値)

철학적 사회학적 의미의 가치는 그 자체가 하나의 사상(思想)이다. 어떤 가치 혹은 어떤 가치관을 갖고 있느냐는 어떤 사상, 어떤 이즘을 갖고 있느냐 와 같은 의미다.

그렇다면 태준이즘을 만들어내는 박태준의 가치 혹은 가치관은 무엇인가. 물론 이때의 가치·가치관은 포스코, 포스텍이라는 대성취를 이룩한 것과 연 관된, 또는 거기에 한정된 가치며 가치관이다. 그것은 한마디로 절대적 사익 (私益)은 없다는 것으로 요약할 수 있다. 이 말은 공산주의 사회의 강령과도 같은 '절대적 사익'의 부정이 아니라 절대적 사익을 절대적으로 추구하는 세 계—그것도 가장 적나라하게 추구하는 사업 조직(business concern)의 세 계에서 그 절대적 사익을 추구하지 않고도 엄청난 성공을 거두는 대조직을 만들어 낼 수 있다는 말이다.

절대적 사익은 절대적으로 추구하는 개인의 이익이다. 상대편을 생각하며 그 상대보다 상대적으로, 또는 비교 우위적으로 추구하는 개인 이익이 아니 라, 가능한 모든 수단을 다 동원해서 최대한 자기 이익을 절대적으로 키우는 자기 이익 극대화 행위다. 사람은 누구나 소유 본능을 갖고 있고, 이 소유 본 능에 의거 자기 이익을 추구한다. 그것도 단순한 이익 추구가 아니라 극대화 하는 이익 추구다. 그것은 극히 자연스러운 행위일 뿐 아니라 당연한 행위로 서 보편성을 띤다. 그 보편성에 가장 잘 맞는 사상이며 제도가 자본주의이며 시장경제다. 사상적으로 제도적으로 이 자본주의 시장경제는 절대적 사익을 절대적으로 추구하도록 허용하는 사회며, 심지어 강요하는 사회다. 물론 법 률이 쳐놓은 울타리 안에서다. 그 울타리 안에서 사익 극대화 행위는 누구나 추구하는 최고의 행위이며 가장 기본적인 행위이다. 그것은 누구에게나 작용하고 누구에게나 수용되는 보편적 행위다.

이 보편적 행위가 세계 어느 나라보다 가장 강하게, 밀도 있게 욕구하고 지향하는 나라가 바로 한국이다. 한국인의 물질주의—한국인의 절대적 사익 추구 행위는 미국의 3배, 일본의 2배로 조사되었다.[16] 그것도 지금과는 엄청난 부의 차이를 보이는 가난했던 지난 세기의 1960년대 1970년대의 한국이 아니라 세계 13대 경제 대국에 드는 21세기 2010년 현재의 한국인의 욕구 추구 실태이다. 그 실태도 빈곤의 시대를 넘긴지 까마득히 오랜, 빈곤의 절정에 이르러 있는 북쪽과 아득히 대비되는 시점에서 보이는 한국인의 욕구 현실이다. 그만큼 한국은 아직도 절대적 사익 추구의 보편성 속에 깊숙이 침잠해 있다.

이 같은 보편성의 세계, 그 세계 한가운데서 그 어느 나라보다 가장 매니아적 돈집착—사익 추구의 열병을 앓고 있는 한국에서 절대적 사익 추구의 반대—절대적 사익은 없다는 명제가 성립 가능한가. 아니 현실적으로 그 같은 주장이 존립할 수 있는가. 다른 말로 그같은 보편성의 세계와 정면으로 배치되는 그같은 특수성의 사고며 행태가 실제(實際)로 살아남을 수 있는가. 여기서 실제의 의미는 절대적 사익을 추구하지 않는 공기업 같은 경쟁력 없는 기업, 국민의 세금으로 연명하는 기업이 아니라 절대적 사익을 추구하는 사기업에 필적하는 경쟁력, 또는 그 이상의 성과를 내는 기업으로서의 존재며 존속 가능성이다. 그것이 가능한가. 그것이 가능하다면, 그 무엇이 그것을 가능하게 하느냐이다.

그 가능의 현실태(現實態)가 포스코며 포스텍이라 한다면, 포스코, 포스텍은 보편성의 세계 속에서 그 존재를 극명히 드러낸 특수성이고, 그리고 특수성의 한 승리다. 그것은 절대적 사익은 없다의 명제를 입증하는 증명서이고, 그것의 실현을 밝히는 증거자료다. 더구나 사익(私益)의 가치를 공익(公益)의 가치로, 그것도 절대적 사익을 절대적 공익으로 바꾸어 놓는 가치전환의 최고 사례다. 그 '절대적 사익'이라는 가장 보편화된 가치를 '절대적 사익은

16) 한국갤럽·글로벌 마켓 인사이트, 「대한민국, 우리는 무엇으로 행복해질까」, 《조선일보》, 세계 10개국의 「행복의 지도(地圖)」조사, 2011년 1월 1일 A4-A5 보도.

없다'는 가장 특수화된 가치로의 전환—그 가치전환을 가져오게 한 것은 도대체 무엇인가. 이 희귀하고도 심지어는 불가사의하기까지 한 그 가치전환은 도대체 어떻게 해서 일어났는가. 그것이 바로 태준이즘이고 동시에 태준이즘을 성립시키는 주요 요소다. 그것은 두 가지로 나눠 볼 수 있다. 그 하나가 무사심(無私心)이라면 다른 하나는 결백성(潔白性)이다.

(1) 무사심

무사심은 사사로운 욕심, 내 개인을 위한 욕심을 갖지 않는 것이다. 반대로 공심(公心)을 갖는 것이다. 공심은 공정(公正)한 마음, 내가 속해 있는 집단이나 조직, 나라의 입장에서 생각하는 마음이다. 그 말은 참으로 쉽지만 행동은 참으로 어려운 것이다. 사람의 사심은 본성이다. 사람은 천부적으로 그 사심을 갖고 태어났다. 그래서 내가 존재하고 내가 존립하는 것이다. 그러나 공인(公人)의 자리에 앉았을 때, 사람들은 예외 없이 그 사심을 버리고 공심을 갖기를 요구한다. 사람들의 공인에 대한 그같은 요구 압력과, 공인들의 식지 않는 사심·사욕 열기, 그것이 어느 시대 어느 나라에서나 일어나는 공사(公私)간 마찰, 쟁투, 괴리, 모순의 역사다. 그만큼 공인의 무사심은 어렵고 어려운 것이다.

무엇보다 무사심의 내재화(內在化), 체질화(體質化)가 지난하다. 나는 사심이 없다고 말하는데 사람들은 믿지 않는다. 그 믿지 못함은 그 사람에게서 그 무사심을 느끼지 못하기 때문이다. 마음으로 그 사람의 무사심이 보이지 않기 때문이다. 진정한 무사심의 소지자만이 무사심의 전달자다. 오직 그 사람만이 사람들에게 무사심을 느끼게 하고 마음으로 보게 한다. 인간은 영감의 동물이어서, 그의 영감으로 무사심을 보고 무사심을 느끼고 무사심을 믿는다. 오직 무사심일 때만 거짓이 없고 위장이 통하지 않는다. 숨기려 해도 숨겨지지 않고, 허식(虛飾)해도 허식되지 않는다.

이런 무사심이 어떻게 절대적 사익 추구를 막고, 절대적 사익은 없다란 명제를 실현시키는가. 말할 것도 없이 이 무사심은 국가나 국가내 주요 조직의 지도자 무사심이다. 지도자의 무사심이 지도자 자신의 절대적 사익 추구를 차단하고, 그 절대적 사익을 절대적 공익으로 만드는 것은 너무나 당연하다. 지도자 스스로 무사심이기 때문에 지도자 스스로가 추구하는 절대적 사익 행위는 처음부터 있을 수 없기 때문이다. 지도자의 무사심과 절대적 사익은 없다의 명제는 논리적으로 동의어 반복이고, 실제적으로도 서로 분리될 수 없는하나의 행위다.

(2) 결백성

이 무사심과 함께 논의돼야 할 지도자의 덕목이 지도자의 결백성이다. 결백성은 맑고 깨끗해서 허물이 없는 성품이다. 맑고 깨끗하다는 것, 그것은 청렴 혹은 청렴성이고, 허물이 없다는 것, 그것은 잘못, 과실이 없다는 것이다. 사람은 누구나 과실이 있다. 허물 없는 인간은 없다. 하지만 맑고 깨끗한 사람이 저지르는 과실은 과실이 아니라 실수다. 과실이라 해도 부작의(不作意)의 과실이고, 작의가 없었던 것만큼 그것을 발견하는 순간 남이 말하기 전에 먼저 알아서 스스로 고치는 과실이다. 그 과실에는 변명도 없고 구실도 없다. 남의 탓은 더더욱 없다. 오직 고치는 것만 있을 뿐이다.

지도자의 결백성이 갖는 맑고 깨끗함, 바로 청렴·청렴성은 마음에 탐욕이 없고 검소하다는 것이다. 마음에 탐욕이 없다는 것은 무사심과 서로 상통하지만 서로 다른 행위다. 무사심이 공심(公心) 공익(公益)을 위한 마음가짐이라면, 청렴은 스스로에 대한 욕심의 자제 행위다. 이 자제 행위는 반드시 검소(儉素)한 행위로 이어져서, 무엇보다 생활이 검소해지는 것이다. 조직 지도자의 생활검소는 조직 성원들에게 모범이 되는 행위이고 귀감이 되는 행위이며, 그리고 조직 성원을 마음으로 이끌고 마음으로 따르게 하는 행위다. 조직 지도자가 아니라도 부를 가진 사람, 권력을 가진 사람, 혹은 높은 지위에 있는 사람이 검소하면 사람들은 모두 그를 우러러보고 존경한다.

그렇다면 지도자 결백성의 요체는 두 가지다. 하나는 맑고 깨끗해서 일반 사람보다 허물이 없기도 하지만, 반면 허물이 있을 경우, 그 과실을 변명하거나 수식하지 않고 바로 수용해서 고친다는 것이고, 다른 하나는 맑고 깨끗해서 일반 사람들보다 청렴한 것은 말할 것도 없고 무엇보다 스스로 욕심을 자제해서 부와 지위, 권력에 상관없이 검소한 생활을 한다는 것이다. 앞의 경우, 조직에 신선한 바람을 불어넣고 조직을 활성화시켜 조직의 정체(停滯)를 막음은 물론, 조직의 목표를 언제나 선명히 부각시킨다는 것이고, 뒤의 경우 검고능광(儉故能廣)[17] 이라는 옛말에서 보듯, 검소하면 일상생활에서든 공적인 조직 세계에서든 남에게 널리 베풀 여유가 있고, 폭넓게 행동할 여유가 있고, 풍족하게 마음 쓸 여유가 있다는 것이다. 어느 것이든 검소는 지도자의 여유를 생산해서 조직기능을 활발하게 재점검하게 하는 것이다.

이 같은 맥락에서 지도자의 그러한 결백성이 절대적 사익은 없다는 명제를 실현시킬 수 있음은 명백하다. 그것은 첫째로 공익과 어긋나고 사익 추구 행위가 일어날 때 지도자의 결백성으로 하여 이에 대한 즉각적인 시정 조치와 새로운 정책 수립을 가능케 하고, 둘째로 지도자의 청렴성이 가져다 주는 검소 행위로 하여 처음부터 지도자 스스로 사익 추구와 거리가 먼 생활을 할 뿐 아니라 사익을 바라보는 시각이 처음부터 완전히 다를 수밖에 없다는 이유에서다. 예컨대 검즉금천(儉則金賤)[18] 이라는 오랜 경험이 이를 입증해주기도 한다.

문제는 지도자의 이 무사심과 결백성이 어떻게 그 많은 조직 성원들의 가치전환을 가져 오게 하느냐 그리고 그 가치전환으로 태준이즘의 형성을 가능케 하느냐이다. 지도자의 가치와 사상이 반드시 조직 성원의 그것이 될 수는 없다. 거기에는 반드시 그렇게 전수되고 이어질 수 있게 하는 연결 고리가 있어야 한다. 더 구체적으로, 지도자의 절대적인 사익은 없다는 가치와 사상이 어떻게 조직 성원들의 가치와 사상이 될 수 있느냐이다. 지도자의 그 절대적 명제가 어떻게 많은 조직 성원들의 보편적 가치인 절대적 사익추구를 절대적 공익추구 행위라는 특수한 가치로 바꾸어 놓을 수 있느냐이다. 그것을 가능

---

17) 검고능광(儉故能廣) 노자(老子) 67장, 검소하기 때문에 널리 베풀 수 있는 여유가 생긴다는 것.
18) 검즉금천(儉則金賤) 치즉금귀(侈則金貴), 『관자(管子)』 「승마(乘馬)」 편, 검소하면 돈을 별것 아닌 것으로 생각해서 절대로 돈에 매달리지 않고, 사치하면 돈을 너무 귀하게 여겨 돈에 완전히 포박된다는 것이다.

케 하는 요인—그 연결 고리는 무엇인가이다.

그것은 감동과 신뢰와 소통이라 할 수 있다. 조직 성원들의 마음을 열고 마음을 움직이고, 진정으로 믿고 열정을 불러 일으키고, 그리고 목숨도 아까워하지 않고 온몸을 바쳐 일하게 하는 원동력이 지도자의 무사심이며 청렴·결백이라는 것이고, 지도자의 무사심과 결백성이 조직 성원들의 감동과 신뢰를 깊게 하고 소통을 원활하게 해서, 마침내 어느 조직에나 있는 보편적 가치를 그 조직만의 특수 가치로 바꾸어 놓는 것이다.

① 감동. "일은 통하는 마음으로 한다." 이 말은 일본 경영의 귀재라고 하는 우쓰미 기요시가 박태준을 처음 만나고 한 말이다. "서로 통하는 마음이 없으면 어떤 일도 되지 않는다"[19] 포철 제1고로가 완성되었을 때의 소감을 그는 그렇게 말했다. 감동하지 않고 통하는 마음은 없다. 통하는 마음은 모두 감동하는 마음이다. 박태준의 성취는 포철 사람들의 감동이 불러온 성취라는 것이다.

"의욕을 가지고 진심으로 그를 따르며 열심히 일하는 종업원들의 모습. 그 모습을 보며 참으로 기쁘고 감격적인 마음을 금할 수 없었다. 진심으로 최고 경영자를 따르는 분위기가 공장 전체를 휘감고 있었다."[20] 포철을 직접 방문하고 종업원들의 일에 임하는 태도며 분위기를 느낀 후쿠다 수상의 소감이다. 의욕에 넘쳐 몰입해서 일하고 그리고 진심으로 지도자를 따르고 생각하는 분위기, 공장 전체를 휘감은 그 감동과 열정을 후쿠다 수상은 느낀 것이다.

"내가 가장 인상 깊게 느낀 것은 종업원들이 너나없이 마음으로부터 그를 따르고 있었다는 것이다. 나는 도저히 표현할 수 없는 감명을 거기서 받았다."[21] 일본 통상대신으로 재직시 포스코를 방문했던 나카소네 수상의 말이다. 그는 포철 사람들이 갖는 감동만이 아니라 일본 정·재계 지도자들이 받았던 감동도 함께 술회했다.[22] "일본 정계나 재계가 이처럼 합심해서 대외 협

19) 우쓰미 기요시(內海淸), 미쓰비시 상사 고문, 『우리친구 박태준』, p.245
20) 후쿠다 다케오(福田赳夫), 전 일본수상, op.cit., p.151
21) 나카소네 야스히로(中曾根康弘), 전 일본수상, op.cit., p157
22) 앞의 책, p.156-157

력에 열성을 보인 것은 매우 드문 일이다. …… 그 계기는 작업복 차림으로 진두지휘하는 그의 정열적인 모습에서 그리고 그의 노력과 성실성에 깊은 감명을 받은 나가노 사장과 이나야마 사장의[23] 마음으로부터 우러난 감동에서 비롯된 것이다."[24] 앞의 우쓰미나 후쿠다 나카소네 모두 감동을 피력했고 그 감동이 포스코의 분위기를 휘덮고 있다고 말했다.

대조되는 것은 처음 포스코 건립에 일본의 정·재계 지도자들이 모두 부정적이었다는 것이다. 그러나 당시로서는 일본의 협력 없이 포스코 건설은 꿈도 꿀 수 없는 일이었다. 그런 그들이 나카소네 수상 말처럼 모두 협력했다. 그 협력도 후쿠다 수상의 말을 빌리면, "일본의 정·재계 인사들이 국경을 초월해서 박태준을 흠모하고 그가 하는 일에 협력했다. 뿐만 아니라 그와의 친교를 모두 자랑으로 생각했다."[25] 할 정도로 절대적이었다.

무엇이 그렇게 만들었는가. 무엇이 일본 정·재계 인사들의 마음을 한국으로 돌아서게 했는가. "일본 재계 지도자들이 진심으로 그를 좋아하는 까닭은 그로부터 이익을 얻어서가 아니다. 그의 인품과 능력에서 존경심이 절로 우러났기 때문이다."[26] 야히로 도시쿠니의 회고담이다. 이어 그는 "제철회사 사장 가운데 전 일본을 통틀어, 아니 전 세계를 망라해도 박태준만 한 사람은 없다. 세계적으로 손꼽히는 제철회사가 서넛 있지만 그 제철회사를 손수 만들어 키운 현직 사장은 박태준 말고는 없다"[27]고 했다. 그의 이 말은 박태준의 무사심 그리고 그의 청렴·결백으로 체화(體化)된 그의 인격과 거기서 나오는 애국심과 사명감, 그리고 전 종업원들의 깊은 감동, 그것이 포스코를 만들었다는 함의(含意)가 있다.

②신뢰. "어째서 부하직원들이 일사불란하게 그를 따르는가." 헬무트 하세크 총재는 자문(自問)하며 대답했다. "사심(私心) 없는 그의 지도력 때문이

---

23) 나가노 시게오(永野重雄) 후지제철 사장, 이나야마 요시히로(稻山嘉寬), 야하다제철 사장
24) 나카소네, op.cit., p157
25) 후쿠다, op.cit., p148
26) 야히로, op.cit., p.186
27) 야히로, op.cit., p.185

다. 그같은 그의 지도력이 없었다면 그렇게 흔들림 없이 많은 사람들이 따르지는 않았을 것이다." 그리고 사람들이 포스코를 기적이라고 말했을 때, 그는 망설임 없이 그의 무사심이 포스코의 성공을 가져왔고, 그리고 그 무사심이 '부하 직원들의 깊은 신뢰와 존경을 쌓게 했으며, 그리고 목숨까지 아끼지 않는 헌신'[28]을 하게 했다고 했다. 이 유럽인—유럽인 중에서도 유럽 금융계의 제1인자인 그의 눈에는 신뢰가 보였고, 부하 직원들의 깊은 신뢰를 읽으며 포스코의 성공을 분석했다.

③ 소통. "노사분규가 한 건도 없었다. 학생시위도 없었다."[29] 레너드 홀슈의 말이다. 1980년대와 1990년대, 한국은 노사분규의 시대고 학생 시위의 시대다. 그런데 어떻게 공장에서는 노사분규가 없고 학교(포스텍)에서는 학생 소요가 없었는가. 그는 그 이유를 소통에서 찾고 있다. "분규가 있었다면 그것은 그(박태준)의 인격에 문제가 있어서가 아니라 커뮤니케이션이 이뤄지지 않은 데서 비롯되는 것이다. 세계의 위대한 지도자들이 종종 겪는 어려움도 바로 커뮤니케이션의 부재로 인한 것이다. 교육 이념이 훌륭하고 시설이 훌륭할지라도 설립자와 학생간에 커뮤니케이션이 이뤄지지 않으면 삐걱거리게 되어 있다."[30] 노사분규도 학생 시위도 없었던 것을 레너드 홀슈는 소통에서 찾았다. 또 다른 유럽인답게 그의 시각은 일본인과 달랐고, 그의 초점은 같은 유럽인이면서도 앞서의 헬무트 하세크와도 달랐다. 하세크가 '신뢰'라면 그는 '소통'이었다.

그러나 그는 박태준(朴泰俊)의 그 무엇이 그러한 엄청난 소통을 가능하게 했는지에 대한 의문은 없다. 오직 단 한건의 노사분규도 단 한건의 학생 시위도 없음에 감탄할 뿐이다. 그 대답은 브라질 최고의 지식인이며 한때 각료직까지 맡았던 엘리저 바티스타에게서 나왔다. "감동을 주지 못하는 말은 소용이 없다. 그(박태준)의 말은 짧고 명료하다. 한마디 말로 축약된 메시지다. 그

---

28) 헬무트 하세크(Helmut Haschek), 오스트리아 국립은행 총재, 『우리친구 박태준』, p.338
29) 레너드 홀슈(Lenard J. Holschuh), 국제철강협회 사무총장, 『우리친구 박태준』, p.269
30) 앞의 책, p.270

감동에 찬 메시지로 그는 상대방을 리드한다."[31]

소통은 감동에서 오는 것이다. 바티스타 말대로 감동을 주지 못하는 말은 소용이 없는 말이다. 소용이 없는 말은 소통력이 없는 말이다. 소통이 되지 않는 메시지는 메시지가 아니다. 소통은 또한 신뢰에서 온다. 소통은 또한 언어로써 한다. 그 언어가 신뢰가 쌓이려면 언어가 마음으로부터 우러나와야 한다. 그것이 진정성(眞情性)이고 그 진정성 있는 신뢰에서만 진정한 소통이 이뤄진다. 그 진정성은 지도자의 무사심과 지도자의 결백성·청렴성에서 나온다. 사심이 있는 진정성이 있을 수 없고 탐심이 내재된 진정성 또한 기대할 수 없다. 태준이즘이 태준이즘이 되는 것은 무사심, 결백성이 생산해내는 이 진정성에서 우러나오는 감동이며 신뢰며 소통에 의해서다. 그는 이 감동, 소통, 신뢰에 의해서 그의 가치를 조직 성원의 가치로 이입하고 전환해서 태준이즘을 발효하고, 그리고 그 성원들과 함께 대성취를 이룩한 것이다.

태준이즘은 사상이다. 바로 박태준(朴泰俊)의 사상이다. 그것은 세 가지로 요약된다. 절대적 절망은 없다, 절대적 불가능은 없다, 절대적 사익은 없다가 그것이다. '절대(絶對)'는 상대할 만한 것이 없는 것이고, 일체의 비교를 초월하는 것이다. 그것은 극한 상황이고, 끝나는 상태다. 천 길 벼랑 끝에 서 있는 것이다. 그런 절대적인 절망에서 어떻게 높이 솟아올랐는가, 그런 절대적인 불가능에서 어떻게 대성취를 이룩했는가, 그런 절대적인 개인 이익 추구에서 어떻게 모두의 이익으로 만들어 냈는가. 그것이 이 글의 요지이고, 태준이즘이 구체화되는 줄거리이다.

문제는 그런 절대적인 상황을 극복하고 이겨내서 전혀 새롭고도 다른 현실을 창조해 내는 것, 그것이 아무리 새로운 역사의 장을 만드는 것이라 해도,

31) 엘리저 바티스타(Eliezer Batista), 브라질 기획부장관, 『우리친구 박태준』, pp.323-324

그것이 어떻게 사상으로 승화돼서 '이즘'이 될 수 있는가, 누구나 지지하고 누구나 거부 없이 수용할 수 있는 웨이(way)—길이 될 수 있는가. 그것을 풀어가는 과정이 이 글의 맥락이고, 그것을 사회과학적으로 입증해 가는 것이 이 글의 목적이다. 그러나 박태준 사상이 어떻게 태준이즘이 되고, 박태준 방식, 박태준 길이 어떻게 태준웨이 혹은 포스코웨이가 되는지는 여기서 다시 되풀이해서 설명하거나 요약할 필요는 없다. 중복(重複)은 췌언(贅言)이 되고, 췌언은 어느 글에서든 금물이다.

다만 본문에 없는 것을 맺음말을 빌려 보탠다면, 그것은 우리 현대사를 어떻게 볼 것인가, 오늘의 우리 역사를 만든 큰 별들은 누구인가 하는 것이다. 건국 60주년이 넘고, 새로운 국가로서 우리 현대사가 정립되는 것도 60년이 넘는다. 확실히 우리는 새로운 국가를 건설했고, 새로운 역사를 만들었다. 비로소 우리의 긴 역사에서 처음 등장하는, 국가다운 국가가 지금의 대한민국이다. 특히 조선조 전근대 사회나 다를 바 없는 북쪽과 비교하면 더욱더 그러하다.

이런 엄청난 역사, 새로운 나라를 만든 사람들이 누구인가. 말할 것도 없이 대한민국 국민이다. 지금의 대한민국 국민은 이전의 우리 선조—그 '우리 민족'과는 전혀 다른 사람들이다. 산업화와 민주화를 함께 이룩한 국민이고, 그것도 140개가 넘는 신생국 중 유일하게 두 개의 혁명을 한꺼번에 완수한 국민이다. 지금의 대한민국 국민은 선진국 국민이나 다름없이 개별적인 사회적 사고를 할 수 있는 사람들이다. 국가나 집단 혹은 공동체와 분리돼 스스로 사고할 수 있는 능력을 가진, 그런 사회적 존재로서 기능할 수 있는 개체들이다.

그러나 개체는 오직 개체일 뿐이다. 아무리 훌륭한 사고를 하는 개체도 유능한 지도자를 만나지 못하면 하루아침에 우매한 대중으로 전락한다. 그것은 우리보다 앞서 선진화를 실현하고 경험한 나라들이 보여준 사례다. 똑똑한 개체들을 우매한 대중으로 만들지 않고 비전을 제시하며 주어진 목표를 향해 끌고 나가는 것은 지도자들이다. 어떤 지도자를 만났느냐가 어떤 국가, 어떤 역사를 만드느냐를 결정한다. 특히 우리의 긴 역사를 되돌아보면, 특히 우리가 그런 민족이다.

우리는 지난 60년의 현대사에서 다섯 사람의 유능한 지도자를 만났다. 그 만남은 대한민국의 행운이고, 국민으로써 우리의 축복이었다. 그 지도자는 정치인으로는 이승만, 박정희이고, 경제인으로는 이병철, 정주영이며, 또 다른 범주로써 박태준이다. 박태준은 정치·경제 그 어느 카테고리에도 꼭 끼워넣기 어려운 위치의 지도자다. 박태준은 경제인도 되고 정치인도 되면서, 정작으로 이승만, 박정희 같은 정치인도 아니고 이병철, 정주영 같은 경제인도 아니다. 정확히 자리매김하면 독보적 위치다.

지난 60년의 우리 역사는 기적의 역사였다. 대한민국 탄생부터 기적의 탄생이었고, 그 존립도 기적의 존립이었고, 성장도 기적의 성장이었다. 이 '기적'을 일구어낸 주역이 이 다섯 사람의 지도자들이다. 그들은 별이었고, 별중에서도 큰 별이었다.

이 다섯 사람의 지도자들 중에서 유독 박태준만을 끄집어내서, 그의 사상 그의 길을 태준이즘으로 명명한 데 대해 많은 사람들은 의문을 가질 것이다. 그것은 박태준의 대성취가 박정희로 인한 것이라는 것이다. 그것을 부인할 사람은 아무도 없다. 그러나 박태준이 없어서도 박정희가 그것을 해낼 수 있었을까. 박태준(朴泰俊)을 찾아낸 박정희의 형안(炯眼)은 분명히 위대했다. 그러나 아무리 형안이 빛났어도, 그 형안으로 또 다른 박태준을 찾아낼 수 있었을까. 박태준 역시 박정희를 만나지 않고서도 그같은 대성취가 가능했을까.

확실히 박정희와 박태준, 이 두 사람의 만남은 우리 현대사의 숙명이었고, 우리 국민으로서는 큰 행운이었다. 마치 류성룡 없는 이순신이 있을 수 없고 이순신을 생각지 않는 류성룡이 있을 수 없듯이, 두 사람의 만남은 우리 현대사에서 가장 '위대한 만남'이었다. 그래서 다시 태준이즘을 생각한다.

참고문헌

박태준. 2004.「쇳물은 멈추지 않는다」.《중앙일보》.

서울대학교 사회과학연구소. 1992.『민족, 인간 그리고 세계』.

안상기. 1995.『우리 친구 박태준』. 행림출판.

이대환. 2004.『세계 최고의 철강인 박태준』. 현암사.

《조선일보》. 2011. 세계 10개국의「행복의 지도(地圖)」조사. 1월 1일 A4-A5.

《중앙일보》. 2011. 1. 4. B1

포항종합제철주식회사. 1988.「창업정신과 경영철학」.

포항종합제철주식회사. 1985a.「제철보국의 의지: 박태준회장 경영어록」.

포항종합제철주식회사. 1985b.「나의 경영철학」.

포항종합제철주식회사. 1992.「4반세기 제철대역사의 완성」.

한국갤럽·글로벌 마켓 인사이트.「대한민국, 우리는 무엇으로 행복해질까」

Robert S. Phillips ed. *Funk & Wagnalls New Encyclopedia*. Volume27. "World War Ⅱ".
pp. 420-448.

송복 연세대 사회학과 명예교수, 미래인력연구원 이사장, 바른사회시민회의 고문

《사상계》기자,《청맥》편집장, 서울신문 외신부 기자 역임
연세대 사회학과 교수(1975 ~ 2002)
한국간행물윤리위원회 서평위원 역임 (1997)
전경련 발전특별위원회 위원(1999)

주요 저서
『동양적 가치란 무엇인가 』(2003)
『위대한 만남: 서애 류성룡 』(2007)
『이승만의 정치사상과 현실인식 』(2011) 외 다수

A Study on Taejoonism as a Principle

Song Bok

I. Why Taejoonism?

Is Taejoonism possible? There is Thatcherism in England and Reaganism in the United States. Taejoonism is coined by putting "ism" at the end of the first name of the founding father, Park Tae-joon, of Pohang Iron & Steel Co. Ltd (POSCO, henceforth). Can Taejoonism be a school of thought, a system of knowledge, a way of thinking, or a mode of execution that is generally and willingly accepted and communicated?

In the past 100 years of Korean history, there were other CEOs who can be counted as the best entrepreneurs, such as, Lee Byung-chull, Chung Ju-yung, Koo In-hwoi, and New Il-han.[1] Don't these names also deserve the suffix ism? If Taejooism is possible, there is no reason why these other CEOs should be otherwise, for they all have their own unique systems of thought and knowledge, or modes of thinking and practice; besides, they all have created something out of nothing.

Why then focus only on Taejoonism? In fact, there is no particular reason. As stated above, there are many other

---

1) Hanguk kyongyongsa hakhoe [Korean Management History Academy] selected these four as the best entrepreneurs in the past 100 years. *JOONGANG DAILY*, (Jan. 4, 2011): B1.

personages who more than deserve ism at the end of their names. Each of them, with his own unique system of thought and methodology and in his own style, worked out so-called "*chaejo ui un* (再造之運; destiny to recreate the nation)."[2] Nevertheless, one crucial point differentiates Park Tae-joon from the other CEOs: all the other CEOs were in the private sector, while Park Tae-joon was the only one who brought up a public enterprise into a business more successful than those in the private sector. It is a widely accepted opinion that the "ownerless enterprises in the capitalist market economy are bound to go under."[3] However, Park Tae-joon has rendered the opinion groundless by raising the status of the ownerless enterprise beyond the level of the privately owned enterprises, in fact, to the level of the super-class enterprises. In the history of the public enterprises all over the world, it is unprecedented.

The rationale behind the coinage of Taejoonism lies in the

2) View of nation frequently appealed and attempted in the traditional society for the purpose of rebuilding or reviving a nation.

3) The most representative example is the collapse of JAL, the then best airline in the world. It was privatized in 1987. With the largest stockholder's share being less than 3%, it became a "private enterprise without the owner" and the government was the de facto owner. In the end, it failed to cope with its debts in astronomical figures and was put under legal management in January 2010.

extraordinary nature of his great achievement. Certainly, POSCO is not only the most "glorious" achievement but the most "special" achievement as well. Samsung, Hyondae, LG, and Yuhan Yanghaeng are all glorious achievements, but not special achievements. It is because their kind of achievement exists universally in any society where the capitalist market economy operates. They can be seen in the United States, Western Europe, and Japan. However, none of them has a company like POSCO. It is a "special achievement" that exists uniquely in Korea.

What made it possible? What factors and what secrets? The keys to POSCO's success are widely known through the testimony of the participants; and the contributing factors have been discussed in the researches conducted by many scholars. However, all of the existing analyses and researches explain by making a causal connection between an individual event and an individual factor. They fail to present a comprehensive view of POSCO's success under the theme of Taejoonism and from the perspective of the thought and philosophical conviction called Taejoonism. Theoretically, Taejoonism is a system through which all the events and factors are put together in a coherent and harmonious context.

II. Common Property Inherent in All Isms

1. Two Faces of Ism

The English-Korean dictionary definition of ism is "*juui*," as in

*kongsan
juui* (communism), *sahoe juui* (socialism), and *chabon juui* (capitalism). A doctrine, tenet, theory, particular type of thought, or behavior of a particular nature can also be called ism. These numerous representations of ism demonstrate its broad extension. All of the various representations, however, have one thing in common, that is, consistency. Consistency is the very core and essence of an ism. The consistent perception, whether it be of one's work or the outside world, and the consistent conduct are the root and trunk of an ism.

Thanks to consistency, theory and knowledge can be systematized; and even a subjective argument can claim its own system. Thanks to consistency, friendship emerges among people; their loyalty to one another deepens; and they can do business together. Most of all, consistency makes it possible to predict people's behavior, which is most crucial in maintaining human society. One can decide what type of business he would like to be in and estimate the future of that business. That is how one can reassuredly plan and work for the future. If the ism held by one's colleagues or superiors is clear and solid, his thoughts and conduct can remain consistent, clear, and solid as well, which will in turn lead to effective communication among the team or group members and possibly, to a greater achievement than expected.

However, the consistency of ism is not necessarily a good thing. Its negativity may outweigh its positivity. The other face of ism may often cause side effects, corruption, and troubles. A good example is its dogmatic nature. Dogmatism means firmly believing what one thinks is true is the irrefutable truth, refusing to accept or tolerate any rational criticism or disproof. The more consolidated an ism is, the more dogmatic it gets, all because of the consistency of the ism.

Therefore, an ism and its consistency are what, much too often, cause one to miss the right timing and great opportunities. Countless organizations perish because they fail to catch the right timing with too much emphasis on consistency. "Idol" is the name Nietzsche gives to any ideology, ism, thought, theory, dogma, or tenet that remains in the fetter of consistency and refuses to change. He contends that the most important role of the intellectuals is to destroy the idol. The collapse of communism, which had been blindly conformed by the communist countries for decades, resulted from their idolization of the ism and refusal to change. The case clearly demonstrates the seriousness of the negative function of the consistency of ism. Hence, the suffix ism at the end of one's name is not necessarily favorable.

The issue here is whether an ism works positively or negatively for a person or an organization. If we hypothesize that an ism is meaningful only when it functions positively, how then should the positive ism operate? The answer is: it should have consistency as its natural property, be an open system, be communicated within and without, and accept changes. Openness, effective communication, and readiness for changes—among the three, openness is the origin of the other two. Openness leads to smooth communication, which in turn leads to changes. It also frees an ism from dogmatism and idolatry. Only then, the ism has not two faces, but one, and becomes a way and a dynamic force.

2. Three Elements Required for the Formation of an Ism

Three elements are required for an ism to function positively and become a way and a dynamic force: the first is a system of thought, the second leadership, and third administrative achievements, including the "great" achievements. Of course, one's unique personality, charisma, clearheadedness, and excellent insight can all be determining factors. All of these can be explained within the scopes of thought and leadership.

(1) Thought

First, one's thought is his opinions and views of society and humans, which are formed, not superficially, but through deliberation and meticulous pursuit; hence more informed and accurate judgments. Through the process of thorough deliberation, pursuit and judgement, the opinions and views are bound to have a logical system that supports them. Thought, as is discussed here, is an outcome of such deliberation and pursuit, and a particular system of judgement and cognition with respect to society and human beings. Therefore, it is in a dimension loftier than that of casual opinions or views.

If one's thought is to be an ism, two characteristics are required that distinguish it from other thoughts: one is uniqueness and the other softness. The former, uniqueness, stems from the originality of his thought. As the saying

"Nothing's new under the heavens" goes, there cannot be a thought original and unique to one person. Nonetheless, it is possible for a person to have his own thoughts, principles, strategies, or behavior pattern that differentiate him from the others; and these characteristics provide uniqueness to his claims or outcries.

His thought is the synthesis of all the characteristics of his and the synthesis creates his own "way"—with his own direction and vantage point. Of course, he is not alone; he has companions and colleagues to share his way with. Thus, his way is an organizational way. He is a member as well as the chief manager of the organization, the goal of which is shared by all members. It is how the POSCO-way, Samsung-way, or Hyundae-way is supposed to be created.

Being unique is the opposite of being ordinary. Anyone can think of and accomplish ordinary tasks. Being ordinary means being universal. The universal can be applied in all directions. It is like the golden mean. If so, being ordinary or universal is a good thing. However, it cannot change the world. It cannot resuscitate recession or stagnation. Only the unique, the unbeknownst to ordinary people, can build a new enterprise, reinstate prosperity in a country, and transform the world. Thus, an original thought, possessed by no one else and identical to none, can create an ism, which serves in turn as the way and the dynamics to bring about the "great" achievement.

The second characteristic required to form an ism is softness. Softness is literally being soft and tender, as opposed to being rigid or solid like rock or iron. Being rigid is being straight, unyielding, and unbending. Being soft is the opposite. The softest, the tenderest thing is water. Perhaps, the old expression "Spring water is the ultimate good"[4] has us believe so. However, humans can never be as soft or tender as water.

Another name for softness is flexibility. Or, from softness comes flexibility, flexibility being the causal result. The flexibility within a system of thought leads to that in thinking and acting and broadens the scope of thinking and acting. Flexibility involves extension and contraction as well as straightening and bending, which is impossible with rock and iron. Rigid and straight rock and iron, which only crack or break, do not have the absorbency or elasticity of softness. They may be able to maintain the consistency of an ism, but they are unable to consider or attempt transformation.

However, the softness and flexibility of thought remove the consistency, especially the negative or reverse function inherent in the consistency. And they transfuse fresh blood into the organization, thereby preventing it from being stagnant. Further, they discourage the bureaucratization of the organization and the authoritarianism and dogmatism of the leaders. Thus, the softness of thought, like the uniqueness, creates an ism and becomes the driving force behind the ism on its way to the great achievement.

(2) Leadership

Uniqueness is also required in leadership if it is to contribute

---

4) Lao-Tsu, Chap. 8, It means the highest good. It is the concept of being good in ancient times, meaning that water is the ultimate good.

to the formation of an ism. In other words, leadership must represent the leader's own distinct style. His unique style could mean his characteristic spirit or vision of the future that is not found in the other leaders.

There are two or three or rarely four types of leadership categorized by different researchers. Among them, the most frequently cited types are the transactional and transformational, or democratic, laissez-faire, and authoritarian leadership.[5] This categorization was made through the theoretical abstraction of various existing leadership traits. In the process of theorization, any impressive leadership in reality tends to be abstracted into either transactional or transformational type, or one of the democratic, laissez-faire, or authoritarian types. Therefore, these categories are not very effective in searching for the leadership styles or traits that can lead to the formation of an ism.

If so, what are the leadership traits or factors that can help form an ism? We may examine at least three of such traits. First, it is inspiration. A leader should be able to inspire the members of the organization. Inspiration is the power of induction that religious or charismatic leaders show to their followers. The power of induction can move both mind and body. Like the electric current, it deeply moves the hearts of the members and encourages them to identify with the leader's intentions and actions. This type of inspiration can often be seen even in ordinary leaders who are not religious or charismatic leaders.

5) For more information on the leadership classification, see James M. Burns, *Leadership*, Harper & Row.

The key is the power of induction exerted on the members. All of the leaders who can move others spiritually and emotionally possess the inspirational leadership. So, inspiration or the power of induction is an essential trait of leadership that can help create an ism.

Second, it is commitment. Commitment is a trait of leadership that encourages people to commit themselves to their work. Concentration means channeling all of one's mental energy only into one's own work, but nothing else. On the contrary, the commitment leadership goes beyond concentration. In addition to concentration, it elicits the spirit of sacrifice that transcends one's ego and the devotion of his entire energy and loyalty to the organization. Can it really happen to selfish humans? Can such commitment develop in the members of a non-religious organization? Further, without the incentive of higher rewards, is it possible to see such commitment and concentration in the modern men who are used to seeking only self-interest? To give birth to an ism, a leader must be in possession of such commitment leadership. Otherwise, no great achievement as the fruition of an ism is possible.

The third trait is morale-boosting. Morale means high spirits. Along with inspiration and commitment, morale-boosting is an essential trait in leadership. Needless to say, it is indispensable for the formation of an ism. It is often said that morale is proportional to the size of material reward and to the expected increase in status. The bigger the reward, the higher the morale; the higher the status, the higher the morale. However, this style of morale-boosting quickly reaches the limit. Whether it is material or status, there is always a limit to the reward. There is no need to continue discussing this style of leadership. The morale that leads to the formation of an ism remains high regardless of the level of material or status reward. The leadership that creates a work space overflowing with high morale and the spirit of challenge will give birth to an ism.

(3) Achievements

One's achievement is the product or fruition of his thought and leadership. Without fruition, there is no ism. The expression Thatcherism was coined because of the prime minister's fruition, her great achievement. The expression Reaganism was created for the same reason. The question is what kind of achievement it is. One's achievement must be tangible and acknowledged and supported by the majority of people. In general, his achievement, including his administrative achievement, is acknowledged and supported within his lifetime. It is not easy to find the examples of ism named after a leader whose achievement is acknowledged posthumously.

The question is how great the achievement is. What is required is "the great achievement"—the trail-blazing, history-rewriting achievement that is accepted by everyone unobjectionably. The achievements evaluated simply as high or remarkable always leave room for objections. In other words, many will refuse to accept the validity of such evaluation itself. The level that the great achievement reaches is such that even the critics or detractors themselves have no choice but to acknowledge and accept its greatness. Only this level of achievement results in an ism. Thus, the great achievement and an ism are one and inseparable. Or, the great achievement is the beginning and the end of an ism.

III. The Idiosyncrasies of Taejoonism

In the section "Why Taejoonism?" earlier, it was argued that the formation of Taejoonism is based on the great achievement of his. Unlike the other founding fathers of enterprises in the private sector, Park Tae-joon turned a public company into a success greater than the prosperous private companies—into a special, not an ordinary, success at that. It is not the kind of special success stories found in an affluent, advanced countries, but a special success emerged out of nothingness typical of the countries at the initial stage of development. Even more surprising is the fact that the special, great achievement was made in an under-developed country that even IBRD, which approved the development possibility of the countries like Brazil or Turkey, appraised as hopeless.[6]

If the blessed great rivers are a great achievement, their maker is Nature, that is, the operator of the earth, wind, and atmosphere. The great achievement is made by a human being and his thought and leadership. Without his unique and solid

6) In February 1969, IBRD decided that "building a steel manufacturing facility in Korea was not a valid project." Korea International Steel Associates (KISA) also refused to approve a loan. IBRD approved a loan for Turkey and Brazil to build steel manufacturing factories. Later, however, both countries failed to carry out their plans.

system of thought, the great achievement is unthinkable; without his unique, superior leadership, the great achievement is impossible. His thought, as both a vivid vision of the future and a value system, puts forth an unwavering faith in what is the supreme at the moment and what can definitely be achieved in the future. His leadership not only inspires others spiritually and emotionally, but also draws the most vigorous energy out of the members of his organization and renders the workplace inundated with high morale.

Taejoonism was built on the foundation of his thought and leadership. If thought and leadership are essential in the formation of an ism, what was at work to constitute Taejoonism and to systemize and maintain it as an ism? And what was his leadership like? Taejoon-way,[7] the embodiment of Taejoonism, was made of his thought and leadership. What was the function of Taejoon-way? How did it establish itself as an organizational way? *

Three thought systems constitute Taejoonism. They are the characteristics as well as the uniqueness of Park Tae-joon's thought. They are also the essence of his thought, revealing Park Tae-joon's true character, and thus distinguishing Taejoonism from Thatcherism and Reaganism. The three systems are called devotion, achievements, and values respectively.

---

* In this section, Taejoonism is discussed in terms of his system of thought, excluding his leadership and achievement.

7) Taejoon-way is usually referred to as POSCO-way.

1. Devotion (*sunmyong*)

"*Sunmyong*" in Korean literally means devoting one's life. One may wonder how devoting one's life can constitute a system of thought. It is because *sunmyong* is, first and foremost, mentality before it constitutes thought. Because of one's mentality, his view of the world changes, his will and consciousness toward his work revive, and his attitude and behavior alter. Then comes thought as an outcome of that mentality. Therefore, the nature of mentality shapes the nature of thought.

Nothing in the world can outdo the devotion of one's life when it comes to extremeness. Everyone lives only once. So, risking or devoting one's life means going to extremes. The point here is to find out what his mentality, psychology, and spirituality would be like after his experience in the crucible of extremes which not every one can access and where, once in it, he has no choice but to risk his life to achieve what he wants. How different is he from those who have never experienced the extreme situations of the degree.

One can imagine a realm of rebirth, resurrection, or transformation that cannot possibly be explained using the intellectual or scientific paradigm of social sciences; that is visible only to the survivors of the crucible of extremes; and that endows those survivors with an unexperienced state of spirituality. Insightful eyes and face shining with life-force can be seen in charismatic or religious leaders, which reveal the state of their spirituality. This state of being or spirituality is what the survivors of the extreme devotion would have acquired.

Almost supernatural abilities and great achievements are quite often witnessed in the people of extreme devotion. I Ching (The Book of Changes) says, "Faced with adversity, change; Change, and prosper."[8] The wisdom in this teaching is none other than the devotion discussed here. In extreme situations, one changes; and if he changes, he will be able to see the way to prosperity. The change mentioned here is not one of the ordinary changes people experience in their daily life. It refers to the kind of change, occurring in extreme situations, where the sky and the earth turn upside down, and one's life is at stake. The change that takes place at the ultimate end of such state is rebirth or resurrection; at the very moment of rebirth or resurrection, the way to prosperity finally opens to him.

Park Tae-joon was one such devotee who had been to an extreme, absolutely impossible situation before he opened the way to success, and who thereafter realized the great achievement. What then gave him the spirit of extreme devotion? The most obvious answer would be the type of DNA he was born with, fatalism, or divine providence. Some believe that his excellent genes, predetermined fate, or blessing from God gave him the spirit. However, these explanations, which are frequently applied to religious or charismatic leaders, are neither objective nor scientific. More objective and scientific explications are those of the behaviorists based on particular socio-environmental factors, that is, where and how he lived his life. What kind of life and how that particular life influenced

8) I-Ching, Kye-sa-ha-chon (繫辭下傳).

him to attain the will or spirit of extreme devotion?[9]

Indeed, he must have felt intense patriotic anguish under the Japanese colonial rule, suffered greatly from his wounded pride, witnessed the ephemeral existence of humans while running through the battlefields, harbored fury, resentment, and visceral hostility, burned with love for his country, survived the deadly watershed event of 5 · 16 military coup, yet another life-threatening extreme situation. Whether it be nationally, ethnically, or socially, he lived the first half of his life in the worst of extreme situations. Pushed to the limit during the period, he might have internalized the spirit of the trans-life, trans-reality devotion. Anyway, living through the adversity, devotion became his ultimate spiritual realm, which was subsequently sublimated into his unique system of thought. "Unique" here signifies that he was to be the only one who attained the spirit of devotion among all the people of his generation who experienced the same Japanese colonial rule and the same Korean war as he did.

In this sense, the social environmentalist explanation of the behaviorists is less than satisfactory because it is not very different from the fatalist or the gene-deterministic interpretation in that none of them can explain why the other people, under that same adverse circumstances, did not arrive at the same result, or why there are so few of them who came

9) It is frequently said in POSCO: "If you fail, you should turn right and plunge into Yongil Bay." The expression is often called "the spirit of the Right Face." Perhaps, these expressions can be a manifestation of the spirit of devotion. However, the spirit of the Right Face is not the same as the spirit of extreme devotion. It should be understood as a warning or fierce readiness for the possible situation.

to have the spirit of devotion. It does not seem particularly useful here to try to answer the question, "How was he able to get the spirit?" What's more effective is the question, "How was his will or spirit of devotion materialized to eventually create Taejoonism and Taejoon-way?"

(1) Absolute Spirit

His spirit of devotion allowed him to attain the absolute spirit, which is the state of consciousness where the subject and the object become one and arrive at a perfect self-awareness. Everyone has both subjective mind and objective mind. One's subjective mind is his own thoughts, opinions, and perspectives he comes to possess according to his position, situation, and standpoint. Thus, his subjective mind has difficulty in seeing facts as they really are and understanding reality as it really is, because his interpretation of facts and reality is already colored by his own beliefs, ideas, and hopes that have been established in accordance with his standpoint. So, he tends to see a fact in relation to his situation and think the distorted fact as the real fact and accept the warped reality as true reality. His objective mind can escape his subjective mind and see the fact and reality from another perspective beyond the subjective self. The absolute spirit is the complete assimilation of the subjective and the objective, which forms the trans-subjective spirit obtainable only when one transcends his subjective self.

Thus, devotion is trans-ego and the absolute spirit where the subjective and objective become one. Taejoonism is the embodiment of the absolute spirit and represented in reality by his expression, "There is no absolute despair."[10] Only those who came out alive from the valley of death of the war and even after the war, crossed the boundary between life and death time and again are able to understand the spirit of devotion expressed in the phrase "There is no despair." This denial is not an ordinary negation of despair, but a manifestation of the absolute spirit, that is, the absolute negation of despair or the absolute belief in the "absolute non-existence" of despair. Anyone can experience a hopeless situation; he may slip into the pit of absolute despair. Nevertheless, will he be able to believe steadfastly in the absolute negation of absolute despair? If so, what makes it possible?

The process of establishing POSCO was dotted with a series of situations of absolute despair, in the most defenselessly exposed way at that. Both in IBRD evaluation for the provision of loans and in the Cabinet meetings regarding the exclusive use of the property claims against Japan, there was nothing but despair. In fact, that absolute despair turned out to be just a tip of the iceberg. In the situation, what made his absolute negation of the absolute despair possible? Needless to say, it was his spirit of devotion, through which he was able to develop the absolute spirit where his subjective and objective mind fused into one and his faith and action completely

---

10) In Park Tae-joon Collection of Works, among the works about his memories of the Korean War, Chotae *chok cholmang un opta* "*There is no absolute despair*"; Ryu Chan-u, *Uri chingu Park Tae-joon* [*Our Friend, Park Tae-joon*], p. 103.

corresponded with each other. The absolute spirit expressed in "There is no absolute despair" is the fundamental principle of Taejoonism and the driving force behind Taejoon-way.

(2) Ultra-Resolution

His spirit of devotion paved the way to his ultra-resolution which differentiates Taejoonism from other isms and Taejoon-way or POSCO-way from other ways. In a nutshell, ultra-resolution is a resolution that makes a decisive choice, for example, a choice between life and death, existence and non-existence, prosperity and perish, success and failure, etc. A resolution can change the passage of a river, the height of a mountain, and even the course of history. Even the ultimate resolution that changes the course of history may not succeed at the first attempt, so new resolutions may have to be made one after another, which is called here "ultra-resolution."

There comes an occasion for anyone to make a resolution in his daily life; and everyone has the ability to do so. However, his resolution never reaches the stage of the ultra-resolution. Even if he makes a wrong resolution, it will not affect the course of his life. Of course, there can be many resolutions that change people's lives, but most of them are accidental rather than inevitable. People are unlikely to voluntarily step into a situation where they are required to make a resolution. Also, they seldom find themselves placed in such "unreal" situations. That is why the resolutions we make in our daily life are not extraordinary. Also, we even have friends and teachers to help us make those ordinary resolutions. It is not difficult to find mentors whose advice we seek.

However, the ultra-resolution is different in that no one can assist a person to make the resolution. Carl Clausewitz, in his *On War*, also states, "No competent counselor can help the leader with his decisiveness."[11] War decides between life and death of tens of thousands of troops, at the least, and between rise or fall of even an entire nation. Such decisions require the ultra-resolution indeed. Determining whether the location of the Steel Company should be Pohang or Samchok, or whether the Second Steel Company should be located in Asan or Kwangyang Bay was not simply a decision on the location of the Steel Company, but was the ultra-resolution on life or death of the company.

The exclusive use, in advance, of the property claims against Japan for manufacturing steel was the crux of the Hawaii Plan, without which there would have been nothing. Any resolution would have been meaningless; and the company would never have come into being. At the time, it was impossible for anyone even to dream of the exclusive use of the fund, let alone turning it into reality. That decision was the ultra-resolution. "Answer for our ancestors' blood" and "The grand one-hundred-year plan for our native country begins here" were his words when he made the ultimate decision to explode the faulty construction. That unimaginable decision was another one of his ultra-resolutions. Ordinary CEOs,

---

11) *On War*, Carl Clausewitz (1780-1831), a General of Preussen, compiled and analyzed the wars fought by Napoleon I and systematized the theory of war. The book was published in 1832 after his death and is considered a classic in the field.

mindful of the budgets, manpower, and construction deadlines, would have turned a blind eye to it. However, the large-scale explosion eliminated the very notion of faulty construction as well as the faulty structure itself. Both decisions were the examples of his ultra-resolutions unprecedented in the history of industry.

Where did they come from? It was not possible without the spirit of devotion, without the willingness to put his life on the line. The ultra-resolutions created and realized by the spirit of devotion are what is unique to Park Tae-joon and his way. Taejoonism and Taejoon-way are packed with ultra-resolutions.

2. Achievement

Achievement means to carry through. In Korean (*haenaenun kut*), it has two other implicit meanings: first, to successfully carry out a task that is generally viewed as too difficult or unfeasible; second, to demonstrate remarkable levels of endurance and perseverance without having a second thought. The two Chinese characters, "songchwi (achievement)" used by Koreans, signify all of the three meanings simultaneously. Whether it is expressed in Korean or Chinese, at their core are "a goal" and the determination to achieve the goal using all possible means. The expression "*haenaenun kut*" or "*songchwi*," however, is not an ordinary achievement, but the great achievement, known as unthinkable and unfeasible to ordinary people.

If so, can the great achievement be viewed as a system of thought? The great achievement means the unimaginably high achievement, but it is not necessarily a system of thought. It doesn't seem appropriate to call it "the spirit of the great achievement," either. Perhaps, it may be called "the will to the great achievement," like "the will to devotion." However, the will alone cannot constitute thought; nor can it be established as an ism. President Dwight D. Eisenhower made the great achievement by winning the war in Europe; and Douglas MacArthur made it in the Pacific War. Nevertheless, no one put the suffix ism at the end of their names. It is because none of their great achievements developed into an ism.

Is it then possible to coin the term "Taejoonism"? Can the great achievement made by Park Tae-joon for POSCO-POSTECH be an ism? Perhaps another question has priority over this question: Is Park Tae-joon's great achievement comparable with that of either Eisenhower or MacArthur? From the viewpoint of the history of humanity or the international great achievement, they are not comparable with each other because of the enormous difference in the scale of achievement. Once the scale of achievement is put aside, what is exactly the difference between Park Tae-joon and the other two? In sum, it is the possibility for the achievement to transform itself into an ism. What then changes the great achievement into an ism? I argue that two kinds of thought can answer the question: "refusal to accept impossibility" and "patriotic sublimation."

(1) Refusal to Accept Impossibility

This Chinese expression means "There is no such thing as

impossibility" or "Absolute denial of absolute impossibility." We often hear people say, "The term 'impossibility' is not in my dictionary," but no one actually believes it because people have learned from their experience that there is more impossibility than possibility in life. Because they live in the empirical world, repeating the phrase does not make it any more believable. Without belief, it is fictitious; therefore, it can never be an ism. In order for it to be an ism, it needs to establish itself as an unwavering faith like a religious faith. As stated earlier, thought, as a type of consistent faith, should remain consistent.

In the 1950s and 1960s, Korea was in an absolutely impossible situation, where the citizens, imprisoned in the hopeless situation, internalized the ethos of impossibility they were experiencing in their daily life, repeating the self-defeating phrases, like "There's nothing we can do," and "We are a hopeless, helpless nation." The situation continued in the 1970s, though to a lesser degree. At the time, serving the nation by means of the steel industry was impossible, let alone stepping in the steel industry itself. It was the then Japanese businessmen and politicians who knew exactly why it was impossible—those who had led the industrialization of Japan and paved the way to the era of prosperity for Japan. These Japanese financial and political leaders assessed the prospects of Korea's development to be absolutely impossible; and they were firm on their assessment, firmer than the United States or even IBRD, the most trusted analytical institution in the world.

When Japan, the United States, IBRD, and even KISA (Korea

International Steel Associates) all insisted on the impossibility, the absolute impossibility at that, of the steel industry in Korea, Park Tae-joon said politely but resolutely to Fukuda Takeo, then Japanese premier, "I can make it! I'll make it no matter what! That's the reason why I was born in this country!" Later, Fukuda Takeo recollected, "I was so surprised by his resolute attitude and thought that this man might be able to make it. Finally, as if to laugh at my prediction, he made it. It was miraculous indeed."[12] The same situation was repeated when he set out to build Postech, despite the long lapse of time since the first episode.

As a person who had crossed the valley of death time and again, he believed that he could overcome any adversity and transform any impossibility into possibility. When his will to reject absolute impossibility developed into his firm conviction, pledge, and faith, his fierce desire to succeed turned into an unyielding will to succeed, into the spirit of success, and finally into a system of thought, an ism. "I can make it! I'll make it no matter what! That's the reason why I was born in this country!"—there is no will more fervent or no pledge more ultimate than this remark of his. He swore by God that he would make it possible. It was a pledge as a total commitment and a conviction as powerful as the rising sun. Thus, absolute impossibility was absolutely impossible for him. When that conviction became one with the meaning of his being in the world, there could be no pledge, no faith stronger than that combination. As a result, his accomplishment became a system

12) Fukida Takeo, *Uri chingu Park Tae-joon [Our Friend, Park Tae-joon]*, p. 150.

of thought and an ism.

During the long war, neither Eisenhower nor MacArthur ever faced, even once, any situation that could be called absolute impossibility. Of course, they had to overcome many difficulties and hardships, but they never fell into the pit of absolute impossibility. Above all, World War II, on the part of the UK and the US, was a winning war. At the time, the GNP per capita was over 6,000 dollars in the US and close to 6,000 dollars in the UK, while it was only around 5,000 dollars in Germany, 3,000 dollars in Italy, and 2,000 dollars in Japan. On top of that, The British-American alliance had on its side France with 4,000 dollars of GNP per capita and Russia was attacking the enemy in the rear, although with much less GNP per capita.[13] The financial power of the Allies was three times as much as that of their enemy. Moreover, in terms of weapons, the numbers of troops, and talented commanders, the Allies had a long lead. So, the success of Eisenhower and MacArthur was just a great achievement, which had no reason or need to develop into a faith or to rearm itself as a system of thought.

(2) Patriotic Sublimation

Patriotic sublimation means to sublimate all of one's affections and desires into the love for his native country. Through the process of sublimation, an achievement changes into a conviction and faith, which then transmutes into a system of thought and an ism. Sublimation represents moving up to a higher realm or the spiritual dimension, that is,

13) Robert S. Phillips ed., *Funk & Wagnalls New Encyclopedia*, Volume 27, "World War II", pp.420-448.

converting one's individual desires and hopes to the social or national desires and hopes. Therefore, the patriotic sublimation is to devote one's body and mind to the prosperity of his native country. There is no ego and in its place, there is only his native country; one's heart beats only for his native country. Compared with the patriotic sublimation, a sense of duty— which means to carry out a given task with all one's might, while taking pride and finding a special meaning in doing so— is much lower in the degree of purity and enthusiasm, both intellectually and emotionally.

The question is if the patriotic sublimation is possible. No matter how earnestly a country teaches its people to be loyal to their native country, it is hard to find citizens who are truly loyal. Even if they are loyal, they do so only with a sense of obligation. Throughout history and across the world, the loyalty to one's nation has always been weak. The loyalty to one's lord seen in the traditional society was based on the then ethical precept of *"pulsa igun"*[14] (meaning, "refuse to serve two lords"). The traditional notion of loyalty is not the same as the modern notion of loyalty; modern loyalty is to be directed toward a country or an institution, not toward an individual. Therefore, loyalty is not for one's boss himself, but for the boss's position or status. And the patriotic sublimation is the loyalty toward one's native country.

How is the sublimation possible? How can one sublimate one's affections and desires into his love for his native country? How can one detach one's personal affections and desires from

14) Typical notion of loyalty in the traditional society.

himself and turn them into the trans-self love for his native country so that it can finally be embodied in a system of thought? If one's native country did nothing for him except giving pain and absolute despair, would the patriotic sublimation still be possible for him? Putting the Japanese colonial period aside, let's go back to the 1950s and 1960s and see what were the poems that the Korean intellectuals, especially students, loved to read and cry out?

> This country I would like to give away to the enemies, to their own defeat
> For a country like this
> We must fight, but whatever for?
> You always make me cry, my homeland
>
> Yu Chi-hwan, "My Homeland", 1951

> Shall I go to a faraway land / Shall I hum a tune of hunger there
> Deeply mortified in this land / I'd rather take insults there
> though more biting still
> 'til they bore into my bones
> Like a blade of weed in the crevice of the stone wall
> in a bystreet of my hometown
> to be plucked or already plucked / Shall I live here
>
> Pak Chae-sam, "Prologue", 1956

Everyone was resigned to the era and the country like this.

"Native country" was nothing but a term in the dictionary and did not exist in reality. The homeland in reality is something "I" want to give away to "I"'s enemy, old foe at that, because the homeland gives "I" nothing but pain. It holds no value at all for "I." The valueless and pain-causing country should be given to the enemy so that the enemy will suffer the same. That was Korea then. Their mortification was so great that they cried out if the land, where their lives were threatened at all times, could truly be called their homeland. How could patriotism be expected from the people of such country? No one could even utter the phrase, "the love for one's homeland," let alone sublimate one's love into the patriotic spirit.

How then was Park Tae-joon able to do it, devoting his entire being, mind and body, to his native country? Toward the utterly miserable country that gave its people nothing but burden, oppression, and pain, for the land that let its people suffer the paralyzing anguish, how could he feel the patriotic sublimation? That seems a mystery or a puzzle difficult to solve or explain. However, it is neither a mystery nor a puzzle because his great achievement is sensible reality that no one can deny.

Yasuhiro Dosukuni describes Park Tae-joon: "He established the great enterprise with his patriotism, burning like a unextinguishable furnace."[15] This description unifies his great achievement and burning patriotism. Yasuhiro's pithy yet

15) Yasuhiro Dosukuni, *Uri chingu Park Tae-joon [Our Friend, Park Tae-joon]*, p188. He was the leader of the Japanese financial world and the president of Mitsubishi Company, Japan's largest general trading company.

moving and penetrating remark articulates, above all, Park Tae-joon's patriotic sublimation and its direct link to his great achievement. As in the case of "Refusal to accept absolute impossibility" discussed earlier, Taejoonism cannot hold its validity without his patriotic sublimation, internalized like religious faith and embodied in the form of the great achievement.

3. Values

The value of a philosophical or a sociological meaning lies in the fact that the meaning in itself is a system of thought. One's view of values can be equated with one's thought or ism.

If so, what is Park Tae-joon's values or view of values that can support Taejoonism? Naturally, the values or view of values in question is examined only in relation to and limited to his great achievement, that is, POSCO POSTECH. His view of values is summed up in the phrase, "There is no self-interest." This is not the same as the communist principle, that is, the negation of the "absolute self-interest." Rather, it means that even within the world of business concerns where the absolute self-interest is absolutely and openly pursued, an enormously successful mega-concern can be created without pursuing the absolute self-interest.

The "absolute self-interest" means the personal profits and benefits pursued absolutely. It is not the self-interest or superiority pursued relatively or comparatively, but the act of private profit maximization, by mobilizing all possible means, with the focus on the absolute accumulation of private gains.

All humans have the instinct of possession; and according to this instinct, they pursue their self-interest and strive to maximize it. It is a natural part of being human, therefore universal. Capitalism and the market economy cater to that universal human nature extremely well. Philosophically and institutionally, the capitalist market economy allows, and even coerce, the absolute pursuit of the "absolute self-interest," as far as the law permits, of course. Within the boundary of the law, the act of maximization of private profit is the ultimate goal for everyone and the most fundamental behavioral orientation. It applies universally to everyone and is accepted by everyone.

Korea is where this universal orientation is most intensely demanded and pursued in the world. The materialism of the Korean people—the absolute pursuit of self-interest—is three times as intense as that of the Americans and twice that of the Japanese.[16] Korea no longer suffers from the poverty of the 1960s and 1970s; it now belongs in the top thirteen economic powers of the world. Nevertheless, the rampant materialism is the current social condition in the country even in the year 2010. Almost half a century has passed since the poverty-stricken era; and South Korean economy is in striking contrast with North Korea that is suffering from the extreme case of poverty. In this context, Korea still remains obsessed with the universal pursuit of the absolute self-interest.

In Korea which suffers from the epidemic of maniacal

16) Korea Gallop · Global Market Insite.
Taehan Minguk, uri nun muot uro haengbok haejilkka [Korea, What Makes Us Happy]; Segye 10 gaeguk ui 'haengbok ui chido' chosa [A Survey on 'The Map of Happiness' for Ten Countries] The Chosunilbo. (Jan. 1, 2011): A4-A5

obsession with money and the pursuit of self-interest, is it possible to cry out the opposite proposition, that is, "There is no absolute self-interest"? Can it subsist? In other words, can the unique proposition, which is in direct confrontation with the world of universality, survive in reality? "Reality" here signifies a public enterprise which does not pursue the absolute self-interest and therefore cannot be competitive. Can the public business, which is funded by the people's tax money, develop its competitiveness comparable or even superior to the private businesses which always pursue the absolute self-interest? Is it possible? If so, what makes it possible?

If POSCO and POSTECH are the manifestation of that possibility, they clearly distinguish themselves within the world of universality; their uniqueness has triumphed. They have proved the proposition, "There is no absolute self-interest" and they themselves are the evidence. Further, they are the best examples of transforming the view of values from the self-interest into the public-interest, from the absolute self-interest into the absolute public-interest. What made the transformation possible? What on earth happened to bring about the enigmatic change in the value system? There are two main ideas to discuss in order to answer the questions: disinterestedness and integrity.

(1) Disinterestedness

Disinterestedness means having no self-interest or greed for oneself and instead, having the public mind. The public mind is the spirit of fairness, which encourages people to think from the standpoint of a group, organization, or country that they belong in. It is easier said than done. Self-interest is part of the human nature. People are born with it and use it to feel and sustain their existence. However, when one assumes a public post, people invariably demand him to replace his self-interest with the public mind. History, regardless of time and place, is interspersed with the conflict, struggle, estrangement, and discrepancy between the people demanding and putting pressure on the public figures and the unabated desire for self-interest on the part of the public figures, vividly demonstrating how difficult it is for a public figure to practice dis-interestedness.

First of all, internalizing disinterestedness is extremely difficult. One may say that he has no self-interest, but people don't believe him because they cannot feel his disinterestedness. Only he who has true disinterestedness in his heart can reveal what is in his heart to others. Humans are the animal of inspiration; as such, they can see, feel, and trust disinterestedness through their inspiration, that is, through their hearts. True disinterestedness does not allow pretension or disguise; nor can it be concealed or affected.

How then can disinterestedness prevent the pursuit of the absolute self-interest and realize the proposition, "There is no absolute self-interest"? Needless to say, disinterestedness discussed here is the disinterestedness in the hearts of the leaders of a country or an important organization in a country. It is quite natural that a leader's disinterestedness prohibit his pursuit of the absolute self-interest and transform his absolute self-interest into the absolute public-interest. Since the leader is disinterested, it is impossible, in the first place, for him to pursue his absolute self-interest. The leader's disinterestedness and the proposition "There is no absolute self-interest" are logically synonymous and, in fact, are not separable.

(2) Integrity

What needs to be discussed along with disinterestedness is integrity. Integrity means a character or a disposition that is pure, honest, and faultless. Being pure and honest is synonymous with being upright and incorruptible. To be faultless, one should not make any mistakes or errors. As a matter of fact, however, everybody makes mistakes. Nonetheless, the fault made by a person of integrity is not a meditated mistake; as such, even before being told by others, he tries to correct it as soon as he recognizes it himself. He does not get defensive or make excuses for himself. Moreover, he never blames anybody else for his own mistake. He only focuses on correcting the mistake.

The integrity of a leader consists of honesty, purity, uprightness, and frugality; in a word, it lacks greed or avarice. Having no greed in one's heart may correspond with disinterestedness; however, they are not the same. If disinterestedness is the public mind that seeks the public-interest, uprightness means being able to control one's own greed. This self-control necessarily leads to frugality, especially frugality in everyday life. The frugal life of a leader can be a role model for the members of his organization, encouraging them to conform to his leadership. Frugality is not only limited to the organizational leaders, but applies to anyone of wealth, power, or high status. If they practice frugality, they are to be respected by all.

Thus, a leader of integrity should satisfy two essential conditions. First, he is honest and pure, so has less faults than the ordinary people. More importantly, when he makes a mistake, he does not attempt to explain it away or make excuses, but tries to correct it immediately. Second, he is upright and much more incorruptible than the ordinary people. Most importantly, he controls his own greed and lives a frugal life regardless of his wealth, status, or power. With his honesty and pureness, he is able to instill fresh energy into his organization, revitalizing the organization and thus preventing it from being stagnated. Further, he always brings the goal into relief. His frugality, as articulated in the old saying, "Kom-go-nung-gwang,"[17] whether it be in his private life or in a public organization, creates room for greater generosity, for a broader scope of activities, and for more presence of mind. In every way, frugality generates room for the leader to pro-actively reexamine the organizational functions.

In this context, apparent is the possibility for the leader's integrity to realize the proposition, "There is no self-interest." First of all, in case the pursuit of self-interest occurs in conflict with the public-interest, the leader's integrity enables the

---

17) Kom-go-nung-gwang (儉故能廣): Lao-tzu, Chap. 67, meaning, "Because of one's frugal life, he can practice greater generosity."

immediate correctional measures to be taken and new policies to be established. Second, frugality as a result of uprightness leads the leader far away from the pursuit of self-interest; in other words, the leader's perspective on self-interest itself is different, in the first place, from that of the ordinary people. The time-honored phrase, "Kom-zuk-gum-chon"[18] has proven to be true time and again.

The question is: How can the leader's disinterestedness and integrity transform the view of values held by so many members of the organization? Further, how does the transformed view of values contribute to the formation of Taejoonism. The leader's view of values and thought do not automatically become those of the members of the organization. There has to be a bridge between them; more precisely, the leader's proposition, "There is no absolute self-interest," must cross the bridge to become the members' own values and thought. How can the leader's absolute proposition change the members' universal pursuit of absolute self-interest into the pursuit of the absolute public-interest? What can bridge the two?

The paradigmatic bridge consists of the ideals of inspiration, trust, and communication. What opens and moves the members' hearts and makes them trust the leadership and enthusiastically devote their life to work is the leader's disinterestedness and integrity. Once the trust of the inspired

---

18) Kom-zuk-gum-chon (儉則金賤) Chi-zuk-gum-gwi (侈則金貴): Guan-Tzu (管子), Part Sungma (乘馬), meaning, "If one is frugal, he makes nothing of money, so he does not get obsessed with it; If one indulges in luxury, he make so much of money, so he becomes enslaved by it."

members in the leadership deepens and the communication lines run smoothly and effectively, the universal values can be transformed into the values unique to that particular organization.

① Inspiration

"Work is as good as done when the members' hearts are connected," said Utsumi Giyoshi, who is called "Genius" in Japan's management circles, when he met Park Tae-joon for the first time. When the construction of POSCO's first shaft furnace was completed, Utsumi gave his impression, "Without the connected hearts and souls of the members, nothing can be done."[19] Without the inspired or touched hearts, there can be no connected hearts. "Connected hearts" are all necessarily touched hearts. Park Tae-joon's achievement was brought about by the touched hearts of the POSCO members.

After his visit to POSCO, where he observed the workers' attitude toward their tasks and the overall organizational atmosphere, Premier Fukuda expressed his impression as follows: "While watching the employees working enthusiastically with genuine trust in his leadership, I couldn't help feeling so happy and being deeply moved. The entire factory was completely filled with the atmosphere of respect for and trust in the chief executive officer."[20] Premier Fukuda felt, at POSCO, the workers' overflowing zeal for and

19) Utsumi Giyoshi, the advisor for Mitsubishi Business Company, *Uri chingu Park Tae-joon [Our Friend, Park Tae-joon]*, p. 245.
20) Fukuda Dakeo, ex-Premier of Japan, op.cit., p. 151.

concentration on their work and their genuine trust in their leader.

"What impressed me the most was the fact that all the employees followed him from the bottom of their hearts. I can never express fully how profoundly I was touched there,"[21] said Premier Nakasone, who visited POSCO as Japanese Trade Minister. He continued to talk about the impressions the other Japanese political and financial leaders got of POSCO,[22] "It is rare that the Japanese political and financial circles show this much enthusiasm and combined effort toward an overseas cooperation. ... It all originated from President Nagano and President Inayama[23] who were deeply moved by his [Park Tae-joon] effort and sincerity while he, in his work clothes, was passionately leading the workers in the field."[24] Utsumi, Fukuda, and Nakasone—all expressed their deeply felt impression and testified to the atmosphere of inspiration overflowing the entire workplace of POSCO, which was created by the touched workers.

What's interesting is the fact that all of the Japanese political and financial leaders were pessimistic about the establishment of POSCO in the beginning. Unfortunately, at the time, no one could even dream of establishing POSCO without the help from Japan. Later, however, as Nakasone testified, all those Japanese leaders were willing to cooperate. The cooperation,

21) Nakasone Yasuhiro, ex-Premier of Japan, op.cit., p. 157
22) Nakasone Yasuhiro, ex-Premier of Japan, op.cit., p. 156-157
23) Nagano Shigeo, the President of Fuji Steel Company; Inayama Yishihiro, the president of Yahada Steel Company.
24) Nakasone, op.cit., p. 157.

according to Premier Fukuda, was an absolute one: "Transcending the national boundary, Japanese political and financial leaders admired Park Tae-joon and willingly cooperated with him for his projects. Moreover, they were all proud of their friendships with him."[25]

What made it possible? What changed the minds of the Japanese political and financial leaders? Yahiro Doshikuni recalls, "The reason why the Japanese political and financial leaders genuinely loved him was not the profits they got from him, but the reverence they felt for his character and ability."[26] He continues, "Among all the CEOs of the steel companies in Japan, in fact, in the whole wide world, no one can be a match for Park Tae-joon. There are a handful of world-renowned steel companies, but Park Tae-joon is the only one incumbent CEO who has established and developed a steel company with his own hands."[27] What's implied in Yahiro's remark is that Park Tae-joon's disinterestedness, character embodying his integrity, patriotism, sense of mission, and the employees deeply touched by his leadership—all of these created POSCO.

②Trust

"Why are all of his employees absolutely loyal to his leadership?" Governor Helmut Haschek answered his own question, "It's because of his leadership free of self-interest. Without it, he wouldn't have that large number of people

25) Fukuda, op.cit., p. 148.
26) Yahiro, op.cit., p.186
27) Yahiro, op.cit., p.185

following him that unswervingly." When people described POSCO as a miracle, he didn't hesitate to say that Park Tae-joon's disinterestedness led POSCO to success and that his disinterestedness persuaded "his employees to feel a profound trust in and respect for him and to dedicate their whole life to their work."[28] This European—the highest-ranking banker in the European financial world—was able to see the POSCO employees' trust in Park Tae-joon and analyzed it to be the key to POSCO's success.

③Communication

"There was absolutely no management-labor conflict. No student protest either,"[29] said Lenard J. Holschuh. The decades of 1980s and 1990s were the era of management-labor confrontations and student demonstrations. However, there was no management-labor conflict at POSCO and no student riot at POSTECH. Why? He found the answer in communication. "If there had been a conflict, his [Park Tae-joon] character wouldn't have been the reason. The reason would have been the lack of communication. Great leaders in the world often experience difficulties stemming from the lack of communication. No matter how great the educational ideology and the facilities are, there's bound to be conflicts without a clear communication between the founder of the school and the students."[30] Lenard Holschuh attributed the lack of conflicts

---

28) Helmut Haschek, the Governor of Austrian National Bank, *Uri chingu Park Tae-joon* [*Our Friend, Park Tae-joon*], p. 338.

29) Lenard J. Holschuh, the Secretary-General of the World Steel Association, *Uri chingu Park Tae-joon* [*Our Friend, Park Tae-joon*], p.269.

and riots to the efficient and effective communication channel. As a European, his viewpoint was different from that of the Japanese. However, his viewpoint was also different from that of Helmut Haschek, another European: Haschek's focus was on trust, while Holschuh's was on communication.

However, Lenard Holschuh never asked how Park Tae-joon had made the incredibly effective communication possible; he was just impressed by the lack of student riots. The answer to the question came from Eliezer Batista, the most renowned intellectual in Brazil who had once been a Cabinet member, "Speeches are useless unless they move people's minds. Park Tae-joon's speech is laconic and clear. It is more like a contracted message. He leads people with his messages, short but moving and inspiring."[31]

Communication begins when people are moved and inspired. As Batista said, words that cannot move the hearts of others are useless. Communication stems from trust. Communication is done via language. If a language is to receive trust, it should come directly from the core of one's heart. In other words, authenticity is required and only within the trusting relationship based on authenticity, the true communication can take place. The authenticity originates from the leader's disinterestedness and integrity. There is no authenticity in self-interest or greed. The validity of Taejoonism comes from the inspiration, trust, and communication, which are born out of authenticity, which

30) Lenard J. Holschuh, the Secretary-General of the World Steel Association. *Uri chingu Park Tae-joon* [*Our Friend, Park Tae-joon*], p. 270.

31) Eliezer Batista, Minister of the Planning Department, Brazil, *Uri chingu Park Tae-joon* [*Our Friend, Park Tae-joon*], pp. 323-324.

is in turn produced by the leader's disinterestedness and integrity. Through inspiration, trust, and communication, Park Tae-joon was able to transfer his view of values into the hearts of the members of his organization. Thus, Taejoonism came into effect and he was able to enjoy the great achievement together with his employees.

IV. Conclusion

Taejoonism is a system of thought, the system of Park Tae-joon's thought. It can be summarized in the three main statements: "There is no absolute despair"; "There is no absolute impossibility"; and "There is no self-interest." "Absolute" means having no match for it, or being above all comparisons, extreme situations, endpoints, and standing on the edge of a cliff. How was he able to emerge from the pit of absolute despair to soar so high? How did he turn that absolute impossibility into the great achievement, or transform the absolute pursuit of self-interest into the enthusiastic pursuit of public-interest? This paper attempts to answer these questions by explicating the process of the formation of Taejoonism.

Even if the process involves overcoming the absolute situations, creating a new and different reality, and writing a new chapter of history thereby, how can it be sublimated into a system of thought or an ism? Or, how can it be a way that is willingly accepted and supported by anyone? This paper tries to demonstrate the process of development using a social science approach. It is not necessary to repeat or summarize the discussion in the main body of this paper. Repetition or redundancy should be avoided by all means regardless of the genre of any writing.

Therefore, I would like to add here something that has not been mentioned so far in this paper: what should be our perspective on the modern history of Korea and who are the main contributors to the chapters of the modern history? It has been over 60 years since the new, modern, independent government was launched and the modern history of Korea began to unfold. We certainly established a new country and history. The Republic of Korea has become a modern state worthy of the name for the first time in its long history. When compared with North Korea which is not very different from the feudal society of the Yi Dynasty, modernity of South Korea seems more striking.

What has been the main dynamic behind the amazing transformation of the country? Needless to say, it has been the Korean people. Koreans as we know them now are completely different from their counterparts, that is, their ancestors of pre-modern times. They are the people who worked on the country's industrialization and democratization simultaneously; they are the people who carried out two revolutions at the same time, which was an exceptional example among over 140 newly emerging nations. Now, the Korean people possess their individual views of society as the peoples of the advanced countries do. They are able to function and form opinions independently as individual social beings outside the influence of their country, community, or any other group they belong to.

Nevertheless, independent beings are just independent beings; so, no matter how great their thoughts are, without a competent leader, they could turn into a mass of ignorant people overnight. Some countries that have succeeded, ahead of Korea, in turning themselves into advanced countries have already experienced the overnight turnabout. It is the leaders who guide the smart individuals toward the set goal by presenting them a vision, without turning them into the uninformed masses. A leader determines what kind of country or history his people will live in, which has always been the case in Korea as we look back on our long history.

In the past 60 years of our modern history, we met five competent leaders. Those meetings were fated to take place and were our blessing. They were Rhee Syngman and Park Chung-hee as statesmen, Lee Byung-chull and Chung Ju-yung as entrepreneurs, and Park Tae-joon who belongs to his own category. It is difficult to put Park Tae-joon in one of the existing categories. He can be viewed as an entrepreneur and a statesman at the same time, but he is neither a statesman like Rhee Syngman and Park Chung-hee, nor is he an entrepreneur like Lee Byung-chull and Chung Ju-yung. To be exact, we have to put him in his own unique category.

Our history of the last 60 years is a history of miracles. The birth of the Republic of Korea is a "miraculous birth," its survival is a "miraculous survival," and its growth is a "miraculous growth." And we have the five leaders who were the miracle workers. They are the stars, the largest and brightest stars.

Some may wonder why I have chosen only Park Tae-joon among the five leaders and named his thought and way Taejoonism. They may say that Park Tae-joon's great achievement would not have been if it had not been for Park Chung-hee. No one denies the fact. However, without Park Tae-joon, could Park Chung-hee have achieved the same? One has to admit that Park Chung-hee was a man of insight to notice Park Tae-joon's character and competence. However, no matter how insightful Park Chung-hee was, there is no saying that he would have found another person just like Park Tae-joon. Park Tae-joon also might not have made the same great achievement had he not met Park Chung-hee.

Park Chung-hee and Park Tae-joon—their meeting was indeed fated to take place in the modern history of Korea. As for the Korean people, it was a great blessing, as the meeting of Yu Seong-ryong and Yi Sun-sin had been centuries ago. It was the greatest meeting in Korea's modern history. So, Here I am, thinking of Taejoonism once more.

Bibliography

An, Sang-gi. *Uri chingu Park Tae-joon [Our Friend Park Tae-joon]*. Seoul: Haengrim Chulpansa, 1995.

Changop chongsin kwa kyongyong chorhak [Foundation Principle And Management Philosophy]. Pohang: Pohang Chonghap Chechol Chusik Hoesa, 1988.

Checholboguk ui uiji: Park Tae-joon hoejang kyongyong orok [The Will to Serve The Native Country with Steel Industry: Quotations from President Park Tae-joon]. Pohang: Pohang Chonghap Chechol Chusik Hoesa, 1985a.

JOONGANG DAILY. (Jan. 4, 2011): B1.

Minjok, ingan kurigo segye [Nation, Man And The World]. Seoul: Seoul National University, Research Center for Social Sciences, 1992.

Na ui kyongyong chorhak [My Management Philosophy]. Pohang: Pohang Chonghap Chechol CHusik Hoesa, 1985b.

Park, Tae-joon. *Soemmul un momchuji annunda [Molten Iron Continues To Flow].* Seoul: *JOONGANG DAILY,* 2004.

Sa pan segi chechol tae yoksa ui wansong [The Complete Twenty-Five-Year History of Steel Manufacturing]. Pohang: Pohang Chonghap Checho Chusik Hoesa, 1992.

Segye 10 gaeguk ui Haengbok ui chido chosa [A Survey on 'The Map of Happiness' for Ten Countries]. The Chosunilbo. (Jan. 1, 2011): A4-A5.

Taehan Minguk, uri nun muot uro haengbok haejilkka [The Republic of Korea: What Makes Us Happy]. Hanguk Gallop Glopbal Market in Site.

"World War II". Robert S. Phillips, ed. *Funk & Wagnalls New Encyclopedia.* Vol. 27. pp. 420-448.

Lee Dae-hwan. *Segye choego ui cholgangin Park Tae-joon [Park Tae-joon, The Top Steel Man in The World].* Seoul: Hyonamsa, 2004.

Song Bok Professor emeritus, Department of Sociology, Yonsei University; Chair, Board of Directors, Future Man Power Studies Institute; Advisor, Citizens United for Better Society

Reporter, *Sasanggye*; Editor-in-chief, Cheongmaek; Reporter, the Foreign News Department, *Seoul Shinmun*
Professor, Department of Sociology, Yonsei University (1975-2002)
Member, Book Review Committee, Korea Publiation Ethics Commission (1997)
Member, Special Committee on Development, the Federation of Korean Industries (1999)

Major Publications
What are Oriental Values? (2003)
Great Encounter / Seoae Seongryong Ryu (2007)
Rhee Syngman's Political Thoughts and Perspectives on Reality (2011)

행장 | 짧은 인생 영원한 조국에 바친 박태준: 박태준 1927~2011
Records of the Life of the Deceased | Park Tae-joon, A Life Dedicated to
his Eternal Fatherland, 1927-2011

연보
Chronology

짧은 인생 영원한 조국에 바친 박태준

박태준 1927~2011

전영기

국무총리, 포스코 회장, 민자당 최고위원, 포스텍 설립자……. 그 어떤 직함도 그의 이름 세 글자보다 빛을 내진 못한다. 박태준, 그는 세계가 인정한 리더였다. 1990년 11월 미테랑 프랑스 대통령은 서울로 특사를 파견해 외국인에게 주는 최고 훈장 레지옹 도뇌르 코망되르를 그에게 수여했다. "한국이 군대를 필요할 때 당신은 장교로 투신했습니다. 한국이 기업을 찾을 때 기업인이 되었습니다. 한국이 미래의 비전을 필요로 할 때 당신은 정치인이 되었습니다." 미테랑의 치사는 박태준의 삶을 꿰뚫었다. 20대의 그는 6·25전쟁에 참전해 치열한 전투를 겪은 '총의 사나이' 였다. 그때 가슴에 새긴 인생관이 '짧은 인생을 영원한 조국에' 였다.

박태준과 박정희

1970년 포철 기공식 때.

1992년 10월 2일 박태준 당시 포철 회장은 광양제철소에서 1만2천 명의 손님을 모시고 '포항제철 4반세기 대역사 준공식' 을 치렀다. 1968년 시작된 포항제철 건설은 연간 2천100만 톤의 생산능력을 확보하게 된 광양4기 설비 준공식으로 마무리됐다. 25년 만의 대역사였다. 그러나 그에겐 더 중요한 행사가 남아 있었다. 이튿날 그는 하얀 와이셔츠에 검은 넥타이, 검은 양복 차림으로 서울 동작동 국립묘지 박정희 대통령 묘 앞에

섰다.

"각하, 불초 박태준, 각하의 명을 받은 지 25년 만에 포철 건설의 대역사를 성공적으로 완수하고 삼가 각하의 영전에 보고 드립니다. ……일찍이 각하께서 분부하셨고, 또 다짐 드린 대로 저는 이제 대임을 성공적으로 마쳤습니다."

그는 생전에 "박정희 대통령에게 임무 완수를 보고한 1992년 10월 3일이 인생에서 가장 기쁜 장면이었다"고 말하곤 했다. 그가 박정희를 만난 건 스물한 살 때인 1948년. 그는 육군사관학교 6기 생도로, 박정희는 탄도학을 강의하던 교관이었다. 인연은 박정희 부산 군수기지사령관이 1960년 박태준을 데려다 인사참모로 쓰는 것으로 이어졌다. 그러나 1961년 5·16 때 박정희는 박태준을 거사자 명단에서 제외시켰다. 대신 "실패할 경우 내 처자를 보살펴 달라"고 부탁했다.

철강인 박태준

"나는 경부고속도로를 책임질 테니 자네는 제철소를 맡게.
제철소는 아무나 하는 게 아니야. 그러나 임자는 할 수 있어."

'쇳물은 멈추지 않는다', 「남기고 싶은 이야기」, 《중앙일보》, 2004년 8월 11일.

1967년 11월 박정희 대통령이 박태준을 종합제철소 건설추진위원회 위원장으로 임명하며 한 이 말은 '철강인 박태준'으로서의 삶의 시작을 의미한다. 박태준은 대한중석 사장, 포항제철 사장을 거치며 '짧은 인생을 영원한 조국에'라는 인생관에 '제철보국(製鐵報國)'을 추가했다.

자금 조달 단계부터 난관이 이어졌다. 그는 1969년 차관 교섭 차 미국을 방문하고 돌아오는 길에 하와이에서 대일청구권자금 일부를 종합제철 건설자금으로 전용하는 '하와이 구상'을 한다. 대통령의 허락을 받기는 했지만 당초

농림수산업에만 쓰기로 한 일본과의 합의가 문제였다. 이 돈을 제철소 건설에 쓰려면 일본 내각의 만장일치 동의를 구해야 했다. 그는 일본 주요 정·재계 관계자들을 일일이 만나 설득했다. 나카소네 야스히로 전 일본 총리는 회고록에서 "보는 이들이 안타까워할 정도로 열심히 뛰어다녔다. 그의 진지한 노력에 일본은 감동했다"고 썼다. 결국 박태준은 대일청구권자금과 은행 차관 등 1억 2천370만 달러로 제철소 건설에 나섰고 1973년 6월 우리나라 최초의 용광로를 준공해 첫 쇳물을 생산했다.

그 과정에서 그의 '우향우 정신'은 전설로 남아 있다. 직원들에게 제철소 건설이 실패할 경우 '우향우'해 동해 바다에 몸을 던져 죽을 각오로 일하라고 독려한 데서 나온 말이다. 그는 2003년 7월 포스코 역사관 개관식에서 당시를 이렇게 회상했다.

"나는 제철소 사업에 실패하면 차라리 영일만에 빠져 죽자며 각오를 새롭게 다졌고 여러분 모두의 혼에 우향우 정신을 불어넣기도 했습니다."

하지만 포스코의 성공 신화 못지않게 기업인 박태준을 돋보이게 하는 건 신앙처럼 고집했던 '소유와 경영의 분리'에 대한 신념이다. 그는 포스코 회장 재임 중은 물론 퇴임 뒤에도 포스코 주식 보유를 철저히 거부했다. 1988년 포스코 직원 1만 9천419명이 발행 주식의 10%를 우리사주로 배정받을 때도 그는 단 한 주도 받지 않았다. 전국경제인연합회 고위 관계자는 "철저히 사욕을 버리고 나라의 부(富)를 쌓는 데 일생을 바친 국가 대표급 전문 경영인"이라고 평가했다.

박태준과 김영삼

1992년 민자당 김영삼 대표와 함께.

박태준이 정치에 입문한 건 53세인 1980년이었다. 신군부 세력이 만든 국가보위입법회의 위원을 거쳐 1981년 민정당 비례대표 의원으로 시작했다.

자의 반 타의 반이었다. 자기가 일군 포철을 외풍으로부터 보호하기 위한 고육책이었다. 그의 정치는 성취보다 좌절이 많았다. 보람은 짧았고, 배신과 분노와 불신은 길었다.

가장 모질었던 건 동갑내기 김영삼 전 대통령과의 악연이었다. 두 사람은 노태우 전 대통령의 3당 합당으로 한솥밥을 먹게 됐다(1990년). 1992년 봄 노태우 대통령은 민자당 대선 경선을 앞두고 박태준 당시 최고위원에게 '당신도 나가 보라'고 언질을 줘놓곤 김영삼 대표 최고위원이 반발하자 불출마를 종용했다는 게 박 전 총리의 생전 회고였다. 그는 정치에 환멸을 느꼈다. 1992년 겨울 대선 후보인 김영삼이 도움을 청했으나 그는 거절했다. 김영삼 대통령 시절 그는 세무조사를 당하고 외국을 떠돌아야 했다.

세월이 바뀌어 1997년 여름. 김영삼은 아들의 비리와 외환위기로 식물 대통령이 됐다. 박태준은 귀국해 포항 보궐선거에 무소속으로 출마, 당선해 명예를 회복했다.

박태준과 DJP

1997년 당선증을 든 김대중 당선인과 함께.

1997년 9월엔 김대중 국민회의 대선 후보로부터 도와달라는 부탁을 받고 수락했다. 김대중-김종필의 이른바 DJP 공동 정권 만들기에 또 다른 축으로 뛰어든 것이다. 그때 김대중 후보에게 '당신은 거짓말쟁이 아닌가' '당신의 색깔은 진짜 어떤 색깔인가' '당신이 집권하면 호남 사람들이 통·반장까지 다 해먹을 거라고 믿는 사람이 많다' 등 다섯 가지 항목의 질의응답을 했다는 '면접시험'은 유명하다.

김대중 대통령 시대, 박태준은 자민련 총재(1998~2000년)와 국무총리(2000년)를 거쳤다. 그는 정치부패를 줄일 선거 완전 공영제와 지역정치를 타파할 중선거구제 도입을 위해 혼신의 힘을 기울였다. 그의 정치 개혁은 결정적 순간 현실론을 앞세운 국회의원들의 집단반발과 공동 여당(새천년민주당·자민련) 오너인 DJP의 발 빼기로 실현되지 못했다. 1980년 시작된 그의 정치생활은 20년 만에 막을 내렸다.

산업화 + 민주화 통합 비전

박태준은 정치를 하면서도 이상과 원칙을 관철하려 했다. 그의 비전은 박정희의 유산인 산업화 세력과 김대중·김영삼이 이끌었던 민주화 세력을 통합하는 일이었다. 산업화 세력에서 부패 성향을 제거하고, 민주화 세력에 먹고사는 것과 성장의 중요성을 알게 하는 것이었다. 지역 구도를 극복하고 부패 환경을 개선하기 위해 혼신의 힘을 쏟았던 것도 '산업화＋민주화'의 통합 비전 때문이었다.

그래서일까. 그는 후세에 남기고 싶은 말로 이런 말을 자주 했다. "독재의 사슬도 기억하게 하고, 빈곤의 사슬도 기억하게 하라."

《중앙일보》 2011년 12월 15일

전영기 《중앙일보》 편집국 국장

《중앙일보》 편집국 정치부 기자(1989)
《중앙일보》 기획취재부 기자(1992)
《중앙일보》 편집국 정치부 차장대우(1995)
《중앙일보》 편집국 정치부 차장(2001)
《중앙일보》 편집국 정치부 부장대우(2006)
《중앙Sunday》 편집국 국장(2008)
2011년 제7회 한국참언론인대상 정치부문 수상

주요 저서
『성공한 권력』(2000)
『창조 CEO 사막에선 지도 대신 나침반을 들어라』(2010)
『다음 대통령』(2010)

Park Tae-joon, A Life Dedicated to
his Eternal Fatherland:
Records of his Personal Life, 1927 ~ 2011

Chun Young-gi

Prime minister, Chairman of POSCO, Supreme Counselor, Founder of POSTECH... None of these titles shines as brightly as his three-syllable name itself. Park Tae-joon was a leader acknowledged by the world. Mitterrand, the French president, sent a special envoy to Seoul to present him with the Commandeur de la Légion d'Honneur, the highest honor given to a foreigner. "You dedicated your life as a military officer when Korea needed the military. You became a businessman when Korea was looking for an enterprise. You became a politician when Korea needed a vision for future." Mitterrand's praise touched the core of Park Tae-joon's life. He was a "man of the gun" who participated in the Korean War and went through intense battles during his twenties. His motto inscribed in his heart during that time was "Let me devote my short life to my eternal fatherland!"

Park Tae-joon and Park Chung-hee

On October 2, 1992, Park Tae-joon, chairman of POSCO, held the "Ceremony Celebrating the Completion of the Quarter-century Grand Construction of POSCO" at Gwangyang Works with 12,000 guests. The construction of POSCO that had begun in 1968 was concluded with the completion of Gwangyang Works Phase 4 (annual crude steel capacity: 21 million tons). It took twenty-five long years. There was, however, another more important event for him to attend after the ceremony. The next day he stood in black suit, black tie, and white shirt in front of the grave of late president Park Chung-hee (no relation) at the National Cemetery in Dongjak-dong, Seoul.

"Your Excellency, your unworthy son Park Tae-joon respectfully reports to your spirit that he successfully accomplished the grand construction of POSCO twenty-five years after he received your order. ... I now successfully finished my great duty that you entrusted with me and I promised to accomplish."

He used to say, "October 3, 1992, the day when I reported back to President Park Chung-hee that I fulfilled my duties, was one of the happiest moments of my life." He met Park Chung-hee in 1948, when he was twenty-one. He was a student at Military Academy and Park Chung-hee was a teacher who taught ballistics. Park Chung-hee later chose him as a member of his human resources staff when he was appointed commander of the Busan Military Supply Complex Headquarters in 1960. Park Chung-hee, however, excluded Park Tae-joon's name from the list of the participants in his coup. Instead, he asked Park Tae-joon, "Please take care of me if my coup d'état fails."

Park Tae-joon, the Man of Steel

"I'll take charge of the Seoul-Busan Highway. Please take over the steel company. It's not for everyone to build a steel company. I know you can do it, though." – "Stories That I Want to Leave: Melted Iron Doesn't Stop,"

JOONGANG DAILY, August 11, 2004.

The above remark made by President Park Chung-hee when he appointed Park Tae-joon as chair of the Committee to Promote the Construction of an Integrated Steel Company in November 1967 was the beginning of Park Tae-joon's life as "a man of steel." Park Tae-joon added the motto "Patriotism by Steel Manufacturing" to a previous motto of his, "Let me devote my short life to my eternal fatherland."

The first hurdle was funding. On the way back from his visit to the US for a loan negotiation, he came up with the "Hawaii plan," a plan to redirect part of the Funds from Property Claims Against Japan to the construction of POSCO. Although the president agreed to this plan, there was a big obstacle, i.e. the agreement with Japan that Koreans would use the funds only for agriculture, forestry and fishery industries. In order to redirect part of these funds, the entire Japanese cabinet would have to sign on to this redirecting plan. He met every political and economic leader in Japan to persuade them. Former Japanese Prime Minister Nakasone Yasuhiro wrote in his memoirs, "He ran around so hard that we felt pity for him. Japan was moved by his sincere effort." In the end, Park Tae-joon succeeded in building the steel company based on 123,7 million dollars composed of part of the Funds from Property Claims Against Japan and bank loans. In June 1973, construction of the first blast furnace in Korea was completed, and produced the first melted iron.

The spirit of "Right Face!" he championed during this period became a legend. "Right Face!" came from his urging his employees that they, like himself, should all be prepared to die in the sea flanking their workplace if they failed in the construction of the steel company. He reminisced about that time in his speech at the opening ceremony of the POSCO Museum in July 2003.

"I proposed that we all drown in Young-il Bay if we failed in our work, inspiring the spirit of "Right Face!" in all of us.

Park Tae-joon as a businessman stands out, however, not so much for his legendary success in building POSCO but for his firm and religious belief in "the separation between ownership and management." He insisted on not owning stocks of POSCO not only during the period of his chairmanship but also after he stepped down. When 10% of POSCO stocks were assigned to 19,419 employees in 1988, he didn't take any. A high-ranking official in the Federation of Korean Industries commented that Park Tae-joon was "a truly professional businessman on the level of a national champion who thoroughly selflessly devoted his entire life to accumulating the wealth of our nation."

Park Tae-joon and Kim Young-sam

Park Tae-joon entered politics in 1980 when he was 53. He began his political career as a member of the National Security Legislative Council formed by the military junta that had just taken power through a coup d'état in 1980 and as a member of the Assembly from the national constituency in 1981. It was an inevitable and reluctant choice for him and a desperate measure to protect POSCO from political pressure. There were more frustrations than achievements in his political career. It was less rewarding and more exasperating. There were betrayals and mistrust.

The worst of it was his bad relationship with Kim Young-sam, a politician of the same generation as Park Tae-joon. They were on board the same ship due to the merger of three parties initiated by President Roh Tae-woo in 1990. Park Tae-joon recollected that President Roh broke his promise to support Park's run for the party nomination race for the presidential candidacy and dissuaded him from running when Kim Young-sam opposed it. He was disillusioned about politics and refused to help the candidate Kim Young-sam when he requested Park's help during the presidential election in the winter of 1992. During Kim Young-sam's presidency, Park Tae-joon had to live in exile and was subjected to a tax investigation.

Time passed and Kim Young-sam became a powerless president due to his son's involvement in corruption and the financial crisis in the summer of 1997. Park Tae-joon returned home and recovered his honor by winning the special election for representative of Pohang North District.

Park Tae-joon and DJP

Kim Dae-jung requested Park Tae-joon's help in September 1997 for his campaign in the upcoming presidential election. Park Tae-joon accepted this request and joined the DJP (Kim Dae-jung and Kim Jong-pil) collaboration to create a joint regime as a third axis. Rumor has it that Park Tae-joon conducted "a screening interview" of Kim Dae-jung before he joined the team, asking five questions including "Are you a liar?" "What are your true colors?" and "Many people believe that people from your region will take over all offices, even the heads of neighborhood associations if you are elected. What are your thoughts?"

During Kim Dae-jung's presidency, Park Tae-joon served as the chairman of the Liberal Democracy Party (1998-2000) and as prime minister (2000). He worked with all his might to establish a completely public financing system for election in order to reduce corruption and to introduce the system of having medium-sized electoral districts in order to break down regionalism in politics. Unfortunately, he couldn't achieve these goals because most politicians opposed them when the time came, claiming that they were unrealistic and because DJP, who were co-owners of the ruling party, reneged. He ended his twenty-year political career.

Vision for the Unity between Industrialization and Democratization

Park Tae-joon attempted to stick to his ideals and principles even when he was a politician. His was a vision to unify the industrialization group—Park Chung-hee's descendents—and the democratization group led by Kim Dae-jung and Kim Young-sam. He hoped to eliminate corruption from the industrialization group and teach the democratization group the importance of economic development. He worked very hard to break down regionalism and improve the corruption-encouraging political environment because of his vision for the unity between industrialization and democratization.

Perhaps because of his vision he often said to future generations, "Let's remember both the chains of dictatorship and those of poverty."

JOONGANG DAILY, December 15, 2011.

Chun Young-gi Editor-in-chief, *JOONGANG DAILY*

Reporter, Department of Politics, *JOONGANG DAILY* (1989)
Reporter, Department of Special Coverage, *JOONGANG DAILY* (1992)
Acting vice chief, Department of Politics, *JOONGANG DAILY* (1995)
Vice chief, Department of Politics, *JOONGANG DAILY* (2001)
Acting chief, Department of Politics, *JOONGANG DAILY* (2006)
Editor-in-chief, *Joongang Sunday* (2008)
Recipient of the 2011 7th Korea True Journalist Grand Award (Political Coverage)

Major Publications
Successful Power (2000)
Creative CEO: Use a Compass instead of a Map in a Desert! (2010)
Next President (2010)

연보 Chronology

1927

경남 동래군 장안면(현 부산시 기장군 장안읍) 임랑리에서 아버지 박봉관과 어머니 김소순의 6남매 중 장남으로 출생(음력 9월 29일).

(29th day of the 9th lunar month) Born as the first son of six siblings to father Park Bong-gwan and mother Kim So-soon in Imrang-ri, Jangan-myeon, Dongrae-gun, Kyeongsangnam-do (currently Jangan-eup, Gijang-gun, Busan).

1931 4세

백부 박봉줄 도일(渡日).

Uncle Park Bong-jul goes to Japan.

1932 5세

천황제 파시즘 체제 등장. 아버지 박도일.

Emperor-based fascism emerge Japan; father Park Bong-kwan to Japan.

1940 13세

5년제 이야마북중학교 입학.

Enters five-year system of Iyama North Middle School.

1944 17세

일본 육사 입교 권유 거부. 와세다대 공대로 진학 결심. 소결로공장에 노력봉사대원으로 배치, 제철과 초면.

Rejects a recommendation to enter the Japanese Military Academy and decides to enter the Faculty of Science and Engineering, Waseda University; assigned to a sinter furnace plant for a compulsory community service work—this was his first encounter with the steel manufacturing industry.

1945 18세

와세다대 기계공학과 입학. 미군의 도월대공습으로 죽을 고비 넘김. 8·15 광맞아 가족과 귀향. 서울에 가서 학업을 할 길을 모색하나 좌절.

Enters the Faculty of Science Engineering, Waseda Univers survives a life-or-death crisis du the Tokyo Raid by the U.S.; ret to Korea with his family after August 15 liberation; tries in vai find a way to continue his studie Seoul.

와 도일하여 아다미에 정착. 이듬해
학교 입학.

s to Japan with mother and
es in Adami; enters elementary
ool the next year.

아버지가 찌구마가와(千曲川) 수력발전소로
옮겨 나가노현 이야마로 이사.

Family moves to Iyama, Nagano-
hyun, where father works at
Chikumagawa Hydroelectric Power
Plant.

초등학교 6학년으로 스키(활강, 점프)대회
참가.

Participates in ski competition
(downhill and jump) as an
elementary school student.

다대 기계공학과 2년을 마치고 중퇴.

s his studies after finishing his
homore year at Waseda
versity (mechanical engineering
or).

귀국 후 취업 좌절로 칩거하다 부산 국방경
비대에 자원. 훈련 중 남조선경비사관학교
(육군사관학교) 6기 생도로 선발되어 입교.
제2중대장으로 탄도학을 강의하던 박정희
대위와 초면. 단기 과정 수료 후 육군 소위로
임관(7월 28일), 육군 제1여단 제1연대 소
대장으로 부임.

Volunteers for the National Defense
Guard in Busan after frustrated
attempts to find work; selected to
enter the 6th class of the South
Korean Guard Academy (the
current Military Academy) while
training for the National Defense
Guard; first encounter with
squadron leader Park Chung-hee
who taught ballistics; commissioned
army second lieutenant on July 28
and assigned to the position of
platoon leader of the first regiment
of the first army brigade.

미군 철수. 육군 대위로 7사단 1연대 중대
장에 부임하여 철원 배치

U.S. military withdraws; promoted
to captain and assigned to
Cheolwon as squadron leader of
the first regiment, the 7th army
division.

한강 이남으로 철수하라는 전문을 받고 후
퇴, 8월에 포항 형산강전투 참전. 이후 북진
하여 청진까지 올라갔다 1·4 후퇴 대열에
오름.

Retreats following an order to
withdraw below the Han River;
participates in the Battle of the
Hyeongsan River in August;
advances north to Cheongjin, but
retreats again during the January
4th Retreat.

육군 중령으로 5사단 참모. 충무무공훈장,
은성화랑무공훈장, 금성화랑무공훈장 받음.
화천수력발전소 방어를 위한 중공군과의 교
전 지휘(부연대장). 5사단의 지리산 잔비 토
벌 작전을 위한 부대 이동 작전 수립 뒤 11
월 육군대학 입교.

Appointed lieutenant colonel and
staff officer for the 5th army
division; receives the Chungmu
Order of Military Merit, Silver Star
Hwarang Order of Military Merit,
and Gold Star Hwarang Order of
Military Merit; commands the battle
against the Chinese Communist
Army to defend the Hwacheon
Hydroelectric Plant (deputy
regiment commander); drafts a
corps movement strategy for the
subjugation of the remaining
guerrillas on Mount Jiri for the 5th
army division; enters Army
University in November.

금성화랑무공훈장 받음. 육군대학
업. 육사 교무처장 부임, 진해에서 ㅌ
육사 이전 계획 수립. 12월 20일 ㅈ
결혼. 후배 장교 황경노와 만남.

Receives the Gold Star Hw
Order of Military Merit; grad
from Army University
valedictorian; appointed de
academic affairs at the M
Academy; drafts a plan to mo
Military Academy from Jinh
Taerung; marries Jang Ok
November; meets junior o
Hwang Kyung-ro.

25사단 71연대장으로 국군의 날 시가행진
부대 지휘. 꼴찌 사단이던 25사단을 최고
사단으로 바꾼 뒤 육군본부 인사처리과장
부임. 박철언과 초면.

Directs the Armed Forces Day
parade as the 71st regiment
commander of the 25th army
division; appointed the chief of the
personnel division at the
Headquarters of the Army after
transforming the 25th army division
to the best division from the worst;
first encounter with Park Cheol-eon.

도미시찰단장 미국 초방.

Visits the U.S. as a member and
head of an inspection team.

부산 군수기지사령부 사령관 박정희의
참모. 박정희 좌천 후 두 번째 도미, ㄷ
군부관학교 3개월 교육.

Appointed a member of hu
resources staff for Park Chung
commander of the Busan M
Supply Complex Headqua
visits the U.S. again after
Chung-hee was demoted.

대령으로 진급.

moted to army colonel.

국방대학원 입교. 첫 딸을 폐렴으로 잃음. 8
월 국방대학원 수료 후 국가정책 수립 담당
제2과정 책임 교수 부임. 11월 국방부 인사
과장으로 전임, 공군 고준식 대령과 만남.
국회에서 국방위 소속 의원 김영삼과 초면.

Enters Korea National Defense
University Graduate School;
daughter dies of pneumonia;
appointed the 2nd process
professor in charge of drafting
national policies after completing
his coursework at the graduate
school in August; becomes the
chief of the personnel division at
the Ministry of National Defense in
November; meets Colonel Go Jun-
sik; first encounter with Kim Young-
sam, representative and member of
the National Defense Committee at
the National Assembly.

장녀(진아) 출생. 10월 박정희 장군(1군단
참모장)과 재회. 25사단 참모장으로 옮김.
'가짜 고춧가루' 사건.

First daughter (except for the
daughter who died a year ago), Jin-
ah, born; meets General Park
Chung-hee (chief of staff at the 1st
corps) again in October; appointed
chief of staff of the 25th army
division; the Fake Red Pepper
Powder Incident happens.

본부 경력관리기구위원으로 근무 중
6 발발, 박정희의 배려로 거사명단에서
. 5월 16일 아침부터 계엄사령부 요원
. 국가재건최고회의 의장 비서실장, 국
건최고회의 재정경제위원회 상공담당
위원 취임. 구라파 통상사절단장으로
초빙, 산업 실태 시찰. 차녀(유아) 출생.
준장 진급.

제1차 경제개발5개년계획에 참여, 무연탄
개발을 통한 국토녹화사업 적극 건의.

Participates in planning the first 5-
year Economic Development Plan
and actively recommends a land
forestation project through developing
smokeless coal.

박정희의 정치 참여 요청을 거부하고 미국
유학 준비. 3녀(근아) 출생, 육군 소장으로
예편.

Prepares to study abroad in the
U.S. after rejecting Park Chung-
hee's invitation to participate in
politics; third daughter (Keun-ah)
born; goes into the first reserve as
a major general.

officially participates in the May
h coup d'état while working at
Career Management Office of
Army Headquarters (his name
s not included among members
he coup team by Park Chung-
's decision); begins to work as a
f member at the Martial Law En-
ement Headquarters; appointed
ef of staff for the chairman of the
ion Rebuilding Supreme Council
council member in charge of
mmerce and industry; visits
rope as head of the Europe
de Delegation to inspect
ustries; second daughter (Yoo-
born; promoted to brigadier
eral.

박정희의 강력한 요청으로 미국 유학 포기, 일본 특사로 홋카이도에서 규슈까지 일본 전역 10개월간 순방. 야스오카와 초면. 대한중석 사장으로 발령(12월 8일), 전무 고준식과 재회.

Gives up the study abroad plan following Park Chung-hee's strong request; makes a ten-month tour of Japan from Hokkaido to Kyushu as a special envoy; first meeting with Yasuoka; appointed president of Korea Tungsten Manufacturing Company (December 8); meets with Go Jun-sik, managing director of this company, again.

육군 경리장교 황경노, 노중열, 홍건유 등 합류. 대한중석 1년 만에 흑자 체제로 전환. 박정희 요청, 일본 최고 제철소 가와사키제철소 견학, 종합제철 프로젝트에 관심. 4녀 (경아) 출생. 박정희 피츠버그 방문, 코퍼스 사 포이 회장과 종합제철 건설에 대한 의사 교환(5월 26일).

Army officers Hwang Kyung-ro, No Jung-yeol, and Hong Kun-yu join the Korea Tungsten Manufacturing Company; turns the company around and balances the budget within a year; visits Kawasaki Steel Corporation, the best steel corporation in Japan upon Park Chung-hee's request and becomes interested in constructing an integrated steel company; fourth daughter (Kyung-ah) born; Park Chung-hee visits Pittsburgh and discusses with Chairman Lewis W. Foy of Bethlehem Steel the possibility of building an integrated steel company in Korea (May 26).

외아들(성빈) 출생. 경제기획원 종합제 설기본계획 확정. 대한국제제철차 (KISA) 발족. 제2차 경제개발5개년계 정, 종합제철소건설 주요 목표로 포함.

Only son (Sung-bin) born; Economic Planning Board de on the basic plan for constructi an integrated steel company; K International Steel Associ (KISA) inaugurated; the se five-year Economic Develop Plan decided with the constru of an integrated steel compar one of its major goals.

박정희, 설비 구매에 관한 재량권 위임(일명 '종이마패'). 도쿄연락소 설치. 포항 1기 건설 착공(4월 1일). 열연공장, 중후판공장 착공(오스트리아 푀스터 차관)

Granted discretionary authority ("paper Mapae seal") regarding the equipment purchase by Park Chung-hee; Tokyo liaison office opens; construction of Pohang Works Phase 1 begins (April 1); construction of Hot-rolling Mill and Plate Mill begins (Foerster Loan from Austria).

재단법인 제철장학회 설립. 효자제철유치원 개원. 제선공장, 제강공장 등 주요 공장 착공. 호주와의 원료구매 협상에서 일본과 대등한 조건의 장기 공급 계약 체결.

Jecheol Scholarship Foundation founded and Hyoja Jecheol Kindergarden opens; construction of major plants begins; reaches a long-term agreement with Australia through negotiations that it will supply raw material under the same condition as Japan.

영일만의 첫 공장으로 중후판공장 준4일), 첫 제품 출하(7월 31일). 포철 품 첫 미국 수출. 본사 포항으로 이전(.'서울사무소'로 존속)

Plate Mill, the first at Po Works, completed (July 4); th shipment (July 31); the first e of plates to the U.S.; headquarters moved to Po (Seoul headquarters become office).

부와 KISA 종합제철소 건설 가협정 조인
1월 6일). 종합제철건설사업추진위원장에
명, 박정희의 '제철 공장 완수' 특명.

entative agreement on the
onstruction of an integrated steel
ompany between Korean
overnment and KISA (April 6);
ppointed chairman of the
ommittee on the Construction of
n Integrated Steel Company;
eceives a special command from
ark Chung-hee to "finish the
onstruction of an integrated steel
ompany".

'포항종합제철주식회사' 사명 확정(영문 약
자 표기 'POSCO') 및 유네스코회관에서 창
립식(4월 1일) 개최, 초대 사장 취임. 고준식,
황경노, 노중열, 안병화, 곽증, 장경환 등 대
한중석의 인재가 대거 합류. 영일만에 건설사
무소(롬멜하우스) 개설. 공장 부지 조성 공사
착수. 사원 주택단지 매입 및 건설 착공.

Pohang Iron and Steel Company
(POSCO) is inaugurated at the
Korea UNESCO House on April 1;
becomes the first CEO of POSCO;
important managerial staff from
Korea Tungsten Manufacturing
company including Go Jun-sik,
Hwang Kyung-ro, No Jung-yeol,
Ahn Byong-hwa, Gwak Jeung and
Chang Gyung-hwan join POSCO;
builds construction site office
("Rommel House") at Young-il Bay,
prepares for the plant site, and
purchases land for the employee
housing complex and begins its
construction.

1월 하순 KISA 차관 약속 사실상 무산 확인.
대일청구권자금 잔여금 포항 1기 건설자금 전
용 발상(하와이 구상). '3선개헌안 지지성명'
동조서명 요청 거부. 연수원 개원 및 기술자 해
외 연수 파견. 한일 각료 회담에서 종합제철 건
설지원 원칙과 대일청구권자금 전용 원칙 합
의. 일본조사단 영일만 방문, 종합제철건설자금
조달을 위한 한일기본협약 체결(12월 3일).

Agreement with KISA terminated (late
January); comes up with the idea of
redirecting part of the Funds from
Property Claims Against Japan to the
construction of POSCO ("Hawaii
plan"); refuses to sign the "Public
Statement in Support of Amending
Constitutions to Allow the President a
Third Term"; opens Training Institute
and sends technicians abroad to be
trained; agreement on the principles
reached at the Korea-Japan Ministerial
Conference regarding their support for
the construction of an integrated steel
company and the redirecting of part of
the Funds from Property Claims
Against Japan to its construction;
Japanese Investigation Committee
visits Young-il Bay; Korea-Japan Basic
Agreement is reached for funding
construction of the integrated steel
company (December 3).

1고로 첫 출선 성공(6월 9일), 포항 1기
비 종합준공(7월 3일), 일관·종합제철공
완공(연산 조강 103만 톤 체제). 포항 2
건설 종합 착공.

he first blast furnace succeeds
une 9); Integrated steel mill
ompleted (annual crude steel
apacity: 1,03 million tons),
onstruction of Pohang Works
hase 1 completed (July 3);
onstruction of Pohang Works
hase 2 begins.

오스트리아 은성공로 대훈장 받음. 공립 지곡
초등학교 유치. 조업 6개월 만에 흑자 체제 확
립, 조업 1주년 흑자 242억 원 실현. 1고로
출선 100만 톤 돌파. 2고로 157만 톤 착공.
수출 1억 달러, 제품 출하 100만 톤 달성(12
월 1일). 제2제철소 건설을 위한 '한국종합제
철' 설립(초대 사장 태완선 전 부총리 취임).

Awarded the Great Silver Medal of
Honor for Services from Austria; takes
over public Jigok Elementary School;
achieves balanced budget within six
months of operation; achieves 24,2
billion won surplus within a year of
operation; the accumulated production
of the 1st blast furnace surpasses one
million tons; the construction of the
2nd blast furnace of 1,57 million-ton
capacity begins; achieves 100 million-
dollar export and one million-ton
shipment (December 1); Korea Steel
Company founded for the construction
of the second steel works (president
Tae Wan-sun, former prime minister).

뒤셀도르프, 뉴욕, 로스앤젤레스, 싱가포르,
상파울루에 연락소 설치. 한국종합제철 인
수합병. 사단법인 한국철강협회 설립 및 초
대 회장 취임.

Liaison offices in Dusseldorf, New
York, Los Angeles, Singapore, and
San Paolo open; merger with Korea
Steel Company; Korea Iron and
Steel Association founded with
Park Tae-joon as its first president.

1976 49세	1977 50세	1978 51세

포항2기 설비 종합 준공(연산 조강 260만 톤 체제 확립). 포항 3기 설비 종합 착공. 학교법인 제철학원 설립 및 초대 이사장 취임.

Construction of Pohang Works Phase 2 completed (annual crude steel capacity: 2,6 million tons); Phase 3 begins; educational corporation Jecheol Hagwon founded with Park Tae-joon as its first president.

세계철강협회(IISI) 이사 피선. 기술 연구소 설립. 제1제강공장 사고, 포스코 '안전의 날' 선포(4월 24일).

Elected a member of the board of directors at the International Iron and Steel Institute (later World Steel Association); accident at the 1st Steel Making Plant; declares POSCO Safety Day (April 24).

미 씨티은행과 정부 무담보 1억 달러 계약 체결. 포항제철공업고등학교 개교 대와의 제2제철소 실수요자 경쟁 종식고 수요자로 확정. 포항 3기 설비 종합 준공 산 조강 550만 톤 체제 확립). 동아일보 해의 인물'로 선정.

Agreement with Citi Bank unsecured $100 million dollar l reached; Pohang Jecheol Techn High School opens; wins competition for the end user of second integrated steel comp against Hyundai; construction Pohang Works Phase 3 comple (annual crude steel capacity: million tons); chosen as the Per of the Year by *Dong-A ILBO*.

1982 55세	1983 56세	1984 57세

마닐라, 뉴델리에 주재원 파견. 광양만 부지 조성 공사 착공. 타노마 탄광 준공.

Sends resident officers to Manila and New Delhi; preparation for the plant site of Gwangyang Bay begins; construction of Tanomah Coal Mine completed.

포항 4기 2차 설비 종합 준공(연산 조강 910만 톤 체제 확립). 광양제철소 준설 매립공사 착공, 광양제철소 개소식. 캐나다 그린힐스 광산 합작개발 준공. 독일 공로십자 훈장 받음.

Construction of Pohang Works Phase 4-2 completed (annual crude steel capacity: 9,1 million tons); dredging and reclamation for Gwangyang Works begin; inauguration ceremony of Gwangyang Works held; Green Hills Coal Mine, joint development with Canada, completed; awarded the Order of Cross for Services by Germany.

광양제철소 1기 열연 공장 착공.

Construction of Hot-rolling Plant Gwangyang Works Phase 1 beg

스트리아 금성공로대훈장과 페루 대공로
장 받음. 포항 4기 설비 종합 착공. 인덕
철유치원 개원. 기업체질강화위원회 구
타노마 사무소 개설.

arded the Great Gold Medal of
nor for Services from Austria and
e Order of Great Cross from
ru; Phase 4 begins; Indok
cheol Kindergarden opens;
mmittee for the Strengthening of
e Company's Long-term
mpetitiveness established; a
son office in Tanomah opens.

포항제철중학교 개교. 밴쿠버, 멕시코시티
사무소 개설. 국가보완위원회 입법 회의 제
1경제위원장, 한일의원연맹 한국 측 회장
피선. 부친 별세.

Pohang Jecheol Middle School
opens; liaison offices in Vancouver
and Mexico City open; elected the
1st Economic Committee chair of
the National Security Legislative
Council and Korean chairman for
the Korea-Japan Parliamentary
League; father passes away.

사단법인 한일경제협회 회장 피선. 포항 4기
설비 종합 준공(연산 조강 850만 톤 체제 확
립). 포철 초대 회장 취임(사장 고준식 취임)
포항제철고등학교 개교. 제11대 국회의원
민주정의당(민정당) 비례대표 당선, 국회 재
무위원장 피선. 포항 4기 2차 설비 착공. 새
정부와의 긴 씨름 끝에 제2제철소 입지를 광
양만으로 확정. 브라질 십자대훈장 받음. 호
주 마운트·솔리탄광 합작개발 착수.

Elected president of the Korea-
Japan Economy Association;
construction of Pohang Works
Phase 4 completed (annual crude
steel capacity: 8,5 million tons);
becomes the first chairman of
POSCO (CEO: Go Jun-sik); Pohang
Jecheol High School opens; elected
a member of the Assembly from the
national constituency (Democratic
Justice Party) and chairperson for
the Finance Committee; construction
of Pohang Works Phase 4-2 begins;
Gwangyang Bay chosen as the site
for the second steel works after
lengthy negotiations with government;
awarded the Ordern Rio Branco
Gracruz by Brazil; joint development
of Mount Thorley Coal Mine in
Australia begins.

공과대학교 설립 착수. 고준식 사장 퇴
사장 안병화 취임). 광양제철유치원, 초
교, 중학교 동시 개교. 광양 1기 설비 종
착공. 제철연수원 백암수련관 준공. 미국
S(유에스스틸)과 합작회사 설립 합의.

STECH founding project begins;
ange of CEO from Go Jun-sik to
Byeong-hwa; Gwangyang
cheol Kindergarden, Elementary
hool, and Middle School open at
e same time; equipment of
angyang Works Phase 1 begins;
egam Training Hall, Jecheol
aining Institute completed;
eement with US Steel to launch
int corporation reached.

USS와 합작회사 UPI 설립. 광양 2기 설비
종합 착공. 광양제철고등학교 개교. 내방객
500만 명 돌파. 포항공과대학교 개교. 포항
산업과학기술연구원(RIST) 착공. UPI 설비
현대화 공사 착공. USX(USS의 변경 사
명) 노조 전면파업 돌입.

UPI, a joint corporation of POSCO
and US Steel, founded; equipment
for construction of Gwangyang
Works Phase 2 begins; Gwangyang
Jecheol High School opens;
POSCO records more than 5
million visitors; POSTECH opens;
construction of RIST (Research
Institute of Science and Technology)
begins; modernization of equipment
at UPI begins; overall strike at USX
(formerly USS) occurs.

포스텍 첫 입학식. 재단법인 RIST 창립 및 초
대 이사장 취임. 포항제철초등학교, 포항제철
서초등학교 개교. 광양 1기 설비 종합 준공
(연산 조강 270만 톤 체제, 전체 1천220만
톤 체제 확립). 영국금속학회 제114회 베서
머금상(5월 13일), 브라질 남십자성훈장, 페
루 대십자공로훈장 받음. 회갑 기념 문집『신
종이산가족』상재. 정부의 공기업 민영화 방
안 확정. 종합 설비관리 전산 시스템 개발.

POSTECH holds its first entrance
ceremony; RIST Foundation
established with Park Tae-joon as
its inaugural chairman of the board
of directors; POSCO Elementary
School and POSCO West Elementary
School open; construction of
Gwangyang Works Phase 1
completed (annual crude steel
capacity: 12,2 million tons);
awarded Bessemer Sold Medal by
the Institute of Materials, Minerals,

and Mining (England), the National Order of the Southern Cross from Brazil, and the Order of Great Cross from Peru; publishes *A New Variety of Dispersed Families*, his collected writings in celebration of his sixtieth birthday; government introduces policy to privatize public enterprise; comprehensive computerized equipment management system developed.

제13대 국회의원 민정당 비례대표 당선. 미국 카네기멜런대학 명예공학박사 학위, 영국 셰필드대학 명예금속공학박사 학위 받음. 한일의원연맹 한국 측 회장 피선. 포철 주식 상장(국민주 1호). 광양2기 설비 종합 준공(연산 조강 540만 톤 체제 확립). 광양 3기 설비 종합 착공.

Elected a member of the thirteenth National Assembly from the national constituency; awarded an Honorary Doctorate in Engineering by Carnegie Mellon University in America and an Honorary Doctorate in Metal Engineering from Sheffield University in England; elected the Korean chairman for the Korea-Japan Parliamentary League; POSCO listed on the stock market (the 1st of its kind); construction of Gwangyang Works Phase 2 completed (annual crude steel capacity: 14,5 million tons); Phase 3 begins.

포항제철소 누계 출강량 1억 톤 달성. 버밍햄대학 명예공학박사학위 받음. 테인리스 1공장 준공.

The aggregate productio POSCO surpasses 100 m tons; awarded an Hono Doctorate in Engineering Birmingham University in Br Pohang Stainless Steel 1st completed.

해외 유랑, 도쿄 13평 아파트 생활 시작. 포철 회장 정명식, 사장 조말수 취임(황경노, 박득표, 이대공, 유상부 등 이른바 'TJ파' 퇴임). 포철 세무조사. 본인, 가족 친인척, 측근들에 대한 전방위 비자금 조사.

Exile; begins to live in a fifty-square-yard apartment in Tokyo; POSCO management change: so-called TJ group, including Hwang Kyung-ro, Park Deuk-pyo, Lee Dae-gong, Yoo Sang-bu, resigns and Jeong Myung-shik becomes chairman and Cho Mal-soo becomes CEO; tax investigation for POSCO and "slush fund" investigation of Park Tae-joon, his family, relatives, and associates.

포철회장 김만제 취임. 포스텍 초대 총장 김호길 별세(4월 30일). 중국의 초청 거부. 모친 별세. 포항방사광가속기 준공. 포스코신문 창간. 포철 주식 뉴욕 증시 상장.

Kim Man-je becomes chairman of POSCO; Kim Ho-gil, first president of POSTECH, passes away; rejects Chinese invitation; mother passes away; construction of Pohang Light Source completed; POSCO Newspaper inaugurated; POSCO listed on the New York Stock Market.

뉴욕 코넬대학병원에 폐렴으로 입원 코센터 준공. 학교법인 제철학원에서 텍 분리.

Hospitalized in Cornell Univ Medical Center in New Yor pneumonia; construction of PC Center completed; POST separated from the educat corporation Jecheol Hagwon.

ᅵ정당 대표 취임. 노태우, 김영삼, 김종필
ᅵ 3당 합당으로 민주자유당(민자당) 출범,
고 위원 취임. 포철 부회장 황경노 취임.
ᅵ엔나, 테헤란 사무소 개설. 광양 3기 설비
합 준공(연산 조강 810만 톤 체제 확립).
랑스 레종 도뇌르 훈장 받음. 국내 최초
구 전용 잔디 구장 포항 준공.

Becomes the chairman of the
Democratic Justice Party; Roh Tae-
woo, Kim Young-sam, and Kim
ong-pil merge three parties into
he Democratic Liberal Party and
ʼark Tae-joon becomes its
upreme counselor; Hwang Kyung-
o becomes vice president of
ʼOSCO; liaison office opens in
ehran; construction of Gwangyang
Works Phase 3 completed (annual
rude steel capacity: 17,5 million
ons); awarded Légion d'Honneur
y France; grass field exclusively
dedicated to soccer completed in
ʼohang for the first time in Korea.

광양 4기 설비 종합 착공. 포스텍 제1회 졸
업식. 노르웨이, 오스트레일리아 최고 훈장
받음. 포항방사광가속기 착공. 캐나다워털루
대학 명예공학박사 학위 받음. 고준식 별세.

Construction of Gwangyang Works
Phase 4 begins; the first com-
mencement held at POSTECH;
awarded the Order of Commander
First Class with Star from both
Norway and Australia; Pohang
Light Source launched; awarded an
Honorary Doctorate in Engineering
by Waterloo University in Canada;
Go Jun-sik passes away.

한국무역협회 '무역인 대상' 수상. 베트남과
포스비나 합작 설립. 윌리코프상 수상. 모스
크바대학 명예경제학박사 학위, 칠레 베르
니르드 오히기스 대십자훈장 받음. 베이징
과학기술대학 명예교수. 광양 4기 설비 종
합 준공 및 '포항제철 4반세기 대역사 준공'
(연산 조강 2천100만 톤 체제 확립). 포철
회장 사퇴 및 명예회장 추대. 민자당 탈당.
남방 정책(중국, 베트남, 미얀마) 시작. 포철
회장 황경노, 사장 박득표 취임.

Awarded the Grand Prize for Trader
from the Korea International Trade
Association; POSVINA, a joint
company with Vietnam, launched;
awarded the Willy Korf Award,
Honorary Doctorate in Economics
from Moscow State University, and the
Gran Cruz de la Bernardo O'Higgins
from Chile; Honorary Professor at the
University of Science and Technology
Beijing; construction of Gwangyang
Works Phase 4 completed in time to
celebrate a quarter-century of POSCO
(annual crude steel capacity: 21
million tons); steps down as the
chairman of POSCO and selected
honorary chairman; withdraws from
the Democratic Liberal Party; begins
southern policy (towards China,
Vietnam, and Myanmar); Hwang
Kyung-ro becomes chairman and
Park Deuk-pyo CEO.

선 앞의 여야 영입제의 거부.

Refuses invitations from both ruling
nd opposition parties to accept a
eadership position before general
lection.

5월 초 귀국, 포항 북구 보궐선거 당선. 김
영삼 정권의 경제적 실정 중점 비판, 비전
역설. DJT연대, 자민련 총재 취임, IMF 관
리 체제의 국가 부도 위기 사태를 수습하기
위해 동분서주. 사보 『쇳물』 폐간(통권 309
호). 베네수엘라 포스벤 합작계약 체결.

Returns to Korea in early May; elected
in the special election for representative
of Pohang North District; criticizes Kim
Young-sam regime's misgovernment of
the national economy and proposes a
new plan; DJT (Kim Dae-jung, Kim
Jong-pil and Park Tae-joon)
collaboration begins; becomes
chairman of the Liberal Democracy
Party; leads the effort to overcome the
financial crisis during IMF system;
Melted Iron, POSCO company
newsletter, ceases to publish (total 309
issues); agreement with Venezuela for
a joint company, POSVEN reached.

'재벌 개혁의 전도사'로 불림.
포철 회장 유상부 취임.

Called "Missionary of Conglomerate
Reform"; POSCO chairman Yoo
Sang-bu inaugurated.

김대중과 주례 회동으로 현안을 조정하며 경제 회생과 정치개혁에 주력. 광양 5고로 완공(연산 291만 톤 증설).

Focuses on the revival of the economy and political reform through a regular weekly meeting with President Kim Dae-jung; construction of Gwangyang Works #5 blast furnace completed (annual crude steel capacity 28 million tons).

자민련 총재 사퇴, 국무총리 취임. 소량의 각혈 시작. 4월 총선의 여권과 자민련 패배. 5월 19일 총리 사임. 신세기통신 지분 SK 에 매각. 포항테크노파크 이사회 창립. 포철 민영화 완료(10월 4일).

Resigns from the chairmanship of the Liberal Democracy Party; appointed prime minister; begins to expectorate blood; resigns from the position of prime minister after the defeat of his and the ruling party; sells off shares of Sinsegi Communcations to SK; forms board of directors for Pohang Techno Park; privatization of POSCO completed (October 4).

뉴욕 코넬대학병원에서 폐 밑 물혹 제거 술. 뉴욕에서 9·11테러 현장 목격. 포철 예회장 재위촉.

Operation to remove tumor from lung at Cornell University Med Center; witnesses 9.11 in N York; reappointed honorary chairm of POSCO.

한일국교정상화 40주년 기념 학술대회 기조연설. 평전『세계 최고의 철강인 박태준』 중국어판『세계제일철강인 박태준』 출간 및 베이징 출판기념회 참석.

Delivers keynote address at the conference commemorating the 40th anniversary of the Korea-Japan Diplomatic Normalization; attends a party held in Beijing to celebrate the publication of his biography in Chinese translation.

포스코청암재단 이사장 취임.

Chairman of the board of directors at POSCO TJ Park Foundation.

포스코 회장 정준양 취임
고려대학교 명예경영학박사 학위 받음.

Posco chairman Chung Joon-Y inaugurated.
Receives an Honorary Doctorat Business and Management fr Korea University.

수술 후 7개월 만에 귀국. 신의주특구 장관
내정설. 사명 '포항종합제철주식회사' (포철)
를 '주식회사 포스코'로 변경(3월 15일).

Returns to Korea seven months
after operation; rumor of unofficial
decision appointing him to the
position of minister for Sinuiju
Special Administrative District;
company name officially changed
from Pohang Iron and Steel Co.,
Ltd to POSCO Co., Ltd. (March 15).

'중국발전연구기금회' 고문으로 초빙되어
베이징 댜오위타이 '2003년 중국발전고위
층논단'에 참석, 중국 경제에 대한 연설.
포스코 회장 이구택 취임.

Invited to become advisor to the
"Chinese Development Research
Fund," attends "2003 Chinese
Development High-ranking Officials
Forum" at Diao Yu Tai Villa Hotel in
Beijing, and gives an address on
the Chinese economy; POSCO
chairman Lee Ku-taek inaugurated.

미국의 세계적 철강 분석 전문 기관 WSD가
포스코를 세계 철강회사 중 3년 연속 경쟁력
1위로 선정. 희수와 금혼식의 해. 『세계 최고
의 철강인 박태준』(이대환 지음) 출간.

WSD, an American organization
specializing in analyzing world steel
industries, selects POSCO for three
years in a row as the most
competitive company in the world;
celebrates his Heesu (77th
birthday) and golden wedding
anniversary; *Park Tae-joon, the
Best Steel Man of the World*, his
biography written by Lee Dae-
hwan, published.

경전 『세계 최고의 철강인 박태준』 베트남어
판 『철의 사나이 박태준』 출간 및 하노이 출
판기념회 참석, 국립하노이대학 특별강연.

Attends a party in Hanoi to
celebrate the publication of his
biography in Vietnamese translation; gives a special lecture at
Vietnam National University Hanoi.

현장 근무, 퇴직 직원들과 19년만의 재회 행
사인 "보고 싶었소! 뵙고 싶었습니다!"에 참
석해 눈물의 명연설을 남겼으며, 이것이 생애
마지막 연설이 됨(9월 19일). 포스텍 구성원
과 포항시민이 성의를 모아 포스텍 노벨동산
에 '청암 박태준 조각상' 건립(12월 2일).

Attends an event entitled "I Missed
You, We Missed You, Too!" a
reunion between Park Tae-joon and
370 retired founding workers of
POSCO nineteen years after his
retirement and gives a moving, and
last address(September 19);
"Statue of Park Tae-joon" erected
on Nobel Hill in POSTECH by
members of POSTECH and citizens
of Pohang (December 2)

12월 13일 오후 5시 20분 향년 84세로 타
계. 청조근정훈장 추서, 사회장으로 12월
17일 서울 국립 현충원 국가유공자묘역에
안장.

Passes away at 5:20 P.M. December
13; Cheongjo Geunjeong Medal
posthumously conferred; buried in
the Patriots Graveyard in the
National Cemetery in Seoul after a
public funeral on December 17.

영역자 약력 About the Translators

전승희 Jeon Seung-hee

《ASIA》 편집위원. 서울대와 하버드대에서 영문학과 비교문학으로 박사 학위를 받았으며 현재 하버드대학 한국학연구소의 연구원으로 재직 중이다. 현대 한국문학 및 세계문학을 다룬 논문을 다수 발표했으며, 바흐친의 『장편소설과 민중언어』, 제인 오스틴의 『오만과 편견』 등을 공역했다. 1988년 한국여성연구소의 창립과 《여성과 사회》의 창간에 참여했고 2002년부터 보스턴 지역 피학대여성을 위한 단체인 '트랜지션하우스' 운영에 참여해 왔다. 2006년 하버드대학 한국학연구소에서 '한국 현대사와 기억'을 주제로 한 워크숍을 주관했다.

Jeon Seung-hee, a member of the Editorial Board of *ASIA*, is a Fellow at the Korea Institute, Harvard University. She received a Ph.D. in English Literature from Seoul National University and a Ph.D. in Comparative Literature from Harvard University. She has presented and published numerous papers on modern Korean and world literature. She is also a co-translator of Mikhail Bakhtin's *Novel and the People's Culture* and Jane Austen's *Pride and Prejudice*. She is a founding member of the Korean Women's Studies Institute and of the biannual Women's Studies' journal *Women and Society* (1988), and she has been working at 'Transition House', the first and oldest shelter for battered women in New England. She organized a workshop entitled "The Politics of memory in modern Korea" in May, 2006.

차세웅 Cha Se-ung

1978년 서울에서 태어나 미국의 위스콘신 주, 메사추세츠 주 및 한국 서울을 오가며 자랐다. 미국 윌리엄즈 칼리지에서 영문학 학사 학위를, 럿거스 대학에서 영문학 석사 학위를 받았다. 현재 보스턴 지역에 거주하며 창작과 번역 활동을 하고 있다.

Born in Seoul in 1978, Se-ung Cha spent his childhood living in Wisconsin, Massachusetts, and Seoul. As a direct consequence, he has been engaged in projects of translation his entire life. He graduated from Williams College, majoring in English Literature, and received MA in English from Rutgers University. He is now working on his MFA (Master of Fine Arts) in poetry at University of Massachusetts Boston.

A Study on Taejoonism as a Principle 특수성으로서의 태준이즘 연구

전미세리 Jeon Miseli

한국외국어대학교 동시통역대학원을 졸업한 후, 캐나다 브리티시컬럼비아 대학 도서관학, 아시아학과 문학 석사, 동 대학 비교문학과 박사 학위를 취득하고 동 대학에서 강사 및 아시아 도서관 사서로 근무했다. 한국국제교류재단 장학금을 지원받았고, 캐나다 연방정부 사회인문과학연구회의 연구비를 지원받았다. 오정희의 단편 「직녀」를 번역했으며 그 밖에 서평, 논문 등을 출판했다.

Jeon graduated from the Graduate School of Simultaneous Interpretation, Hankuk University of Foreign Studies and received her M.L.S. (School of Library and Archival Science), M.A. (Dept. of Asian Studies) and Ph.D. (Program of Comparative Literature) from the University of British Columbia, Canada. She has taught as an instructor in the Dept. of Asian Studies and worked as a reference librarian at the Asian Library, at UBC. She was awarded the Korea Foundation Scholarship for Graduate Students in 2000. Her publications include the translation "Weaver Woman" (*Acta Koreana*, Vol. 6, No. 2, July 2003) from the original short story "Chingnyeo" (1970) by Oh Jung-hee.

청암 박태준 ⓒ아시아

발행일 2012년 3월 21일
펴낸이 방재석
펴낸곳 아시아
지은이 이대환 외
편집 정수인, 박신영, 김선경
출판등록 2006년 1월 31일 제319-2006-4호
인쇄 한영문화사
디자인 끄레어소시에이츠

전화 02-821-5055 **팩스** 02-821-5057
주소 서울시 동작구 흑석동 100-16
이메일 bookasia@hanmail.net
홈페이지 www.bookasia.org

ISBN 978-89-94006-38-3 03800
*값은 뒤표지에 있습니다.